the UnDeRDOgS

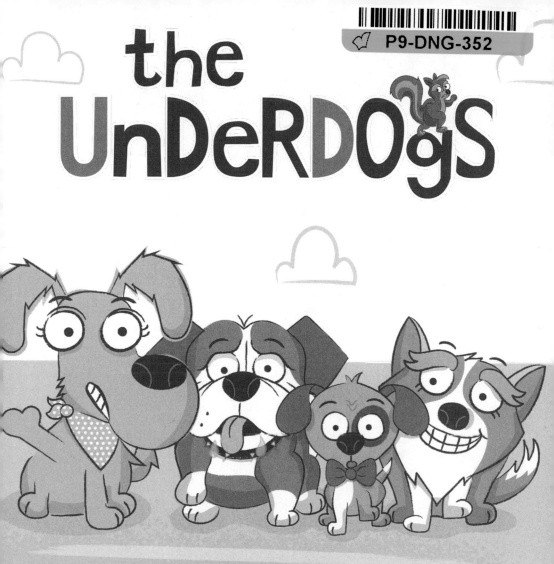

By Tracey West

ILLUSTRATED BY Kyla may

SCHOLASTIC INC.

Library of Congress Catologing-in-Publication Data available

ISBN 978-1-338-73272-6

1 2021
Printed in the U.S.A.   23

First printing 2021
Book design by Jessica Meltzer

For my dog PeeWee,
my best friend for seventeen years and the
inspiration for Peanut. —T. W.

I dedicate this book to my Mum,
who taught me how to love dogs. —K. M.

Table of Contents

—

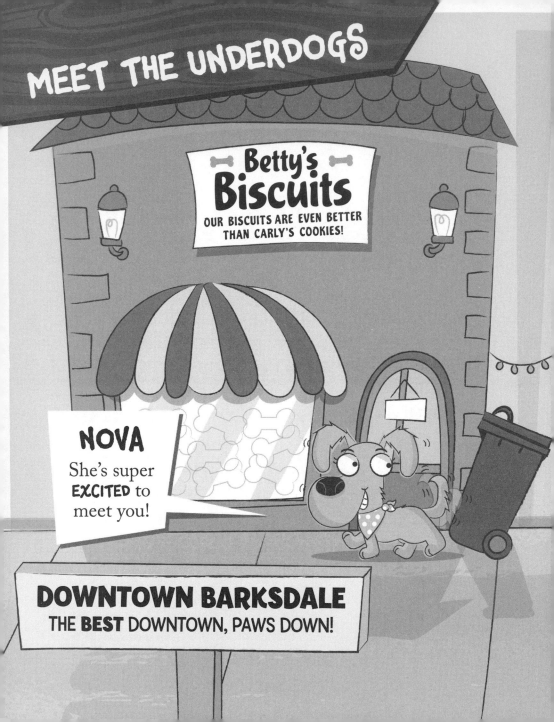

CHAPTER 1

ON YOUR BARK, GET SET, WOOF!

Nova's three best friends stared at her, waiting for instructions.

Duke flexed his powerful muscles.

Peanut's whiskers twitched with excitement.

Harley's fluffy tail wagged back and forth.

"Okay, Team Comeback! Today is the day we practice for our Agility Exam!" Nova announced.

Harley frowned. "Is that why you asked us to come to the park today?"

"There's no point in practicing," Duke said.

"Yeah, we've failed this test every year the last three years," Peanut added.

Nova knew that Peanut was right. Each year, students at Barksdale Academy took nine K-9 exams. Nova and her friends had never passed a single test.

Failing had never bothered Nova before. She had always known that she and her friends were doing their best. But her three sisters were so good at everything—just like everyone else in Barksdale. And for once, Nova wanted to be good at something, too.

"I know," Nova said. "But this time's gonna be different. I can feel it from the tip of my nose to the tip of my tail. This is the year we're going to ace the test! Are you ready to practice?"

"Ready!" her friends cried.

Nova grinned. "Good. Now, on your bark, get set . . ."

Harley raced off toward the trees.

Nova stopped her stopwatch. "Harley, come back!"

Harley skidded to a stop. "Whoops! Sorry, Nova." She ran back to the starting line.

"Let's try this again, Team Comeback," Nova said. On your bark, get set . . ."

"WAIT!" Duke cried. "I think I hear a bear!"

"That's not a bear, it's a lawn mower!" Nova told him. "Mr. Poochwell is mowing his front lawn."

"Are you sure?" Duke asked. "That sounds like the growl of a bear. A big, scary bear with sharp claws."

"I'm sure," Nova said. "Let's try again. On your bark, get set . . ."

"EXCUSE ME," Peanut piped up, raising his paw. "But how exactly does this work? When you say 'on your bark,' does that mean *we* bark before we take off?"

"No," Nova said. "*I'm* the one who barks. I'll say, 'On your bark, get set,' and then I'll bark, and that's when you all start the agility course."

"But that doesn't make sense," Peanut said. "Shouldn't you say, 'on *my* bark'?"

"Peanut, you know how this works," Nova said. Then she saw that he was grinning.

"Yeah, I do," Peanut said. "Just messing around. Come on, let's start!"

"Are you sure nobody has anything else they want to say?" Nova asked. "Because I am going to start the count again, and this time I don't want anything to stop us."

GOOD to go.

NO MORE JOKING AROUND.

I'M SURE.

"Okay," Nova said. "On your bark, get set . . ."
"NOVA!" Peanut yelled.
Nova sighed. "What is it, Peanut?"

Peanut pointed. "There's somebody on the course."
A small dog with feathery ears was sniffing around
the agility course.

"It's Athena," Nova said. "I'll handle this. Then we're going to practice, and nothing is going to stop us!"

CHAPTER 2

MY FUR!

Nova walked up to the little dog on their course. Athena had her nose to the ground, sniffing. She was always investigating something.

"Hi, Athena," Nova said to her friend.

Athena didn't answer. She just kept sniffing.

Nova tapped her on the back. "Athena!"

Athena jumped. "Oh, Nova, it's you!"

"Yes, it's me," Nova said. She nodded over to Harley, Duke, and Peanut. "We're practicing for the agility test. So if you wouldn't mind—"

"You made this course yourself?" Athena interrupted. She looked around the park where Nova had

set up the practice course. There were obstacles made of empty milk jugs for the pups to zigzag around. There were ramps made of wood planks for them to climb. And there was even a Hula-Hoop hanging from a tree for them to jump through.

"Yes, I worked pretty hard on it," Nova answered proudly.

"Why not just use the agility course at Barksdale Academy?" Athena asked.

"We wanted some privacy," Nova answered. "And I'd appreciate it if you could—"

Athena nodded toward the hoop. "You know, Nova, there's a breeze blowing today. It could change the angle of the hoop, which would alter the trajectory of—"

"Athena, we really need to start practicing," Nova said. "Can we talk about this later?"

Athena shrugged. "Sure, Nova."

"All right, Team Comeback, let's try this again," Nova said. "On your bark, get set, **WOOF!**"

Harley, Duke, and Peanut took off as Nova's loud bark rang across the field. Harley quickly took the lead. She zigged and zagged around the milk jugs.

"GO, HARLEY!" Nova cheered. "You're making great time."

"Thanks, Nov—**SQUIRREL!**" Harley yelled. Once again, she ran off toward the trees.

"Harley, no!" Nova called after her.

Peanut made his way through the obstacle course next. He ran to the ramp and climbed up it. Then he slid down the other side.

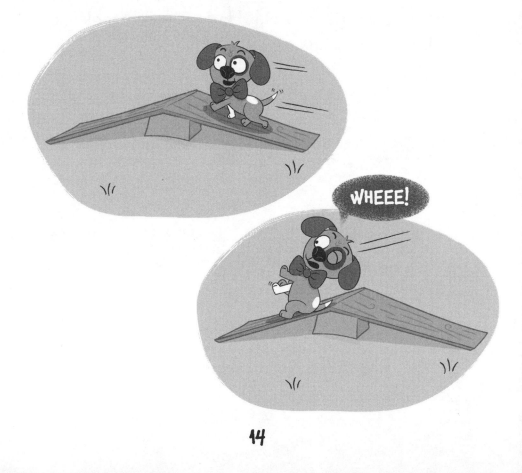

"Keep going, Peanut!" Nova cheered.

Peanut ran to the hoop. Then he skidded to a stop.

"I'm not jumping through that," he said.

"Why not?" Nova asked, but then she saw that Duke was sitting in front of the ramp. He wasn't moving.

"Duke, what's wrong?" Nova asked.

"It's too high," Duke replied.

"It's not that high," Nova replied.

Duke shook his head. "I am *not* going up there."

"Fine," Nova said. "Go around it for now."

"WILL DO!" Duke replied. He ran around the ramp and zoomed toward the hoop.

HUFF! PUFF!

"Duke, do not go through that hoop!" Peanut warned.

"Why not?" Duke asked. "It's not as high as the ramp. I'm not afraid." He huffed and puffed as he ran toward the hoop.

"There's a big mud puddle on the other side," Peanut said. "And I am not about to get my fur dirty for some silly practice."

"HUH?" Duke asked. He couldn't hear Peanut over his own huffing and puffing. **"HERE I GO!"**

Duke jumped through the hoop.

He landed in the mud puddle. Mud splashed up and rained down. It got all over Peanut.

"MY FUR!" Peanut wailed.

Athena looked at Nova. "That's what I was trying to tell you," she said.

Harley ran up. "The squirrels in this park must be drinking rocket fuel for breakfast. I can't catch them!" she reported. Then she looked at Duke and Peanut. "What happened?"

"A mud puddle happened," Peanut said. "A stinky, smelly, nasty mud puddle. And Duke jumped right into it!"

Duke shook his head and his body. More mud flew off.

"Sorry, Peanut," he said.

Nova bounded over to them. She tried to run around the hoop, but she tripped through it instead.

SPLASH! She landed in the mud puddle, too.

"Puddle party!" Harley yelled. She jumped into the mud next to Nova.

Nova shook the mud from her fur as she climbed out of the puddle. "I'll admit, we just got off to a bumpy start," she told her friends. "But that's what practice is for—making mistakes! Let's get back to the starting line and try again. Go, Team Comeback!"

Two perfectly primped dogs with freshly washed fur and long, curly ears were standing behind Nova.

"Mandy and Randy! How long have you two been watching?" Nova asked.

"Long enough to see that you and your team have no chance of passing the agility test," Mandy said.

"Yeah, no chance," echoed her twin brother, Randy.

"We do, too, have a chance!" Nova shot back.

"Statistically, there is a very small chance," Athena pointed out.

"You're not helping, Athena," Nova whispered, nudging her friend. Then her voice got louder. "You'll see, Mandy and Randy. This year we're going to practice really hard. We're going to ace all our K-9 exams. We might even win Best in Show!"

"HA!" Mandy laughed.

"YEAH, HA!" Randy laughed.

The twins started laughing so hard that they rolled onto their backs. They laughed and laughed and laughed.

Finally, they stopped and got back on their feet. The perfect pooches didn't have a speck of dirt or grass on them.

How do they do it? Nova wondered.

"That's pretty funny, Nova," Mandy said. "A bunch of underdogs becoming Best in Show? Here in Barksdale? That'll never happen."

"Yeah, never!" Randy said.

Then the twins jogged away.

"Can you believe those two?" Nova asked.

"Actually, I can," Duke replied. "Let's face it. We *are* underdogs, and underdogs never win!"

CHAPTER 3

A BUNCH OF RUNTS

Nova frowned. "That can't be true, Duke," she said. "I'm sure underdogs win sometimes . . . Don't they?"

Duke shook his head. "Nope. Not here in Barksdale, anyway. Here, everyone is the best at *something*. Everyone but us."

"Duke's right," Peanut said.

"Yeah, we're a mess," Harley agreed.

Athena cleared her throat. "I know I'm not technically a part of your team, Nova, but I think Duke, Peanut, and Harley have a point. The four of you started at Barksdale as a **BUNCH OF RUNTS**."

"Hey!" Peanut growled.

"I'm not being mean; I'm being factual," Athena explained. "Each of you is the smallest member of your family—the runt. Everyone at Barksdale Academy thinks you are underdogs because that's what you are. You remember what happened in our first year of school."

Nova groaned. "How could I forget?" she asked. Her mind drifted off into a . . .

FLASHBACK

Nova, Duke, Harley, and Peanut were the smallest pups in the whole school. Right away, everyone started to call them runts. And runts did not have a good reputation at Barksdale Academy.

"Runts may start out small, but they can learn to do big things," Principal Finefur said, and that was that. "Give them a chance."

But things went wrong right away.

THEY MADE A MESS! They ate like animals and chewed up their textbooks.

THEY DIDN'T BEHAVE! They barked all day and ran when they were supposed to walk.

AND THEY COULDN'T COMPETE! When it came time to take their K-9 exams, they were clueless. Everyone competing in the exams hoped to be named Best in Show at the end of the year. The competition was fierce! But Nova, Duke, Harley, and Peanut failed each exam:

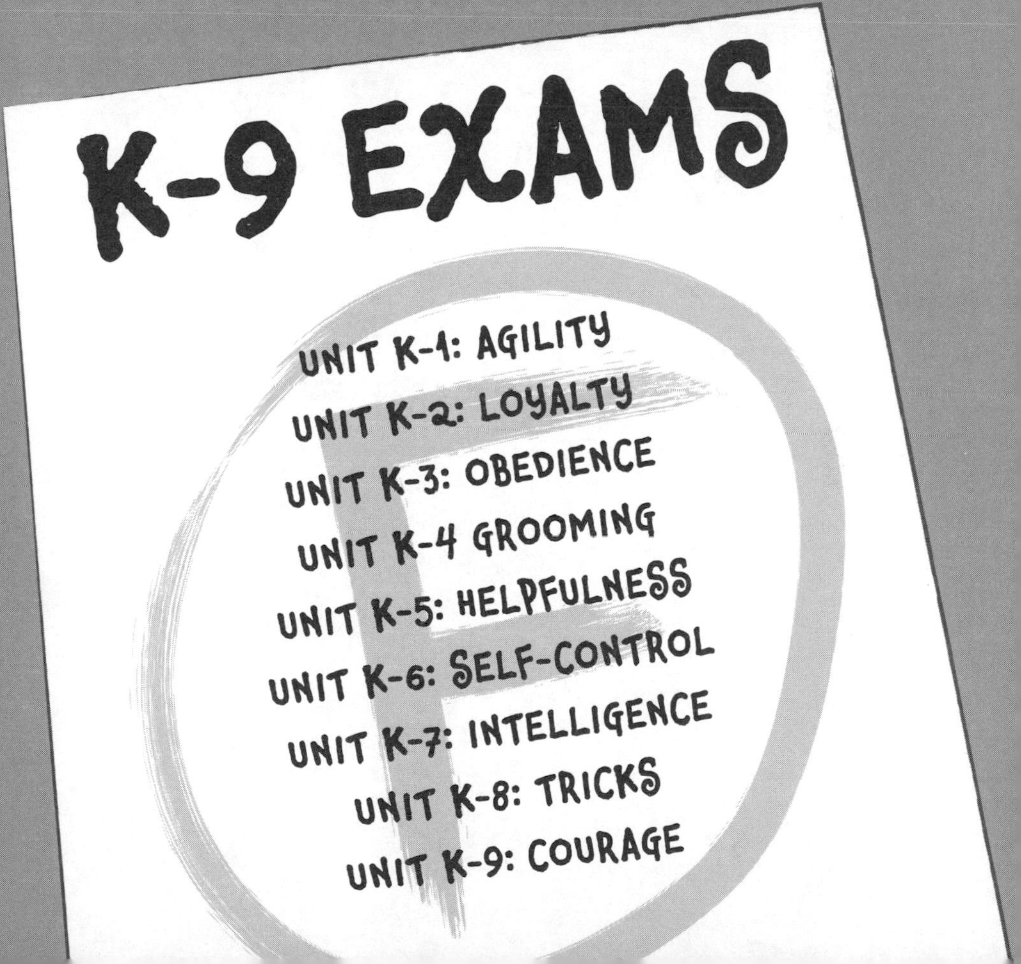

K-9 EXAMS

UNIT K-1: AGILITY

UNIT K-2: LOYALTY

UNIT K-3: OBEDIENCE

UNIT K-4 GROOMING

UNIT K-5: HELPFULNESS

UNIT K-6: SELF-CONTROL

UNIT K-7: INTELLIGENCE

UNIT K-8: TRICKS

UNIT K-9: COURAGE

Some of the other dogs laughed at them. Some of the other dogs made fun of them. But all of the other dogs started calling them **THE UNDERDOGS**.

CHAPTER 4

WHAT'S THE POINT?

"**H**ey, Nova, are you having a flashback?" Harley asked. "Your eyes have that glazed-over look."

"It's over," Nova said. "And yes, Athena, we *were* a mess when we first got to Barksdale Academy. When you're the runt of the litter, you get ignored. Nobody expects anything from you. So, when we came here, we didn't know much."

"Nothing at all, really," Athena pointed out.

"Hey!" Peanut said. "At least I knew how to groom myself. I wasn't totally hopeless in that test."

"Right. And everybody forgets how fast I am," Harley said, running in a circle.

"And how strong I am," Duke said.

"Exactly!" Nova said. "So what if we've never passed a single test? We've gotten a little better every year. And now is our chance to prove everybody wrong, once and for all."

UNDERDOGS CAN WIN!

"But practicing is boring," said Peanut.

"And no matter how hard we train, everyone else will still be better than us," Duke added. "What's the point?"

"Duke is right," Harley said. "Why can't we just keep being underdogs? It's not so bad."

"Come on, pups, we can do this!" Nova urged. "We're not runts anymore. We've grown up. We can do awesome things. And this is the year that we can show everyone just how awesome we are. I can feel it. That's why Team Comeback needs to get back out on that practice field!"

Peanut looked at his fur. "I need a bath first."

"And I don't see the point in training until we lower the height of that ramp," Duke said.

Nova turned to Harley. "What about you? You're with me, right?"

"I think—**SQUIRREL!**" Harley darted off toward the trees again.

Nova sighed. "I guess we can try to practice another day."

"Great! I'm off to the salon!" Peanut said, and he trotted off.

"I think I'll go see if I can order bear repellent online," Duke said, and he walked away, too.

Nova watched her friends leave. She shook her head. "That was a great practice course. We just needed more time! But they wouldn't even give it a chance."

"It was a nice attempt, Nova," Athena said. "But statistics don't lie. You pups are probably always going to be underdogs."

Nova frowned. "That doesn't seem fair."

Why can't I dream about being Best in Show, too, just like my sisters? she wondered. *Why do I always have to be an underdog?*

CHAPTER 5

GRANNY'S PUP TALK

Nova walked home.

Normally, when Nova went from one place to another, she didn't just walk. She ran. She bounded. She bolted. She sprinted. And when she was feeling full of confidence, she swaggered.

But today, Nova was not feeling full of confidence. She felt down, defeated, and dejected. So, she didn't run, or bound, or bolt, or sprint, or swagger. Instead, she walked very slowly, with her tail pointing toward the ground instead of wagging happily.

Nova walked through town. Normally, she would stop and sniff the air in front of Betty's Biscuits and try to guess what delicious flavor Betty was baking. But today, she didn't feel like it.

She walked past the Bubbles and Bows salon. Normally, she would go in and chat with Raven, the fur stylist, and catch up on all the gossip in Barksdale. But she didn't feel like doing that, either.

Nova didn't stop for a slice of peanut butter pizza at Chef Wolfgang's Bistro. She didn't stop to smell the roses at Fiona's Flower Shop. Instead, she made a left onto Bark Avenue, and then a right onto Dogwood Lane, and then she walked up to a yellow house with pretty flowers planted around it: the home of the Goldenfur family.

Nova's older sisters, Nina, Nadia, and Natasha, were playing catch on the lawn. They swiftly and gracefully raced around the yard, tossing a ball to one another.

Nina spotted Nova. **"CATCH, LITTLE SIS!"**

Nova looked up, startled. The ball came zooming toward her. She leaped up in the air. She caught the ball in her mouth . . . and then came crashing down on top of the prickly rose bush.

"OUCH!" Nova cried, and the ball fell from her mouth and rolled back toward her sisters.

"Better luck next time," Nina said.

"You'll get the hang of it someday," Nadia added with a nod.

"You okay?" Natasha asked.

Nova didn't answer her sister. She pulled the thorns out of her fur and trotted inside the house. She walked past the shelf that held her sisters' trophies.

BEST IN HELPFULNESS
Natasha Goldenfur

BEST IN AGILITY
Nina Goldenfur

BEST IN TRICKS
Nadia Goldenfur

Nova sat at the kitchen table and sighed. "I'll never be the best at anything."

Then she felt a soft paw on her cheek.

"What's the matter, my little Nova?"

"Nothing, Granny," Nova replied, but she sighed again.

Her grandmother sat next to her. "Come now, Nova, you're a sad pup if I ever saw one. If you'd like to tell me how you're feeling, I'll listen."

Granny Goldenfur gave great pup talks, and she was famous for her funny old sayings. She always said things like:

I'D RATHER HEAR A FUNNY TALE THAN HAVE A FLUFFY TAIL.

A BONE IN THE PAW IS BETTER THAN TWO BONES IN THE GARBAGE.

THE SQUEAKY MOUSE ALWAYS GETS CAUGHT BY THE CAT.

Her sayings sounded funny, but they always made sense when Granny said them.

Suddenly, the words started spilling out of Nova.

"I'll never be best at anything like Nina, Nadia, and Natasha!" Nova cried. "I don't want to fail the K-9 exams again this year. I want to pass them. Maybe I even want to be Best in Show! But my friends don't think we should even bother trying. What if they're right?"

"There's an old saying that practice makes a pup perfect," Granny Goldenfur said.

Nova nodded. "Exactly! That's why I want to practice for the K-9 exams."

"Well, I don't like that saying very much," Granny said, and Nova's eyes widened in surprise.

"What do you mean?" Nova asked.

"There's no point in practicing to be perfect," Granny replied. "Because I think you're already perfect the way you are, my little Nova."

Nova sighed. "No, I'm not. If I were perfect, I'd pass the K-9 exams."

Granny shook her head. "That's not the point. Stop worrying about the exams. It's okay to try, and to train, and to learn. But try to be the best Nova you can be. Don't worry about comparing yourself to anyone else."

Nova sat up a little straighter.

BE THE BEST NOVA I CAN BE. I LIKE THAT!

Granny Goldenfur patted her on the head. "Now, that's the Goldenfur spirit!"

Nova stood up. "Look out, Barksdale! I am going to try, and train, and study more than any pup you've ever seen!"

"That's not exactly what I meant," Granny said, but Nova had already bounded out the door.

CHAPTER 6

B-O-R-I-N-G

"**G**OOD MORNING!"

Nova ran up to Harley, Duke, and Peanut, wagging her tail.

Whap! Her tail wagged so hard that it knocked over Peanut.

Nova skidded to a stop. "Whoops! Sorry, Peanut!"

"No problem," he said, jumping back on his feet. "Your tail is soft and fluffy."

The four friends talked as they walked to school. A little fly buzzed around them. *Buzzzzzzzz . . .*

"Glad to see you're in a good mood," Duke said. "You looked kinda sad when we left the park yesterday."

"I was, but I'm not anymore!" she replied. "I'm on a mission. A mission to become the best Nova that I can be. And since we're a team, maybe you pups want to be the best Harley, the best Peanut, and the best Duke that you can be?"

"I honestly don't see how I can get any better," Peanut said.

"It's a cool idea, Nova, but—" Harley stopped talking, distracted by the fly.

Buzzz . . .

"What would we have to do?" Duke asked.

"Try, train, and study more than we ever have before," Nova replied. "I already started. This morning, I ran ten laps around the block before breakfast!"

Duke frowned. "I don't know. That sounds kind of hard."

"I need my beauty sleep," Peanut added.

Harley snapped back to attention. "I think an early morning run sounds great! That's when most of the birds are hopping around. And—**GOTCHA**!"

Harley jumped up, caught the fly in her mouth, and gulped it down.

Peanut stuck out his tongue. "Ew, Harley. That's gross! Why would you eat that?"

"Why wouldn't I? Sky raisins are delicious," Harley informed him.

"Sky raisins?" Peanut asked.

"Yeah, those tasty treats that fly around. That's what Pop calls them, anyway," she replied.

Duke whispered to Peanut, "Should we tell her?"

Peanut shook his head. "Nah. I'd hate to ruin her fun."

The four friends had reached the school.

"Anyway, you don't have to go on a run like I did," Nova said. "The whole idea is to just try to be your best. We can all do that in our first class this morning."

Peanut frowned. "History of Barksdale! But that class is so boring."

History of Barksdale was taught by Ms. Finella Finefur, the principal of Barksdale Academy. She knew every single detail of Barksdale's history and loved to talk about it. And talk, and talk, and talk . . .

"I know it's boring, but we can all try to pay attention better," Nova said.

Harley nodded. "Sure, Nova. I can pay—ooh, look! Another sky raisin!"

Nova, Harley, Peanut, and Duke entered the school. Most students were hurrying through the halls, trying to get to class before the bell rang. Other students were still hanging around the lockers, chatting. A small group of pups had gathered around Mandy and Randy, as always.

"Good morning, Underdogs!" Mandy called out as the four friends walked past.

"Yeah, Underdogs!" Randy echoed.

Peanut stopped. "Hey, Randy. What's over there?" he asked, pointing.

Randy turned his head. "Where?"

"Ha!" Peanut laughed. "Made you look!"

Mandy rolled her eyes. "Very funny," she said in a voice that meant she didn't think it was funny at all.

"Why, thank you," Peanut replied.

Duke put a paw on his friend's shoulder. "Come on, Peanut. We've got to get to class."

"You're right! We're gonna be late!" Nova cried, and she raced forward. She zoomed down the main hall, made a right at the gym, and jumped through the doorway of room B-3.

As she sailed through the air, she realized she was probably going to crash into her desk. And crashing into desks was *not* doing her best.

Nova veered to the right and skidded to a stop along the floor just in time. She let out a big sigh of relief.

Crash averted! she thought, and then she gave herself a pup talk. *Keep it up, Nova. Keep being your best!*

EMERGENCY!

The other students entered the classroom. Besides Harley, Duke, and Peanut, Athena, Randy, and Mandy were also in the class. So was Nova's friend Ollie. He rolled into class using the wheels strapped to his back legs. He spun in a circle and then slid up to the desk next to Nova.

The bell rang, and Principal Finefur trotted in. She was smaller than most of her students, with long, straight fur cascading down her sides. It brushed against the floor as she walked. She stood in front of the classroom and adjusted her eyeglasses with her paw.

"Good morning, students!" she greeted them.

"GOOD MORNING, PRINCIPAL FINEFUR!"

"I have an exciting lecture planned for you this morning," the principal continued. "As we learned yesterday, there are 317 different streets in Barksdale. Each one of them has a different name. How did they get those names? I am about to tell you. First, Main Street. It used to be called Weimaraner Road, but nobody could ever get the spelling right. So, the town held a meeting . . ."

Nova tried to pay attention. She really did. But Peanut was right. Principal Finefur's lectures could be B-O-R-I-N-G.

By the time Principal Finefur got to talking about Terrier Terrace, Peanut tossed something at Nova. She looked to see a folded-up note on her desk. She opened it.

Nova wanted to laugh, but she held it in. She needed to focus so she could do her best in class. *Is everyone else having trouble focusing, too?* she wondered.

She turned and looked at Duke. He was asleep, and drool dripped from his mouth. *Drip . . . drip . . . drip . . .*

Next to Duke, Harley was staring at the open window. A squirrel nibbled on a nut in a nearby tree, and Harley's whiskers twitched.

Nova sniffed the air coming through the window and smelled . . . roses. *The rose bush by the front pathway must have bloomed this morning,* she thought.

She sniffed again and smelled . . . a mouse. *It's definitely a mouse looking through the garbage can outside. A combination of fur and stale cheese.*

She sniffed a third time and smelled something farther away . . . smoke. *Wood smoke,* she thought. *Coming from Main Street . . . like something is on fire!*

EMERGENCY! EMERGENCY! THERE'S A FIRE ON MAIN STREET!

BAM! She jumped over her desk, knocking it over. She bolted for the classroom door.

BAM! She toppled the books on Athena's desk and tipped over the wastebasket. Then she raced through the halls toward the front entrance.

BAM! She knocked over a mop bucket, and the water sloshed all over the floor.

BAM! She bumped into Coach Houndstooth, who was carrying a bag to the gym. He dropped it, and the balls inside spilled out and rolled everywhere.

Nova charged through the door and ran to Main Street, jumping over bushes and rocks and fire hydrants to get there as fast as she could. She could see plumes of gray smoke in the blue sky the closer she got. She followed her nose to the source of the smell, and stopped in front of Chef Wolfgang's Bistro. The chef was outside.

"Chef Wolfgang!" Nova cried, racing up to him. "Your restaurant's on fire!"

Chef Wolfgang smiled. "Oh, Nova, don't worry. The bistro isn't on fire. I just installed a brand-new outdoor pizza oven and fired it up. Let me show you."

CHEF WOLFGANG'S
BISTRO

Nova followed him to the side of the building, where wood burned in a brick oven. Smoke floated out of the oven's chimney and into the sky. Nova's mouth opened, and she stared at it.

"I . . . I'm glad your restaurant's not on fire," she finally said.

"Thanks for trying to warn me," Chef Wolfgang said. "Now, shouldn't you be in school?"

School! Nova thought, and her race to the bistro came back to her. The knocked-over books, and trash, and mop water, and balls . . .

Nova sighed. "Yes, I'd better get back."

"Come back later for a free slice of pizza!" Chef Wolfgang called after her as she ran.

When Nova returned to Barksdale Academy, Principal Finefur and the rest of her classmates were in front of the school.

"Nova, is everything all right?" the principal asked.

Nova nodded. "Yup," she said. "Turns out it was just Chef Wolfgang's new pizza oven."

Some of the pups started to giggle.

"You ran out of hcrc for a pizza emergency?" Mandy asked. "What was the matter? Not enough cheese?"

Randy snorted. "Yeah, not enough cheese?"

Nova's eyes filled with tears, and she ran into the building.

What good is being the best Nova I can be if that just means I'm the best at making a mess?

CHAPTER 8

R-R-R-READY OR NOT!

"All right, pups! Five laps around the track!" Coach Houndstooth barked.

Ace Swiftrunner led the pack. Ace was the fastest dog in the school and the best at everything he tried. He was especially good at being nice. When everyone else had made fun of the Underdogs, Ace hadn't joined in. Instead, he had become their friend.

73

Behind Ace was Ollie, zipping along on his wheels. Ollie had moved to Barksdale a year ago. Ace and Ollie had quickly become besties, maybe because Ollie was good at everything, too.

The rest of the students jogged along at their own speed. And all the way at the back of the pack, Nova moped along.

Mandy and Randy hung back until she caught up.

"Hey, Nova, I hear there's a **HAMBURGER EMERGENCY** in town," Mandy teased.

Nova sighed. "Very funny, Mandy."

"And I heard there was a flood emergency, too," Randy added.

Mandy frowned at her brother. "That's not how it works. It has to be food or it's not funny."

"Uh, okay," Randy said. "Nova, I hear there's a **BANANA EMERGENCY**."

Mandy shrugged. "Better. Anyway, Nova, you'd better be careful running laps in case you knock something over!"

Harley, Duke, and Peanut jogged back to Nova. **"LEAVE NOVA ALONE, MANDY AND RANDY!"** Harley said. "She was just trying to be helpful."

Peanut nodded. "Yeah, she can't help it if she knocked over a desk, and the garbage, and books, and a bucket of water, and—"

Duke nudged his friend. "You're not helping, little dude."

Mandy and Randy raised their snouts in the air.

"Good luck, Underdogs!" Mandy said as they jogged away.

"Yeah, you'll need it!" Randy added.

After everyone ran their laps, they gathered in front of Coach Houndstooth.

"Today, I've got some tips for you for the agility course," he began. "I know for some of you the course will be r-r-r-ruff, but today I'll show you how to get r-r-r-ready! Ace, come on up here and help me demonstrate."

The spotted dog bounded over to Coach Houndstooth. "Ready, Coach!"

"Ace, weave through those orange cones," Coach ordered. He started his stopwatch.

Ace sprang into action, weaving through a line of orange cones set up on the athletic field behind the school.

Harley leaned toward Nova. "I can do that, too," she whispered, and then her eyes fixed on a stand of trees on the side of the field. "I'm just as fast as— **SQUIRREL**!" And she raced away.

"Notice how Ace gets power from his back legs, but changes direction with his front legs," Coach Houndstooth pointed out. "Ace, the r-r-r-ramp!"

The athletic dog raced to the ramp and reached the top in one swift move, then jumped down the other side.

Duke shivered. "That ramp is so high!"

"Once again, Ace is getting his power from his back legs," Coach Houndstooth explained. "Next, the hoop!"

Ace sailed through the hoop, landing gracefully on his four feet.

"Notice how he's controlling his muscles, even when he's midair," Coach Houndstooth said. "That's the key to keeping your balance. Great job, Ace!"

Nova sighed. "He's amazing. I don't think I could ever make a smooth landing like that."

Ace trotted back to Coach Houndstooth.

"Look how muddy his paws are after that!" Peanut sniffed. "Why does agility training have to be so messy?"

"To help prep for your agility exam, let's work on strengthening those back legs," Coach announced. "Line up and give me some squats!"

Nova watched her friends as they lined up for the exercise and thought about the last few days.

Maybe my friends are right, she thought. *What's the point of training for the agility exam if we're not cut out for it? I can't run without crashing into everything. Harley loses concentration every time she sees a squirrel. Duke is afraid of heights. And Peanut won't do anything that's too messy. Unless there's some way to fix all this . . .*

Maybe there is*!*

After school, Nova spoke to Harley, Duke, and Peanut. "Are you pups ready for another training session with me?" she asked.

"Sure, Nova!" Harley replied.

"If it makes you happy," Duke said.

"Not really," Peanut answered, and Duke growled at him. "I mean, sure!"

Nova ran around them, excited. "Great! Because I think I know how to solve all our problems!"

CHAPTER 9

FOCUS, HARLEY!

"One . . . two . . . three . . ."

Nova counted as she slowly walked across her backyard the next day. Granny Goldenfur was digging in the garden when she noticed Nova walk by.

"Nova, why is there a plate of biscuits on your head?" Granny asked.

"I'm practicing," Nova replied. "I can't do my best in the agility exam because I'm always crashing into things. I need to learn how to control my movements. Four . . . five . . . six . . ."

Granny nodded. "I suppose that's one way to do it," she said. "But I like the way you move. You're fast, and you're always smiling, and you look like you're having fun."

"Usually I am," Nova said. "But having fun is not going to help me pass the K-1 agility test. Seven . . . eight . . . nine . . ."

"Maybe not," Granny agreed. "But you know what I always say. I'd rather have a good time than be on time."

"What does that have to do with me?" Nova asked. "Ten . . . eleven . . . whoa!"

Nova tripped on Granny's rake. The plate of biscuits flew off her head. Biscuits rained down everywhere. Granny jumped and gulped one down. She caught the rest in her paws.

"I make a mess out of everything!" Nova cried, flopping down on the grass.

"No use crying over spilled biscuits," Granny said, and she handed Nova one. "Now, would you like to help me plant these daisies?"

"I wish I could, but I've got to meet my friends in the park," Nova told her. **"SEE YOU LATER, GRANNY!"**

Nova grabbed her backpack and ran off.

Maybe my practice didn't turn out so great, she thought. *But wait until my friends see what I've got planned for them!*

Harley, Duke, and Peanut were waiting for Nova when she arrived.

"We set up the course, just like you asked," Harley said, nodding toward the milk jugs, the ramp, and the hoop. "Should we head to the starting line?"

Nova shook her shaggy head. "Nope. New plan today. We're going to work on making each of us better, one at a time. Harley, you're up first."

"YIPPEE!" Harley cheered, running in a circle. "What do I have to do?"

"Just wait here for now," Nova told her. "Duke and Peanut, follow me."

The two dogs followed Nova behind a bush. She took two furry costumes out of her backpack.

"What's this?" Duke asked.

"I need you two to dress up like squirrels," Nova explained. "So we can help Harley learn how to concentrate."

Duke frowned. "Are you sure that's going to work?"

"I'll do it!" Peanut cried. He slipped the costume on and began to strut back and forth. "I'm a squirrel supermodel—work it!"

Duke sighed and put on his own costume. Peanut took one look at him, dropped to the ground, and began rolling with laughter. "**HA HA HA HA HA HA HA!** Duke the squirrel! This is great!"

Duke's eyes narrowed. "You're wearing the same thing, Peanut."

"I know, but I'm squirrel-sized," Peanut pointed out. "You look like a giant squirrel. Mega Squirrel! Squirrelsaurus! Squirrelzilla!"

Duke chuckled and started stomping his feet.

GIVE ME ALL THE NUTS OR I WILL DESTROY YOUR CITY!

"All right, enough joking around," Nova instructed. "Wait here. I'm going to give Harley a pup talk. When she starts on the course, run out and try to distract her."

Peanut saluted. "Aye, aye, Squirrel Boss!"

Nova rolled her eyes and trotted over to Harley.

"Okay, Harley," she began. "I want you to run the course. There might be some squirrels who will—"

"**SQUIRRELS?** Where?" Harley asked.

"Nowhere—not yet, anyway," Nova continued. "Harley, when you see a—a furry, nut-eating creature—then I want you to focus. When your brain says '**SQUIRREL**,' I want you to think, '**FINISH**.' Got it?"

Harley nodded. "Finish. Finish. Finish. Got it."

"On your bark, get set, **GO**!" Nova yelled.

Harley took off running. She zigzagged through the milk bottles.

"Duke, now!" Nova yelled.

Duke ran out of the bushes. "Nothing to see here but me, a hungry squirrel looking for acorns. I really, really love acorns."

Harley stopped. She looked at Duke.

"Harley, finish!" Nova yelled.

"Finish. Finish. Finish," Harley said, and she kept running.

"Peanut, now!" Nova yelled.

Peanut ran out in front of the ramp. "Look at me! I'm a squirrel with tiny ears and a ridiculously fluffy tail!"

Harley paused on top of the ramp. Her right eye began to twitch.

"Harley, finish!" Nova cried.

Harley ran up the ramp. Peanut moved to the side.

"Peanut, Duke, go to the finish line!" Nova instructed.

Duke and Peanut ran to the finish line as Harley continued the course.

"Finish, Harley!" Nova cheered. "You can do it!"

"Finish. Finish. Finish," Harley chanted as she neared the finish line. Duke and Peanut stood next to each other, right in front of it.

Harley's eye twitched again. Her tail wagged.

"Finish. Finish. **SQUIRREL!**" she shouted, and she lunged after Duke and Peanut. The two dogs raced to get away from her.

"Harley, it's Peanut, your friend!" Peanut cried as Harley snapped at his furry tail. "Your one-hundo-percent canine friend who is NOT a squirrel."

Harley chased Duke and Peanut across the park, and Nova sighed.

"Stop, Harley! We need to keep practicing!" Nova yelled as she ran after her friends.

My plan for Harley didn't work. But I won't give up!

CHAPTER 10

YOU CAN DO IT, DUKE!

Harley caught up to Duke first. She pinned him to the ground.

"Harley, snap out of it. It's me, Duke!" he wailed.

Harley stopped. She sniffed.

"Oh, hi, Duke," she said, jumping off him. "Why are you dressed like a squirrel?"

"It was Nova's idea," he replied, getting to his feet.

Peanut came around, holding the squirrel costume in his mouth. He dropped it on the grass.

"Thanks a lot, Nova," Peanut said. "Harley almost ate us for lunch!"

"I don't *eat* squirrels," Harley corrected him. "I just like to chase them. And catch them. And play with them. And nibble on their furry tails. And . . ." Her eyes glazed over as she thought about it.

"All right, so maybe that wasn't the best idea," Nova admitted. "But you almost had it, Harley. You almost crossed the finish line."

"I guess you're right, Nova," Harley said. "I'll do better next—**SQUIRREL!**"

She raced off to chase a real squirrel. Nova looked at Duke and Peanut.

"Okay, which one of you wants to go next?"

Duke looked down at the ground. Peanut whistled and looked at the sky.

"Come on, it won't be so bad," Nova said. "Follow me to the bleachers. Duke, you're up!"

Duke and Peanut exchanged worried looks, but they followed their friend to the park's athletic field. Metal bleachers, ten rows high, were there for fans to watch Barksdale competitions.

"Duke, we're going to work on your fear of heights," Nova announced.

Duke gulped and looked at the bleachers. "Really?"

"We'll take it slow," Nova promised. "Start by stepping onto the first row of the bleachers."

"Really? Way up there?" Duke asked.

"Dude, that step is as tall as you are," Peanut pointed out.

Duke took a deep breath. "Okay, I got this."

He put one paw on the first row. Then another. Then he hoisted himself up.

"I'm doing it," he said. Then he looked down. "Oh no. I'm getting dizzy!"

"Close your eyes, Duke," Nova urged him. "Take some deep breaths. Then open them again. You'll see that you're not so high up."

Duke closed his eyes and took deep breaths. He opened them.

"Okay," he said. "This isn't so bad. The ground isn't too far below me. And you and Peanut are right there."

"We sure are, buddy!" Peanut said.

Nova wagged her tail. "Great job, Duke! Now climb up to the next row."

Duke eyed the second row. "Hmm. Maybe we could, you know, take this even more slowly? I could come back tomorrow and start fresh."

Nova didn't want her friend to give up. "Give it a try now. You can do it, Duke!"

"Go, Duke!" Peanut cheered.

Duke slowly climbed up to the second row. He closed his eyes. He took some deep breaths. "Hey, this isn't so bad," he said.

Nova smiled. "See? I told you. Now, go to the third row."

Duke stepped onto the third row of the bleachers. He closed his eyes. He took some deep breaths. While he did that, a little bird flew onto the bleachers next to him. Duke opened his eyes.

"Okay, I'm—wait, what's this bird doing here?! I must be flying in the sky! I'm too high. **TOO HIGH!**"

"It's okay, Duke!" Nova cried. "You're not very high at all. The bird just flew *down* from the sky."

Suddenly, the bird flapped its wings. Duke panicked and ran down the bleachers. He flopped onto the ground, landing right on top of Peanut.

"Sorry, little dude," Duke said.

"That's okay," Peanut replied, squeezing out from under him. "I've always wondered what it felt like to be a pancake."

Harley ran up. "What did I miss?"

Nova focused on the positive. "Duke climbed up to the third row of the bleachers! It was awesome."

"Yeah, until he saw a bird and thought he was high in the sky and freaked out," Peanut muttered.

Nova spun around. "Good news, Peanut. It's your turn next! I think you're going to love what I have planned."

Peanut shook his head. "Oh noooo, Nova. Whatever you've got in mind, I am not going to do it!"

CHAPTER 11

JUMP IN, PEANUT!

"If I had to climb into the sky, then you have to do your thing, Peanut," Duke said as they followed Nova across the park.

"I'm not making any promises," Peanut replied. "I have a feeling that what Nova has planned for me is much worse."

Nova led them to the park caretaker's shed, where Athena was waiting for them. She was holding a hose and soaking a patch of dirt with water.

Harley's ears twitched with excitement. "Ooh, I love a good mud puddle!"

Athena stopped the hose. "I think it's at just the right consistency, Nova. Wet enough to splash around in, but not so wet that the mud won't stick to your fur."

Nova grinned. "Excellent!"

Peanut began to slowly back away.

"You don't have to jump in right away, Peanut," Nova explained. "But I thought if you saw how much fun getting messy was, you might change your mind. Now I'll just jump in and—"

Harley leapt in the air and landed in the mud puddle first. Mud splashed out, and Peanut took another step back.

WHEEEE!

"You don't know what you're missing, Peanut!" Harley called out. "This mud is super squishy and just the right temperature. It's awesome!"

Peanut shook his head. "No, thank you."

Duke stepped into the puddle and started to stomp around. "Just stick your feet in, little dude. It's fun."

"Thanks, but no thanks," Peanut replied.

Nova jumped in next. She rolled around in the mud, then got back on her feet and shook her fur, sending mud particles flying everywhere.

"It feels great, Peanut!" Nova said. "And when you're all done, you just wash off and you're clean again."

But Peanut did not budge. "No to the one hundredth power, no!"

Nova sighed. "I don't understand, Peanut. Why won't you just give it a try? Don't you want us to pass the agility exam?"

"There's got to be some other way!" Peanut insisted. "I do **NOT** like being messy."

Then the little dog ran away.

"Peanut, it's okay! Come back!" Nova called out.

Nova, Harley, and Duke sat in the mud puddle sadly. After a moment, Nova climbed out.

"Please hose me off, Athena," she said.

"Sure," Athena replied, and she began to spray Nova with water. "Poor Peanut. It's a shame the school isn't more agile when it comes to the agility exam."

"What do you mean?" Nova asked.

"Well, 'agility' means to move quickly and easily. It means you can change direction when you're running without slowing down. Maybe it's time the test changed direction so that more of us would be better at it," Athena explained.

Duke walked out of the puddle. "You mean you have trouble with the test, too?"

"Sure," Athena replied. "I get caught up in my head, thinking about the best way to approach the ramp with maximum speed. But that ends up costing me time. I never finish fast enough."

"Hmm," Nova said thoughtfully. "The school isn't going to change the test. And we can't change ourselves for the test. Unless . . . "

I'VE GOT IT!!

Duke frowned. "Um, Nova, none of your ideas today really worked."

Nova shook her head. "No, this is different. Wash up, and then go find Peanut. I know what we need to do!"

CHAPTER 12

THE K-1 EXAM

"**W**elcome to the K-1 Exams for our fourth-year pupils!" Principal Finefur announced.

The students of Barksdale Academy clapped and cheered. The three younger classes had all finished their K-1 exams, and now it was time for Nova, Harley, Peanut, and Duke to compete. They waited in front of the bleachers on the school's agility field.

"This is it," Nova said, taking a deep breath. "It's now or never."

"You'll be competing in teams of four," the principal continued. She and Coach Houndstooth sat behind the judges' table at the end of the obstacle course. "One at a time, each member of the team will go through the course. You'll be judged on total speed,

and your ability to get through the course without knocking over any obstacles."

Mandy and Randy were sitting behind Nova. "Guess that means Nova will never pass the test," Mandy said loud enough for Nova to hear. Nova ignored her.

Coach Houndstooth took the microphone from Principal Finefur. "First up is a team that contains some of the school's best athletes. They call themselves Team Awesome. Come on up, Ace, Ollie, Mandy, and Randy."

"That's a cool name," Harley whispered to Nova. "Kinda better than Team Comeback, don't you think?"

"It's okay," Nova whispered back. "I thought of an even better one."

The four dogs in Team Awesome climbed down from the bleachers and lined up behind the starting line of the agility course.

"R-r-r-ready, Team Awesome?" Coach Hound-stooth asked.

"Ready, Coach!" they replied.

THEN ON YOUR BARK, GET SET, GO!

Randy took off first for the team. He wove through the cones, climbed up and down the ramp, jumped through the hoop, ran through more cones, and then pulled a rope to ring a bell at the end of the course.

That was the signal for the next teammate, Mandy. She completed the course perfectly. So did Ollie, who came next. Ace took off last, and he ran through the course so fast that he became a blur of spotted fur.

"Excellent time!" Coach Houndstooth congratulated them. "A school record. And flawless execution."

Principal Finefur flipped the scorecard for their team: **100!**

Nova's tail twitched nervously. *I guess we know which team will win Best in Show,* she thought. *I'm pretty sure my plan will work. But what if it doesn't?*

Three more teams went through the course. Some dogs knocked over cones. Athena and some other dogs were slow. One pup even tripped going through the hoop. But the teams all got good scores: 83, 95, 87.

"How many points does our team need to pass?" Duke asked.

"Sixty-five," Nova replied.

Duke's eyes got wide. "But we've never gotten more than ten points before!"

Nova's tail began to twitch nervously again. "I know."

"Next up, we've got a team that calls itself Team Underdog," Coach Houndstooth announced. "Come on down, Nova, Harley, Duke, and Peanut."

"Nova, why did you call us Team Underdog?" Duke asked as they made their way to the field. "I thought you didn't like it when Mandy and Randy called us that."

"I know," Nova said. "But I realized it shouldn't bother me. We *are* underdogs. And we're going to be the best underdogs we can be, right?"

Harley grinned at Nova. "You can count on me."

"I'm an underdog, and proud of it!" Peanut added. "Now come on, gang. **LET'S DO THIS!**"

They made their way to the starting line. First Duke, then Peanut, then Harley, and finally Nova. Nova's left front leg bounced up and down nervously.

"Ready, Underdogs?" Coach Houndstooth asked.

"READY!" they replied.

"On your bark, get set, go!"

Duke took off first. He swiftly wove back and forth through the cones. When he got to the ramp, he ran right around it!

The dogs in the bleachers reacted with surprise. Principal Finefur frowned.

"What's he doing? He can't just skip it!"

But that's exactly what Duke did. He jumped through the hoop, ran through more cones, and rang the bell.

Peanut took off next. Everyone in the bleachers gasped.

"What's he wearing?"

In fact, Peanut was wearing a plastic suit that covered him from the tops of his ears to the tip of his tail. Granny Goldenfur had made it for him. The little dog trotted along the course, moving slowly and making squeaky noises as he moved. Principal Finefur frowned again. But Peanut finished!

Ring! The bell rang, and Harley took off. Nova looked to the bleachers. Ace ran out, just like she had asked him to, holding a stick with a stuffed squirrel dangling from it. He ran in front of Harley as she made her way through the course.

"SQUIRREL!" Harley yelled, and she moved faster than Nova had ever seen her. She was right on Ace's heels! Principal Finefur frowned and shook her head.

Ring! Nova launched from the starting line.

Don't knock anything over! Don't knock anything over! she told herself.

And she didn't. She weaved through the cones. She climbed up and down the ramp. She gracefully sailed through the hoop.

"Go, Nova!" Athena cheered from the stands, and some of the dogs began to clap.

Joy filled Nova as she ran through the last line of cones.

"**I DID IT!**" she yelled, and then she jumped up to ring the bell . . .

. . . and soared right past it, landing on the judges' table!

The table knocked over with a clatter. The score-cards toppled to the ground. Principal Finefur and Coach Houndstooth jumped out of the way.

Nova landed. The joy left her. She deflated like a popped balloon.

Oh no! I've ruined everything!

CHAPTER 13

THE FINAL SCORE

Some dogs in the bleachers started laughing. Principal Finefur and Coach Houndstooth picked up the judges' table. Nova moved to help them.

"No, that's okay," Couch Houndstooth told her with a kind smile. "We've got this. Wouldn't want you knocking ever-r-r-ything over again!"

Harley, Duke, and Peanut gathered around Nova.

"It's okay, Nova," Duke said, putting his paw on her shoulder. "You did great."

"Yeah, really great!" Peanut agreed. "Until you crashed."

"I'm sorry, pups," Nova said with a sigh. "We'll never pass now."

Harley shrugged. "That's okay. We've never passed an exam before!"

Principal Finefur faced them.

"That was quite the performance," she said. "I had to take points off for refusal to climb the ramp. Points off for unauthorized clothing. Points off for not ringing the bell. Points off for destruction of school property."

Nova hung her head.

"But . . ." the principal continued, "all of you finished the course. Your time was not bad. And you received some extra points for creative problem-solving. Here is your final score."

She flipped the scorecard: 66.

The four friends stared at the card, frozen, with their mouths opened.

"We . . . we passed!" Peanut said.

They hugged one another and began to jump up and down.

Principal Finefur cleared her throat. "Very nice, Underdogs. Now please return to the bleachers."

Nova, Harley, Duke, and Peanut ran back to the bleachers and sat down.

"What are you all so happy for?" Mandy asked.

"Yeah, what?" Randy added. "You got a terrible score."

Peanut hopped up between them. "Listen up, you two. We're happy because we passed. And we did it *our* way!"

Then he climbed back down and sat next to Duke. The four friends cheered on the students in the other classes. Then Coach Houndstooth and Principal Finefur stepped out from behind the table and faced the students. Couch Houndstooth held a trophy.

"And now it's time to present the award for Best in Agility for the K-1 Challenge," he announced. "While fourth-year student Ace Swiftrunner did have the fastest individual time, we had to deduct points for his interference with another challenge."

Nova looked over at Ace. He'd been so nice to help them, but that had cost him the trophy. He shrugged and smiled at her.

"So, the trophy goes to . . . Ollie Woofur!"

Everyone clapped and cheered as Ollie rolled out to accept his award.

"Very well done, everyone," Principal Finefur congratulated. "Our next challenge will be in three weeks. Now, go enjoy some pizza, courtesy of Chef Wolfgang!"

The students all climbed down from the bleachers. Nova, Harley, Duke, and Peanut walked toward the pizza table.

Athena trotted up. "Great job, Underdogs!"

"Yeah, Underdogs, congrats!" Ollie said as he rolled past them.

Nova grinned. "I guess our name is going to stick with us," she said. "Now the Underdogs just need a plan to pass the K-2 exams . . ."

"Can't we just enjoy our victory for a little while?" Harley asked.

Nova nodded. "You're right," she said. "Who's ready to celebrate?" Nova cheered. She jumped up, pumping one paw in the air. Then she started to fall backward . . . onto the pizza table.

Duke, Harley, and Peanut grabbed her and pulled her back before she crashed into the table.

"Thanks for saving me. I don't think I'll ever be Best in Show," Nova said, but then a Granny Goldenfur–like thought popped into her head. "But you know what's better than Best in Show? Best friends like you!"

Nova held out her paw. "How about a team cheer?" Harley, Duke, Peanut, and Nova touched their paws together.

TRACEY WEST has written more than 300 books for kids, including the *New York Times*-bestselling Dragon Masters series for Scholastic Branches. The canine companions Tracey has known during her life have all served as inspiration for the Underdogs. She currently lives in New York state with her husband and four adopted dogs.

KyLa May is an Australian illustrator, writer, and designer. She is the creator and illustrator of the Diary of a Pug and Lotus Lane book series and illustrator of *The Sloth Life: Dream On*. Kyla has also contributed her imagination and talent to six animated TV series, as well as toys and gifts for children of all ages. Kyla lives by the beach in Victoria, Australia, with her three daughters, three dogs, and two cats.

Keep reading for a sneak peek at

We're Not the Champions, the next book starring

Chapter 1
SCAREDY-DOG

Duke the bulldog panted in the warm afternoon sunshine. He watched his friend Nova walk to the end of the diving board.

"I call this move the Butterfly!" she announced, jumping up and down.

She bounced off. **BOING!** She launched into the air, flapping her arms.

Whoa, that looks scary! Duke thought.

SPLASH! Nova landed in the lake. Water droplets shot up as she hit the water. Then she swam to shore and climbed onto the grass, shaking her golden-yellow fur.

"Be careful, Nova!" cried Peanut. The little dog was stretched out on a beach towel next to Duke. "I don't want to get my fur wet!"

"You don't know what you're missing!" Nova replied, and she shook her head again, hitting Peanut with one last sprinkle of water.

"Aaaargh!" Peanut cried.

Duke laughed. "It's just water, Peanut."

"Oh yeah?" Peanut asked. "Why don't you jump in, then?"

Duke frowned. Peanut knew why Duke wouldn't jump in. He wasn't afraid of water. But heights—yikes!

"Hey, look at me!" Harley called from the diving board. "I call this one the Flipperoo!"

Harley launched off the board using her short, powerful legs. She somersaulted in the air.

SPLASH! She slammed into the water. Then her head popped up.

"What do you think of that one?" she asked as she doggy-paddled to the shore.

"I liked it," Nova replied, and she bounded toward the diving board. "I want to try it!"

Harley shook the water off her fur, and Peanut frowned.

"I keep getting wet!" he complained.

"Well, maybe you shouldn't have come to the lake, then," Duke teased.

Peanut leaned back and slid his sunglasses over his eyes. "It's Saturday! Lake Barksdale is the place to be."

Duke gazed around. Sunlight glittered on the dark blue surface of the lake. On one side was a sandy beach, and on the other side, a grassy meadow. Dogs swam in the water, dug in the sand, played volleyball on the shore, and snacked at picnic tables. The welcome sign informed visitors that Lake Barksdale was:

THE BEST LAKE FOR SWIMMING!
THE BEST LAKE FOR PICNICKING!
THE BEST LAKE FOR HAVING FUN!

Typical, Duke thought. *Everyone and everything*

in Barksdale wants to be the best. And everyone and everything in Barksdale is *the best. Everyone except us.*

Duke, Peanut, Nova, and Harley were four friends known as the Underdogs. They weren't the best at anything. Except, maybe, at being themselves. And that was just fine with Duke.

Nova tried to somersault off the diving board. But instead of curling her body into a ball, like Harley had, her legs spread out in all different directions. She landed on the water with a **SPLAT** instead of a **SPLASH!**

She ran out of the water, laughing. "I'm going to need some practice," she said. "Hey, Duke, you wanna try the diving board?"

"I think I'll just get my feet wet," Duke replied.

"Aw, come on, it's not even that high," Nova urged.

Duke didn't answer right away. Nova had recently tried to help him get over his fear of heights—one of the many things he was afraid of. It hadn't worked, but Duke had been proud of himself for trying.

"*Weeellllll*," he said slowly, "it *is* hot. And jumping in would cool me down."

Harley pulled Duke off his blanket. "You don't have to do anything fancy. I'll give you a push if you want."

"No, you definitely don't have to push me," Duke said, suddenly feeling nervous. But he followed Harley and Nova up to the diving board on the end of the dock.

Harley took off. **"THE ROCKET!"** she yelled. She bounced on the end of the board once . . . twice . . . and the third time, she shot straight up into the air. Then she landed in the water feetfirst, with her arms down at her sides.

Nova giggled. **"THE JELLYFISH!"** Nova called out, charging off the board. She wiggled her legs in a silly way as she sailed across the water.

The two pups paddled in the water, waiting for Duke.

"Come on, Duke!" Nova shouted.

"You can do it!" Harley yelled.

Duke slowly walked to the edge of the board. He looked down into the deep lake. His heart began to beat fast, and he froze.

"Nope," he said. "Just nope. I thought I could do it, but I can't."

"That's okay, Duke!" Nova told him.

Duke slowly backed up off the board—and bumped into something furry.

He turned around to see two twin dogs with floppy ears—Mandy and Randy Fetcherton.

"What's the matter, Duke? Scared?" Mandy asked.

Randy pointed. "He's a scaredy-dog!"

They started laughing, and some of the other dogs on the beach joined in.

"SCAREDY-DOG! SCAREDY-DOG!"

Married to the Money

by

INDIA

Novels by India

Dope, Death and Deception

Still Deceiving
(the sequel to *Dope, Death and Deception*)

The Real Hoodwives of Detroit

The Real Hoodwives of Detroit 2

Gangstress

Gangstress 2

Detroit City Mafia

Coming Soon

The Rich Wives Association

This book is dedicated to my mom, Brenda. Although I've said thank you a million times, it never seems like enough. You've had my back since birth, and you're still holding your baby girl down. I owe you my all and would give you the world if I could. I've watched you hurt, worry, struggle, hustle, and overcome life's obstacles. No matter what you're going through in your own life, you're always available when I need you. Words can't describe how much I appreciate all the lessons you've taught me. You're the best and I'm very grateful for you! Mom, you inspire me. It's because of you I know the true meaning of an independent woman.

Acknowledgments

Let me start by saying to God be the glory! From the bottom of my heart, I want to thank each and every last person who supported me. Without you all, there would be no me and that's for real. I would especially like to thank those who went extra hard for team India as well as my family and friends. I'm overwhelmed by the love and support you all have shown me during my journey. It's because of you my books exist. Had I not received those encouraging words and well-wishes, I never would have penned my first novel. Now I'm several years in the game and your support is still relentless. God gave me something special when He gave me all of you. Michael Jr., A'yanna, Brenda, Lacy, La'mari, Jason, Cassandra, Michael Sr., Jesse, Tia, Mama Ping, Darielle, Dejuan, Joe, Uncle Rob, Auntie Bunny, Auntie Erica, Auntie Nita, Grandma Arcola, Ariel, Destiny, Alicia, Toya, Auntie Nae, Anjela Day, Michele Moore, N'Tyse, Ms. Diane, Robert, and a host of others. If I forgot you, please blame it on my mind and not my heart.

Love Always,
India

P.S. If you have a dream, go after it. You never know what you're capable of, and you might end up surprising yourself. Your vision may not always go as planned, but never give up. The only thing that beats a failure is the fact that you tried. People may not always agree with or like what you do. Remember you cannot please everyone. As long as you stay true to yourself and trust in God, you will prevail. A few people counted against me and said my dreams wouldn't come true. The nonbelievers said I wouldn't do it, couldn't do it, and shouldn't do it. I could have let the negativity hurt my feelings. However, by belief, I knew I could do it. With faith, I knew I would do, and with God I did it! So can you. Now let the church say amen.

Preface

Money is a motherfucker. It's good for changing lives and the people who live them. Some are changed for better, others for worse, but they are changed nonetheless. Money turns close friends into fast enemies and almost always buys you false admirers. I'm sure you already know the ones who smile in your face but really couldn't care less about you. Money messes with your mind and is known for making people do some crazy shit. It's funny, because people will give up everything for a chance to "have it all." Now what sense does that make? Hell, some people will sell their souls and their mamas, too, for a chance to taste the good life. Through my pain and tears, I must admit I was one of those people.

Greed is a sin, and I was guilty of it. Not only did I lose the most important people in my life, I also threw away my blossoming career as well as my identity. On the road to riches I lost myself, my morals, and my common sense. I let a man change me in the worst way. It's sad that I didn't do it because I loved him, but because I loved what he could do for me. People say money is the root of all evil. I just had no idea. Maybe I was too busy popping tags to pay attention. However, now that I look back on it, there is no fur coat, diamond necklace, luxury car, mega house, or dollar amount worth the price of my life, which is ultimately what I paid to live the glamorous life.

My name is Chanel Franklin, and this is my story.

Chapter One

I woke up this morning feeling like money. The pink silk sheets felt great against my naked skin. I turned toward the clock and noticed it was 8:00 a.m. I smiled because it was my twenty-seventh birthday, and I knew the day would be fabulous. As I rose from the bed and headed toward the bathroom, my phone rang.

"Hello." I was smiling as I stared at the sexy face on my call screen.

"Happy birthday, Ms. Jackson," My fiancé, Dominic, teased in his usual husky tone.

I rolled my eyes because this asshole knew I hated my old last name of Jackson. At birth, I was named Chanel Erica Jackson, but I had changed it a few years ago to Chanel Erica Franklin . . . because I was married to the Benjamins! Yes. You heard me right. Money was my reason for breathing and the motive behind everything I did. Therefore, it was only fitting to be named after a Franklin instead of a punk-ass Jackson, whose worth was only $20. Shit, truth be told, Jacksons couldn't do nothing for me except fill up my gas tank.

"Dominic, why are you messing with me, and where are you?" I rolled my eyes and pressed the speakerphone button. He should've been right here when I woke up, to cater to my every need. Hell, on my birthday I expected him to do everything for me, right down to wiping my ass if I asked him to.

If you think I was high maintenance, you're right. I was a 26—excuse me—27-year-old woman who knew what she wanted. I went after the finer things in life, and that was a fact. I was looking for Prince Charming because I wanted it all. Now I ain't saying I was a gold digger, but I wasn't messing with no broke nigga, and you can believe that.

"I had to go into the office early, baby. My bad," Dominic answered. He sounded really sorry, but I didn't care. My damn birthday was a national holiday in my house. He should've taken the day off like I'd told him to do in the first place. Sometimes his ass made me sick because he was so selfish.

"Are you being serious right now?" I smacked my lips and leaned down to run hot bathwater into the soaker tub. "I thought you were taking the day off to be with me," I whined. This was something I often did when I didn't get my way.

"I would if I could, but I can't because I need my job and we need the money. Don't forget we have a wedding to plan and the bills that come with it," he reminded me.

"Whatever. One damn day off would not have put a dent in your paycheck." I was pissed. I was sure he knew it when I hung up. If he didn't have time for me on my birthday, I didn't have time to finish the conversation.

Just as I was starting to brush my teeth, I was startled by a presence in the doorway.

"Damn, is that how you do me when you don't get your way?" Dominic walked into the bathroom and stared at me through the mirror on the medicine cabinet. I didn't say anything to him, just continued to brush my teeth. Wrapping his muscular chocolate arms around my small waist, he squeezed me lovingly. After leaning down to rinse my toothpaste-covered mouth, I turned around to face him.

"I thought you had to work." Looking up at him with my brown eyes and perfect eyelashes, I batted them for special effect.

"I do, but I wanted to make sure your day started off right." He gave a half-smile that made my panties moist. I wasn't wet because of his smile, although baby boy was fine. I was wet because I knew presents were about to be given.

"Here are your gifts, baby. Happy birthday!"

Pressing my full lips against his, I smiled and ran my hand down his freshly shaven bald head. Then I snatched my gifts.

The first one was inside a burgundy box, and I knew it was jewelry. Removing the lid, I revealed the most beautiful pair of diamond earrings I'd ever been given by anyone. The clarity was perfect, and I knew they cost between $2,000 and $3,000. Next, there was a card, but I didn't bother reading it. The $2,000 spilling from it onto the ceramic tile caught my attention instead.

"See, that's the smile I love to see." Dominic turned me to face the mirror so I could see my reflection.

"Well, keep giving me gifts like these and this smile will never go away." I was half kidding around, but he knew I was also half serious.

"Girl, you're something else, but I love you." He leaned in for another kiss and then walked toward the bathroom door.

I took in the sight before me and bit down on my bottom lip. Dominic was sexy as hell. He was six feet four inches tall, around 245 pounds of solid muscle, and the color of cinnamon toast. His face was that of a model's, and the large tattoo of the word "loyalty" across his broad shoulders was just enough to put the cherry on top.

"I love you more, Dom." I called him Dom for short, and I said I loved him because I honestly did. He was the man of my dreams, and I could barely wait the thirteen months until I would be his wife. We'd been together since college, and nothing could rip us apart. We were a power couple and a force to be reckoned with. I was a senior banker at Greensway Banks, with hopes of putting my degree to better use in the investment banking world. Dominic was a chief account executive at Farris, Mueller and Finch. We lived in a three-bedroom dream home in a gated community in the West Chester area just outside of Cincinnati, Ohio. I drove a fire red Nissan Maxima, and Dom was pushing a triple-black Lexus. Our bank accounts were chunky, and life was grand, although things didn't start out that way.

Dominic Breon Lacey was a kid who was raised in the system after his 16-year-old mother took him back to the hospital forty-eight hours after birth. She left him swaddled up and crying on the nurses' desk, never to be seen or heard from again. Dominic didn't have the best of anything in his youth, which made him hustle hard on the streets of Lima, Ohio as a teenager. He pounded the pavement with pounds of crack cocaine to provide for himself when the system failed to do so. When everybody else tricked their hustle money at the strip club on Fridays, Dom stacked his bread right down to the raggedy pennies, with high hopes for a better tomorrow. After saving what he thought was enough to pay for college tuition, he boarded a Greyhound bus to Cincinnati and never looked back.

I, on the other hand, was a hood chick from the cutthroat streets of Detroit, Michigan. Although both our moms had us at young ages, my story was slightly different because my mother, Porscha, was my girl. She had my sister, Kristian, at 13 and me at 15. Things may not have always been the best for us, but we never went a day without food, clothes, a roof, nor electricity. Porscha did what she had to do, bottom line. We grew up more like friends, and even now most people thought my mom was my sister because of how she looked, dressed, and talked. Our yellow skin tones matched to a T. Her coal black hair was naturally curly like mine, and she still had a body to die for. They say apples don't fall far from the tree, so I thanked the Lord often that my tree was one well put-together motherfucker! To sum it up, my mama was a cold piece of work, and I was proud to walk in her footsteps. Porscha was 42 years old and had never worked a day in her life, yet she drove a 2019 Jaguar. She owned a condo on the riverfront, overlooking the Detroit River/Canada border. My mama also rocked enough jewelry to open up her own pawn shop. She schooled me to the game early, and it was because of her that I could sniff out money like a bloodhound.

Ever since I was a small child, my mama had planted the gold-digger seed in my head. However, I decided to upgrade to platinum status and take a different approach to my life. Instead of waiting around for some nigga to come save me, I chose to somewhat save my damn self. I had big plans for my life, and leaving Detroit was necessary. I wanted to see the world beyond the city limits, but my money only took me as far as Cincinnati. I enrolled in Cincinnati State University and set out on a mission to get rich or die trying.

I wasn't the sharpest kid in class, but I obtained my associate of applied business degree to guarantee consideration of placement in the corporate world. I needed that piece of paper to find my future partner and climb the corporate ladder. Unbeknownst to me, my future partner had been my friend and study buddy since freshman year. Dominic asked me to be his girl, and of course my answer was yes. He was heading places in life, and I was riding shotgun. Years later, here we stood, stronger than ever and destined for great things.

Chapter Two

Much to my disappointment and despite my protests, Dominic headed off to work. Still, I managed to hustle another $500 out of him before he left. Feeling vindicated, I stepped into the tub and began to plan my day. Just as thoughts of Macy's and Saks entered my mind, the cell phone rang again.

"Hello."

"Happy birthday, Chanel. What are we doing today?" my friend Trina asked. Trina was cool, and if I had to say I had a best friend, she'd be it. I was the type of girl who hung around all boys growing up because girls had entirely too much going on. I had never chased a skirt, as my mom would have said. I always followed the money and the boys who had plenty of it. Somehow though, Trina had managed to find a place in my life.

"Girl, I don't know. It's my birthday, so what do you have planned for me?" I pressed the speaker button and lay back in the watermelon-scented bubbles.

"I thought we could go down to Kenwood Mall. You know, do some shopping, have dinner, and hang out."

"Okay, call Noel and it's a date," I said as my line clicked. Shaking my hand dry, I tapped the screen on my phone without saying bye. "Hello."

"Happy birthday, Chanel baby," my mama said in a tone that let me know she was still half asleep.

"Thanks, Mama. What's up?" I smiled, genuinely happy to hear from her.

"Ain't nothin' up. I was just calling to say happy birthday, and now I'm gonna roll my ass over and go back to
sleep," she said as it sounded like she was moving around
in the bed.

"Are you still coming down here this weekend?" She'd
been promising to visit my sister's new home and take
me out for my birthday. Just the thought of Kristian
moving down to Cincinnati from Detroit had really
burned my biscuits. She just couldn't let me shine all by
myself.

"Come down there? For what?" she asked flatly like she
didn't remember.

"Mama, you promised!" I started to whine but was cut
off by her giggle.

"Girl, I know, and I'll be there even though that little wench I created couldn't care less if I showed up,"
Porscha groaned.

"Well, you're not just coming for her. You're coming for
me, and I have this fly spot we could go to get massages,
a mud bath, and the whole nine," I said, using my red
loofah to lather up my body with the wonderful-smelling
suds.

"Are you paying?" she asked, this time a little perkier.

"Damn, Ma, it's my birthday!" I said, not believing her
blatant disrespect of protocol.

"Well, you better call somebody and see what they got
on it. I ain't paying nothing!" she replied. "Don't Dom
have a job? He should be able to treat us, right?"

"You are a trip. I hope you know that." I rested my head
on the pink bath pillow.

"Whatever." She smacked her lips just as my line
clicked yet again.

"Let me answer this, and I'll hit you back, 'kay?" I said
and clicked over before she had a chance to reply. "Hello."
I knew it was another birthday wish, so I didn't check the
caller ID.

"Hey, little sis. Happy b-day," Kristian said in a dry tone.

"Hey, thanks," I replied just as dryly. Don't get me wrong, I loved my sister, but she worked my nerves sometimes. She always went against the grain on everything and thought she was the shit because her husband was a lawyer.

Together they'd moved down here from Detroit about three months ago. Her husband had just started his own practice downtown, and she'd used her business degree to open a secondhand store. I frowned at the thought of her consignment shop. Who in the hell would pay to wear other people's clothes?

Kristian was the total opposite of Mom and me, which irritated the crap out of me. Not to mention how she annoyed me by constantly bragging about married life and motherhood. I kept telling her that I wasn't jealous one bit because I was married too—to the money, that was! I also told her that my future husband and I didn't want any of them dirty little crumb snatchers running around no time soon. Honestly, I lied a bit on that one, because Dom couldn't wait to have children, but he missed the memo that I wasn't the one. I didn't have time to change diapers, wipe runny noses, and clean up vomit. I was too fabulous for a diaper bag, and come hell or high water, Jesus Himself couldn't make me trade in stilettos for flat shoes.

Kristian always called me a high-maintenance gold digger, and I always called her a low-budget hater. She was just as pretty as Mom and I were, but she hid her beauty. She wore her hair in one long French braid, hid her face behind a pair of glasses from the nineties, and wore clothes two sizes too big. I didn't know how her husband Deon even found her attractive, but to each his own, I guessed.

"We should maybe do lunch or something today," Kristian chimed in after a moment of awkward silence.

"Yeah, we should. You pick the place, and I'll be there," I said and closed my eyes to enjoy my bath.

"Let's meet at Applebee's at noon, my treat."

"Make it two. I have a nail appointment." She and boring-ass Applebee's could wait until I was finished.

"You're the b-day girl, so two it is," she gave in.

"For sure. See you later!" I said and hung up, dropping the phone to the side of the tub. I lay there for a minute and ran down my plans again in my head.

Out of nowhere I became horny, so I slid my fingers down into the warm water and reached for my vagina. I was thinking about Dom as I rubbed my clit in circular motions, which caused me to twitch. My nipples were hard and erect. I could tell my vagina was getting wet, and not because I was submerged in water, if you know what I mean! Although I was home alone, I still refused to let out a moan because I was a little embarrassed to let the sound escape my mouth and flow freely into the universe. I licked my lips and thought of me and Dominic tonight as I finally had a mediocre orgasm.

Boom, boom! I heard, snapping me out of my zone. I jumped up from the tub and wrapped the pink bath towel I had sitting on the side of the tub around me. I walked to the door with attitude in every step.

"Who is it?" I yelled before I got all the way to the door. At first, I thought it was Dom coming back to surprise me again but thought against it when he didn't use his key.

"It's me, Tone," I heard as I snatched the door open to see Dominic's frat brother and our next-door neighbor Antonio standing on the porch.

Antonio had lived next door to us ever since we moved in two years ago. He had been bugging me since our college days. He used to have a big crush on me and never stopped trying to be with me until Dom snatched me up and shut it down. Even now Tone flirted jokingly, but from time to time I thought he was a little jealous. Dominic laughed it off because he knew his boy wasn't my type. For one, his ass was a cop. Second, he was broke. Third, he was broke, and finally, he wasn't all that attractive. Although he was a pain in the ass, he was also a good friend to have.

"Damn, girl, I ain't know you was gon' come to the door naked and shit," he said, grabbing his dick, and I gagged. Tone was a five-foot, eight-inch tall dark-skinned man with pink lips. He could've made himself look a little better if he put more thought into his appearance. Yet here he stood in a cutoff gym shirt, faded basketball shorts, dingy socks, and some old-ass Reeboks.

"Gross!" I turned to walk back into the foyer, letting the door smack him as he entered.

"You are mean!" he said after locking my door.

"Well, your ass is annoying, so we even!" I said, tiptoe-ing across the cold wood floor back into the bathroom. The house was a ranch-style home, so everything was on the same level.

"Where D at? I thought I saw his car in the drive-way," Antonio called out. He was probably in my custom kitchen, his favorite room in the house, looking for something to eat.

"He was here, but they called him into work." I stepped into the third bedroom, which had been converted into a walk-in closet/dressing room for me.

Moments later, I returned wearing a white halter top that was trimmed in gold and the matching capris. I was fresh to death with my gold red-bottom sandals, gold charm bracelet, gold necklace with my name, Chanel, trimmed in diamonds, and my Chanel earrings with the C's on them. I walked into the bathroom and sprayed

Chanel No. 5 perfume on my clothes. After putting on my MAC lip gloss and sweeping my fingers through my long curls, I was the shit. After blowing myself a kiss, I turned off the bathroom light and headed back into the kitchen with Tone.

I loved the way I looked, and I wasn't ashamed of it. Like Trina said in her song: number ten in the face, slim in the waist, fat in the ass.

I kept my shit tight, bottom line. I stayed in the gym and nail and hair salons, and of course I did it on someone else's dime. Sometimes it was Dominic's bill, and other times it was one of the many men who flirted with me daily. Engaged or not, I didn't mind using what I had to get what I wanted. As long as Dom didn't find out my secrets, I would continue to let my beauty pave the way to a fabulous future. Whoever said looks don't pay the bills was obviously ugly.

"What up, Tone?" I asked as I joined him at my kitchen nook while he ate a bowl of cereal.

"Nothing much. What's up with you, birthday girl?" He was stuffing his face with a big spoon of Cap'n Crunch.

"I'm about to head out with the girls for some retail therapy." I grabbed a banana and peeled it back. I knew the shape of the fruit against my plump lips would turn him on, but I was hungry.

"Damn! Dom is one lucky man." Tone stared at me intently. "What a nigga got to do to get service like that?"

"Boy, stop! You couldn't afford these lips." I punched his shoulder. "Anyway, let yourself out. I have to go, and I hope you leaving some money for all the food of mine you be eating." I raised an eyebrow.

"Go on with that shit. As a matter of fact, I put more groceries in this motherfucker than you!"

He was telling the truth, but I couldn't resist asking for some money. It was something that just came naturally. "Let me hold something." I put my hand out.

"Do I look like your man?"

"You look like my dear friend from next door who wants me to have a good birthday." I smiled and he shook his head.

"All I got is a fifty-dollar bill. That's way less than what you need to do what you're trying to do." He pulled out the money and put his empty cereal bowl into the stainless-steel sink.

"You're right, fifty dollars is chump change." I frowned, and he smiled because he thought he had me. "However, fifty dollars is just enough to fill my gas tank and get a car wash." I cracked up laughing and snatched the money from his tight clutches.

"You are the most money-hungry person I've ever come in contact with." Shaking his square head, he walked toward the door

"I should teach you a lesson or two! Money makes the world go 'round. Without it, you're nothing! That's the top and bottom line."

"Money is also the root of all evil! Don't you know that?" He stood on the large wraparound country porch, and I pulled the door closed behind me to lock it.

"Evil or not, money is necessary! Maybe if your broke ass had some, you'd have better luck with women." I laughed. Tone waved me off and left without another word. I was glad, because I was ready to get my birthday started right.

Chapter Three

Brushing off Antonio's negativity, I walked over to my baby and got inside. Immediately I turned down the music that was still blasting from the night before. I loved my car and treated it like a child. It was only a Maxima, but one day I would have something more expensive, so for now I practiced. The interior was black leather, trimmed with dark red as well as red suede on the seats, and I had a TV in the dashboard. My windows and sunroof bordered on being illegal because they were so dark. I also had red neon lights around the bottom and they looked awesome at night. I topped it off with my personalized license plate, which read PAPR CHSR, an abbreviation for "paper chaser." I flipped through my music collection and decided to play something to get me in the mood. As I pulled off, I turned up the bass and nodded in agreement with my homeboy Plies singing my anthem, "In Love With Money."

As I made the twenty-five-minute drive from the suburbs to the inner city, I became homesick. Most of the large brick two-story homes reminded me of Detroit. They trashed Detroit on television, but I loved my city and represented it every chance I got. I disliked how the media only took pictures of the slums and ghettos, then put those images in magazines or on television for the world to see. There were still some very nice neighborhoods standing and prominent citizens who lived there. Detroit may not have been as rich and glamorous as other cities, but it made the best of us, and I was proud to call it home.

Before I knew it, I was parking in front of the Candy Shop, where my nail tech Bre' worked. Placing my Dior shades on, I grabbed my bag and headed inside the salon for my appointment. The place was beautifully done in pink, white, and purple with a huge mural painted across the wall. It depicted women of all ages getting their hair, nails, or makeup done.

"Hey," I said to Angel, the receptionist, as I walked in. Once I signed my name, I took a seat on one of the white leather sofas with pink and purple accent pillows. Crossing my legs, I picked up one of the magazines from the purple end table beside me.

As I waited, I glanced up occasionally to see that all eyes were on me, and it was starting to piss me off. I pulled out my cell phone and was about to call somebody to make small talk when I noticed a big chocolate nigga walk in and approach the counter to speak to Angel. I looked out the window to peep what he was driving, and my panties got wet when I noticed the customized 2020 745, or "Quarter to Eight," as we called them back home. It was cocaine white with some big-ass chrome rims shining all the way into the shop. I got up and stood behind him at the counter.

"Hold up, Terry. What can I help you with?" Angel asked me with an attitude.

"Angel, where is Bre'? How long does she expect me to wait? Is there anyone else available?" I played the game of Twenty Questions while the two of them looked back at me. I honestly didn't want to keep waiting, but I only really approached Angel to get a better look at the chocolate stranger. He resembled Morris Chestnut, only a little taller and a tad more thugged out. I glanced over his attire of tan Polo shorts, brown loafers, white wife beater, and a light blue Ralph Lauren button-up. I was so slick with my shit that I added up his jewelry in my head and came up with the sum of $10,000 before Angel had even answered my questions.

"It might be another ten or fifteen minutes." She frowned as if she knew what I was doing in my head.

"Okay, well, I'm going to make a phone call really quick, just in case she comes looking for me," I said and stepped outside. I only walked outside so that I would be there when fine-ass Terry came out of the salon. His ass had a small bank, and I could smell it!

After pretending to be on my phone for way too long in my opinion, I was just about to head back inside when I heard the door open. I smiled a seductive smile as I turned around. The smile quickly faded as he and the girl I presumed was his chick exited the salon. "Thanks, boo, for getting my hair and nails done," she said and turned to kiss him.

"It ain't shit to a boss!" he said as he looked at me over her shoulder. I turned back toward the parking lot just as they broke their embrace. I felt defeated that I lost my chance with this one, but I was unfazed nonetheless. I had a thoroughbred at home. Hell, I was checking for this fool just for sport.

"Excuse me," he said, causing both me and his chick to look up at him.

"Yeah?" I said.

"You dropped this in the shop when you walked out," he said and handed me a flyer that had a note scribbled on it.

"Thanks," I said and walked back into the shop, not wanting his girl to trip or suspect anything. I sat down in the same spot I had occupied when I first got there to look over the paper. It read:

You look sexy as hell! I couldn't holler at you because I'm with ol' girl, but if you want to fuck with a nigga, hit me up. 513-515 . . .

"Come on, Chanel. Sorry I'm late. My bad, girl," I heard Bre' say, and I put the paper back in my bag. Walking toward her station, I dismissed the dirty look Angel was giving me.

"Damn, your ass needs to start being on time!" I said, half joking but half serious.

"I know, boo. My bad! I got caught up with my baby daddy," she said, smiling, and I frowned. I'd known Bre' and her baby daddy since my freshman year at Cincinnati State because that was how long she'd been doing my nails. Back then she worked out of her house, and his lazy ass stayed in bed or playing Xbox all day. I knew then that he wasn't shit and wouldn't be shit. I didn't understand why he had her wide open. The nigga couldn't do shit but give her a wet ass and some babies. He worked as a waiter and drove a Ford pickup truck, a 2010 at that!

"Tell that nigga he be fucking up your money!" I responded as she began to do my pink and white fill-in. I watched her as she put the white and pink acrylic on my natural nails then shape them in a square style.

"I know, but—"

I cut her off with the quickness. "But nothing! It's one thing to mess with a broke nigga, because that's your business. You like it, I get it. But it's another thing when you let him stop your cash flow. Girl, your babies depend on you to bring in the money for food and bills. What will you do if your clients start taking their business elsewhere because you're always late?"

All Bre' did was hunch her shoulders, and I could tell I had either hurt her feelings or made her think. "What's the big plans for today?" she asked, trying to lighten the mood.

"Me, Trina, and Noel will probably hit the mall."

"That's what's up. I'm surprised you ain't hitting no parties for your birthday."

"I guess that's kind of played." I shrugged my shoulders. "If I happen to go, then I do, but it ain't like back when I started college and couldn't wait until the next party or ice breaker," I said, thinking back to my younger days.

"Those were the days. Now I got kids and bills." Bre' shook her head. "Do you want kids?"

"Hell no. I ain't fit to be nobody's mama right now, but maybe down the line when I get settled."

"Damn, Chanel, how much more settled could you be? You have Dom, a nice salary, a beautiful house, and a college degree."

"All that is true, but I need more. I have a nice salary, but it could be better. I have a beautiful house, but it too could be better, and Dom is Mr. Right, but I need him to be Mr. Richer!" We cracked up laughing for a few minutes at that one. Then she asked me, if I did get pregnant, what would I want it to be, and what would I name it?

"I definitely want a girl! It's too rough for dudes out here. They have to be balling. Even though I will raise a boss, I don't want my son under that kind of pressure. When I have my daughter, I'll name her Cash'aye, Mercedes, Cashmere, or something expensive. Hell, I don't know." I giggled.

"You and your mama with those names," she said, buffing my nails. I laughed because I knew she was referring to my and my sister's names. Both of us were named after famous labels: Chanel and Christian Dior. My mom used a K instead of the Ch in Kristian's name but let mine stay the same.

  As I stood to wash my hands, I smiled and said, "Yeah, but with names like ours we are destined for success."

Chapter Four

In less than two hours I was back in the car on my way to meet my sister at Applebee's. I picked up the phone to call this nigga Kenny I'd met a week ago in Detroit at Payday's strip club. I was in the city visiting my mother when Trina suggested we go check out the strip club. I sat in the establishment and peeped the scene to see who was dropping the most money. That was when I saw him up in VIP. He was throwing twenties and fifties, and it was turning me on. I told my girl to hold my purse while I went to say hello, and she agreed. Once I made my way up to him, I leaned down close, placing my double D's at eye level, and whispered in his ear, "Why don't you quit tricking your dough on these hoes and spend some on a real bitch like me?"

He glanced up at me, and I could tell my bluntness surprised him. He smiled and patted the seat next to him, gesturing for me to sit down.

"What's your name, honey?" he asked.

"Chanel."

"I'm Kenny," he said, eyeing me seductively.

Dude wasn't a ten, but a real strong eight. I wasn't looking to hook up, but I did need a new sponsor for the red Giuseppe shoes coming out on my birthday. Dominic didn't have the money because he'd just paid the mortgage. I had enough in my secret stash, but I would pass out before I spent $2,500 of my own money on a pair of shoes.

"Kenny, what are you doing in a place like this?" I spoke into his ear. I was trying to be sexy, but it was too loud in there with T-Pain playing over the speakers.

"Shit, baby, if I had a woman like you at home, I wouldn't have to patronize places like this," he said, giving me his full attention and placing the wad of money he held in his hand back into his Armani slacks.

I pretended not to notice the dancer on stage giving me the middle finger and rolling her eyes. I smiled because she was pissed. I'd just cut off the majority of her dough for tonight. It was because of women like me that most strip clubs made it mandatory that women were no longer allowed inside without a male escort.

"Well, consider yourself lucky, because I showed up just in time," I said, and we both laughed.

We left the club that night and went to breakfast at IHOP. We talked for what seemed like hours. He then paid the bill and put an extra $400 on the table. I asked why he was leaving so much. That's when he told me it was mine and to buy myself something for my birthday. I was calling him now to thank him for the manicure and pedicure he'd just paid for and whatever else I was sure to pick up. I also wanted to see if I could still squeeze those shoes out of him.

"Who dis?" he asked, answering my call on the second ring.

"This is Chanel," I said, waiting for him to reply. After a second of waiting, I reminded him, "The one from Payday's."

"Oh, what up doe?" he asked with familiarity.

"You busy?"

"Handling some business, but I got a minute. What's up, baby girl?" He sounded better than I remembered.

"Nothing much. I was just calling because I wanted to say thank you again for the birthday gift."

"It's nothing. When will a player see you again?"

"I should be back in town in a few weeks, and I would love to see you. Maybe next time breakfast will be on me." Sometimes you have to let these dudes know you don't always have your hand out.

"That sounds like a plan." I heard a few voices in the background calling for his attention to come check something out.

"Okay, baby, I'm going to let you go. I can tell that you're busy. I just wanted to say thank you."

"No problem. Anytime you're back in the D, holla at me and I'll show you a good time. Be easy, shorty." Kenny hung up the phone.

I erased the number from my call list and slipped the phone back into my purse. I didn't have to worry about him calling me back because I'd dialed him restricted.

Pulling into the Applebee's lot and parking next to my sister's Honda, I checked my appearance in the rear-view mirror, then stepped out of my ride. I walked inside to see my sister, her husband, and my 2-year-old niece, Deona. She was the prettiest baby, and I loved her to pieces. Although my sister would protest, I vowed to show her the ropes when she came of age. I couldn't have her wasting all that beauty like her mother.

"Happy birthday," they said in unison, and my niece clapped her tiny hands. We were shown to a booth close to the front door and given menus.

"What do you have planned tonight? I know it's big!" Deon said. When I looked up at him, I noticed how toned and buff he'd become since I'd seen him about a month ago. He was dressed in a white V-neck Dockers shirt, brown khakis with a matching Gucci baseball cap, belt, and loafers. He was looking all that and a bag of chips, but I quickly got over it when he asked the question again.

"My bad. I was checking out this cutie who just walked past the window," I said, thinking fast.

"You know you need to stop that!" Kristian chimed in. Her Goody Two-shoes ass was already about to work my nerves, and we hadn't been there five minutes.

"Stop what, Kristian?"

"You are engaged! How would you feel if Dominic did some of the same things you do behind his back?"

I pondered her question for a second, then responded, "Well, for one thing, I'm not married yet. Secondly, I don't know what Dominic does behind my back. For all I know, he could be out fucking some trick right now. Lastly, as long as I don't find out, he is all good with me."

Kristian rolled her eyes, and Deon looked on awkwardly. "Chanel, all I'm saying is you have a good thing, so why mess that up with one of these fly-by-night, good-for-nothing dudes?"

"I'm a grown woman, and I handle my own, believe that! I know what I should and shouldn't be doing, Kristian! I don't need you or anybody else telling me how to run my relationship. Dominic ain't complaining, so why should you?" I was about ready to get up and leave her right here looking stupid.

"You're right! You are grown, and nobody can tell you anything. Don't come calling me when all hell breaks loose."

Dismissing her two cents, I turned to Deona and held a conversation with her until our waitress came back.

"Are you guys ready to order?" She gave us a huge smile.

"Yes," we said in unison.

"Can I get an order of nachos and some of those boneless wings for the baby?" Kristian said.

"And for you, sir?" she asked Deon.

"Um, the riblet dinner would be good, thanks."

"And for you, ma'am?"

"Let me get a fried chicken salad with French and ranch dressing," I said and handed her my menu.

"Okay, what are you guys drinking?" she asked, and we all requested water. When she left, we were all quiet again.

"Chanel, you still haven't answered my question about your birthday plans," Deon said, breaking the silence.

"I'm sorry. Dom had to work, so me, Trina, and Noel are going to hang out later."

"Sounds like fun." His comment was followed by a few minutes of awkward silence.

Biting my tongue, I tried to break up the tension between my sister and me. "Yeah, it will be fun. You guys should come. We're going to Kenwood for shopping and maybe drinks later." I hated her attitude, and I was sure she hated mine, but at the end of the day we were sisters, and I really didn't like to fight.

"Chanel, you know we just opened two businesses, and every dollar counts. I wish we could be careless with money like you and your friends, but we can't, and you know we don't drink," Kristian interjected and shut my invitation down. I'm not going to lie, my feelings were a bit hurt, but like with everything else, I brushed it off and rolled with the punches. Me and Kristian had always had a strained relationship. She stayed in her lane, and I stayed in mine.

"Well, maybe next time," I added and looked out the large picture window.

"Baby, we should go and get out. I'll treat you to a new outfit. We can afford it, and you deserve it," Deon protested.

I watched as Kristian cut him a look, and I shook my head. Instead of adding her input on my relationship, she should've been paying hers a little more attention. My sister was going to push him away real soon if she wasn't careful. Deon was a really cool dude. I could tell he wanted to let loose every once in a while, and I felt bad for him because Mrs. Serious wasn't having it.

Ring. Ring. "Hello," I answered.

"Hello my ass. Did you forget about calling me back?"

"Hey, Mama. My bad. I had to go and get my nails done."

"Where you at now?" she asked like a detective.

"At Applebee's with—" I was cut off by my sister whispering for me not to mention I was there with them. "Um, I'm with Bre', my nail tech. She wanted to take me out for my birthday," I continued with my lie. For some strange reason my sister and mom didn't get along at all, but they tolerated each other while in each other's presence. It had always been that way, and I didn't think it would ever change. Porscha was mad cool, but Kristian thought she was just flat-out embarrassing. My mom made no effort to conceal that she didn't give a damn what anyone thought of her, especially not someone she brought into this world.

"Damn, all she could afford was Applebee's? She could've at least taken you to Benihana for the lunch special."

I smiled because Porscha didn't know she was really putting her daughter on blast. "It's all good, but what's up?"

"I just called to tell you I'll be flying down on Friday, and you need to be at the airport at noon."

"Mom, why in the world would you catch a flight here when all you had to do was drive or take Greyhound?"

"Chanel, I'm not worried about that little $690. It's nothing to a boss."

"I can't believe you paid all of that money for a forty-minute flight." I was at a loss for words. I was high maintenance, but damn! I would never pay that much money to fly from Detroit to Ohio unless it was an emergency. Hell, the car ride was only three and a half hours, and you could arrive with gas still in the tank.

"Girl, bye! I know you know I ain't never, ever riding on no Greyhound bus, and my Jag is too precious to take that trip on those raggedy roads."

"All right, Mom, I'll see you when you get here."

As I ended the conversation with my mother, the waitress came back with drinks and was followed by someone carrying the food. "Dang that was fast! Excuse me while I go wash my hands. Kris, watch my bag please," I said and slid out of the seat.

As I made my way toward the back of the restaurant, I noticed several waiters and busboys checking me out. I laughed to myself, because it would never happen in a million years. While I was in the bathroom, I decided to go ahead and pee since it appeared freshly cleaned. I was just about to wipe when I heard a tap on the door. "Someone is in here," I said in an annoyed voice. I was pretty sure they could see my feet.

"It's me," I heard in a whisper.

Peeking under the stall, I saw shoes that belonged to Deon. "What the hell are you doing?" I asked and opened the door.

"Chanel, I need you!" He barged into the handicapped bathroom, which I used for the extra space, and locked the door.

"Are you crazy?" I asked. "Get the fuck out of here."

"Come on, just one time," he begged.

"What?" I asked as he pulled his seven-inch penis out. My eyes bulged as the reality of what was going on hit me. This nigga and his nonsense were about to get us both caught up.

"Please let me hit it really quick. Your sister ain't giving up nothing, and I need some pussy. Please, baby, you been on my mind lately with your sexy ass! I'll pay for it. Just name your price." He walked up closer to me and backed me up against the wall . . . literally.

I talked shit, but for real I wasn't with this, especially with my sister right outside. "Listen, this is some bullshit! You married her, and you knew how she was, so deal with it. I'm not about to fuck you with your wife, *my sister,* less than fifteen feet away! I wouldn't even do it if she were in another country. Now let me out!" I yelled.

Instead of opening the door, he frowned. "Look, you little bitch, don't act all high and mighty with me, especially when I know you fuck for money. Your sister told me about you and your money-hungry ways. So like I said, how much?" He pulled out his wallet and removed a few Franklins, putting them up to my face. I was sick to my stomach and felt even sicker when the restroom door opened and I heard my sister's voice.

"Chanel, are you in here?"

"Yeah, here I come. I just felt sick, that's all. Go back to the table," I called over Deon's shoulder. It took everything in me not to expose this rat for what he was, but if I did, with my track record, I would end up looking like the guilty party.

"Do you need me to come in there?" She was concerned.

"No, I got it. Here I come."

"Well, while I'm in here, I might as well come in there and change the baby's diaper." She moved closer toward the stall door, and I almost pissed myself.

"I don't think that's a good idea because I just messed this one up with vomit. As a matter of fact, can you hand me a few more paper towels?" Deon backed up against the changing table, and I stretched my hand over the top to retrieve the items.

"Okay, I hope you're all right! I'll be waiting at the table." With that she walked out.

I quickly made my way to unlock the stall door, and I snatched the fistful of money Deon was still clutching up against his chest. I peeled off two twenties and threw them back at him.

"Take that and buy a pocket pussy from a toy store for days like this, you bastard!" I said while washing my hands. "If you ever try some shit like that again, I'll have you handled!" I threatened and headed out the door.

I couldn't believe the nerve he had. This incident definitely made Deon less appealing to me, and I could no longer stand to be around him. I also could not stand to look in Kristian's poor face for much longer. After playing with my food and trying to make small talk for a few minutes, I excused myself from the table. "Kris, I'm not feeling well. I think I need to go lie down."

"Do you need me to do anything for you?"

"No, I'll be cool. Thank you for the birthday lunch." I blew a kiss to my niece and rolled my eyes at Deon when he sat back down at the table. "Call me later, Kris," I said before bolting out the door.

Chapter Five

Just as I started the car, my cell phone rang. Peeping the caller ID and seeing that it was my girl Trina, I answered. "Hey, girl, I'm on the way."

"I was wondering what the holdup was."

"Where are you guys now?" I needed to know where I was headed before I left the parking lot.

"I'm at my apartment waiting for you. Noel is on the way. Hurry up, because I'm ready to get the party started."

"Okay, okay, I'm coming." I put the pedal to the metal and zoomed over to be with my friends.

"Well, it's about time, birthday girl!" Trina exclaimed from the patio of her downtown Cincinnati apartment as she watched me exit my car. It was about 3:45 p.m. when I pulled into Trina's apartment complex. As I reached for my purse, Noel pulled up beside me in her black BMW.

"Happy birthday!" she exclaimed and came over to hug me. "Now let's party!"

I nodded, ready to unwind because it had been a long day for me, and I was sure it was for her as well. Noel was a second grade teacher and had been my homegirl since junior year in college. We stayed in the same dorm room and had become fast friends, although we were slightly different and from different walks of life. I was a refined hood chick, but Noel was straight-up prim and proper. My mama wasn't broke, but Noel's parents were both doctors, and money was never an issue. I applied for grants and student loans to pay for my education. Noel, on the other hand, had her tuition paid for before she could walk. I'm not taking anything from my girl, but sometimes she was so far removed from reality, it was embarrassing. Nevertheless, she was cool peeps, and I usually liked being around her.

Trina, on the other hand, was my main girl, as I stated earlier. We met during the wintertime at Northland Mall in Southfield, Michigan about ten years ago. We both walked into an accessory store at the same time. I barely looked at her because I was on a mission to do as much damage as I could with a credit card given to me by a dude I used to mess with. That nigga had just cheated on me, and I was about to clean his ass out. Yes, at 17 I was still a hot mess.

Anyway, I was picking up everything in sight, even the stuff I wasn't feeling and didn't even want. I must've not been paying attention, because I ran right into her, causing her to fall down and drop all of her items.

"Shit, my bad. Let me help you," I'd said, bending down to help her pick up her stuff. I was peeping some of the price tags on her merchandise, and I told her I liked her style. I'd added up $2,000 worth of stuff in my head. She'd stood to fix herself up as I continued to hand things up to her from the floor. I'd looked up to ask her where she found this particular makeup palette, since I was sure that it wasn't from the store we were in. That was when I noticed her putting the items in her purse and the big-ass bubble coat that she had on. "What are you doing?"

"What does it look like?" She'd looked at me like I was crazy.

"Girl, you shouldn't be stealing. What if you get caught?" I got up off the floor, no longer helping her retrieve her stolen property.

"I won't get caught if you don't say shit," she'd said with a bit of a warning in her voice, and then she walked away.

I shook my head at the girl because she was really pretty and had a nice shape. With a little more finesse and polish she could probably get any baller to spend some paper on her. She'd put me in the mind of a hood-ass Gabrielle Union, only with more curves. I'd brushed it off and continued to mind my own business. Moments later, I'd approached the register, and that was when I saw the girl hemmed up by security. The sales clerk told me to hold on one moment, and then she walked over toward the commotion. I watched as they removed every last item that I'd just helped her pick up.

"Get the fuck off me," she'd yelled.

"What is your name?" the clerk asked.

"Michelle Thompson," she said, and the clerk was about to say something when the security guard held her wallet in the air and said that her name was actually Trina Carter. "Well, Ms. Carter, your name rings bells in this mall for stealing, but no one has ever been able to detain you. Today is my lucky day." The clerk had smiled liked the Grinch who had just stolen Christmas.

"Please, I have kids, lady!" Trina said. I stared on and assessed the situation. The young girl looked to be around my age, and I'd found it hard to believe she had one baby let alone kids, as she'd just stated, but I could've been wrong.

"So do I, and I go to work every day." The clerk tossed the insult over her shoulder to Trina, who was still hemmed up, struggling to get out of the security guard's grip.

"But if I go to jail, nobody will be there to care for them," she pleaded.

"Not my problem, Ms. Carter. I'm calling the police," the clerk had said and then came back behind the register to retrieve the phone. As she picked it up, I placed my finger on the hang-up button. She looked up in awe, and I smiled.

"Please don't send her to jail. Just add her total to my bill," I'd said politely.

"Do you know her?" She looked at me with curiosity.

"No, but I don't want to see a young girl with kids go to jail," I'd said honestly.

"She is known for this, and she has to pay." The outraged clerk removed my finger from the hang-up button.

"Yeah, but not today. Please just add her stuff in with mine, and I'll also throw you an extra hundred for allowing her to keep the stuff from the other stores." I pulled out the credit card and a hundred-dollar bill.

"She cannot get away with this," the woman had insisted.

"Fine, make it two hundred for looking the other way." I watched as she hesitated for a minute. Needless to say, after a little more persuading, a bill of $3,482.56, and an extra $300 in cash, Trina and I had finally walked out of the mall scot-free.

"Thanks, girl, for hooking me up," she'd said, squeezing me tight.

"I ain't hook you up. I hooked your kids up." I shook my head.

"Oh, I don't really have kids, but thanks again." She'd had the nerve to reach down for her bag of things that I'd just footed the bill for.

"What? Are you serious?" I was pissed.

"Yeah. I just say that for sympathy." She shrugged her shoulders.

"Why do you steal?" I really wanted to know the answer to that question.

"Because it pays my bills," she'd snapped.

"You are too pretty to be a thief! You should try something different."

"Like what, stripping like you?" she'd asked with a straight face.

"I'm not a stripper, sweetie." I cut her an amused look.

"You ain't got to lie. Look at you, and look at what you just spent in the mall at a damn accessory store."

I was about to reply when a white Navigator pulled up right beside us and slammed on the brakes. Before I had time to react, two chicks had jumped from the car and gotten in my face. "Which one of y'all is Chanel?" the driver had wanted to know.

"That's me, and you are?" I asked and put my bags down on the ground because I knew where this was headed. In the streets, you had to be ready to lay hands at a moment's notice.

"Bitch, I'm Kionna. Are you fucking with my man?"

"Who the fuck is your man?" I'd asked, really wanting to know.

"James off of Seven Mile."

"Li'l dick, five-minute James?" I asked just to piss her off.

"This bitch got mad mouth," her friend had chimed in.

"Yeah, I know James. He just ate my pussy last night, then left a stack to pay my bills and send me on this shopping spree today." I pointed to the bags on the ground.

"Now I'm going to have to fuck you up for real," she said, reaching into her purse. In Detroit everybody was packing a weapon except my dumb ass! Seeing the weapon shook me up, but I didn't let on.

"You need to be talking to James and not me, bitch."

"Your ass needs to be taught a lesson, and I'm going to make sure you learn not to fuck with nobody else's man. You ain't shit without that pretty face," she'd said and then lunged on top of me, knocking me to the ground with a four-inch blade really close to my face. I was scared shitless and frozen still. Now please don't get it twisted. I could fight, and I'd kicked my fair share of ass. On the other hand, I'd never had anyone put a knife to my face and threaten to disfigure me, so I was caught off guard.

"Cut that bitch, Kiki," her ugly-ass friend had added.

She raised her arm and was almost down to my cheek when we heard a bang.

"Get off of her right now or else," Trina had said, holding a 9 mm handgun. I had forgotten she was back there but was so thankful that she was.

"Are you gon' shoot me?" Kionna asked.

"I will if I have to," Trina had said.

Kionna got up off of me. I quickly rose to my feet and grabbed my bags, and Trina followed me to the Durango I was driving at the time.

"So that's how you get your money," she'd teased.

"Better than stealing and going to jail."

We'd both laughed hard and had been tight ever since.

Eventually, Trina stopped stealing and joined my team as a bad bitch on the paper chase. She even followed me to Ohio from Detroit, although she didn't enroll in college. Throwing caution to the wind, she came out here to see what life had to offer, and to my surprise, she'd done well for herself. One month after touching down, Trina took a waitress position at Don Romano's, a very upscale, swank restaurant located downtown. Within a year, she went from serving to being served by the owner, Giorgio Romano himself. He had a thing for pretty black girls, and she had a new thing for anybody with money. Eventually, they both grew to love each other after creating a beautiful son named Sergio. Unfortunately, Giorgio couldn't take the mixed child nor his black mother home to his old-school Italian family.

Thinking up a master plan, Trina told Giorgio that as long as he kept her comfortable and paid her bills, she would keep their love child a secret. Without argument, he set her up in a three-bedroom condo apartment, provided her with car service since she didn't have a license, and made sure her bank account had a deposit every Friday. Me and my girl had made it a long way from the blocks we were raised on, and I knew the best was yet to come.

"Come on, y'all, before the drinks are gone," Trina called from her patio, snapping me from my daze as Noel and I walked over to the first-floor patio from the parking lot.

"Welcome to the hot spot." Trina posed in the doorway like the model she could've been. Trina was five feet nine inches tall with dark skin and almond eyes, and she was very curvaceous. Her hair was styled in a long, luxurious wet and wavy lace-front. I'm not talking about the lace fronts from the beauty supply store. I'm talking the kind that costs $3,500 and takes a month to make because each individual strand of hair is bleached at the root, hand tied, and double knotted onto a mesh-like material. Her lashes were perfect, and as always, her makeup was flawless. My girl was one of the prettiest girls I'd ever laid eyes on. She was also the tallest, but she used what God gave her and made it work.

After stepping onto the patio, we walked through the gated door into her condo. As we walked into the Japanese-inspired living space, I slipped off my shoes and slipped into one of the nine pairs of house shoes she had waiting by the door. Trina never liked anyone to walk into her home with their shoes on because of the vibe it may bring. Don't ask me why, but it was something she picked up while traveling abroad with Giorgio.

"I thought we were going out for dinner and to the mall." I sniffed the air and smelled something cooking.

"Trina, I know you didn't cook, so what gives?" Noel must've gotten a whiff of the wonderful aroma that was gracing my nostrils too.

"Well, we were going to go out, but I decided to stop by Don Romano's for takeout."

"Whew! You had me nervous for a second," Noel admitted, and we all laughed.

"Whatever, bitch!" She walked to the freezer, retrieved two frozen wineglasses, and placed them down on the table before pouring some Moscato.

"Where is my glass?" Noel asked.

"Thank you," I said while putting my chilled glass up to my lips. It was just the way I liked it.

"Noel, I ain't fooling with you. One minute you don't drink, and the next minute you do. Which one is it today?" Trina impatiently held the bottle, waiting for a response.

"I have to sip something with the birthday girl, so pour me just a little."

After Trina poured Noel's drink, she told me to take a seat and she would be right back. Without hesitation I did as I was told.

"Here you go. Happy b-day." She returned holding a big white box with a gold ribbon. I put the glass down and immediately opened the package. To my shock, it revealed an oversized gold metallic LV bag.

"Oh, my God. This purse is bad. Thank you so much, Trina!" I yelled with excitement.

"Only the best for my girl," she said and watched me admire my gift.

"I might have to change my outfit today just to wear this bag." I truly loved it.

"Girl, I know you have tons of options in that closet of yours already, but I saw you admire this last week, and I wanted you to add it to your collection." She sipped from her glass.

"Thank you, boo. This means a lot."

"Okay, I was going to wait until after dinner, but here is mine." Noel pulled a small gift bag from her Hermès purse and handed it to me.

"Oh, my goodness! Thank you so much, Noel. This is right up my alley." I reached over and hugged her. It was a Visa gift card. I didn't know how much was on it, but with Noel's background, I knew it wasn't going to be a disappointment.

"I bought it because I thought we were going shopping today, but you can use it whenever."

"You girls are the best!" I raised my glass, and they did the same for a toast. "Cheers to my birthday gifts." I laughed and they did too.

At the sound of my stomach growling loudly, Trina hopped up to get dinner and told us to have a seat. Sitting down at the four-seat dinette set, we dug into our meal of lamb chops, herbed potatoes, and Parmesan asparagus. We discussed work, current events, and celebrity gossip. Shortly afterward, the conversation turned to men, as it always did.

"Noel, when are you gon' get a man?" Trina asked, and I listened intently. Noel was a natural beauty with no hair extensions or makeup. She was caramel brown, two shades darker than me. My girl was about a size eight. She hid her cute, modest shape beneath unflattering clothing. Her hair was dreadlocked perfectly with blond coloring on the ends. Her smile was to die for, and her eyes were a greenish hazel. The last time I'd seen Noel with a man was senior year in college, and that was seven years ago. At one point I'd thought she might've played for the other team, if you catch my drift.

"I'm so focused on my students and getting my lesson plans ready that I don't have time to date," she said while forking a piece of potato off of her plate.

"Girl, bye!" Trina snapped. "I know your bed gets a little lonely sometimes, and so does that kitty cat!"

I looked over at Noel, who was turning red from embarrassment. I tried to kick Trina under the table, but her legs were folded Indian style up in her chair.

"I'm not lonely! As a matter of fact, my silver bullet keeps me very satisfied." Noel placed her napkin down on her plate, indicating the end of her meal.

"A bullet?" Trina frowned. "Child, please. You need a man to blow your back out every now and again." Trina reached up for a five, and I gave it to her because I was in total agreement.

"Noel, you mean to tell me that you haven't had sex in seven years?" I asked.

"Nope! I'm a born-again virgin. The next man I sleep with will definitely be my husband." She smiled like she was in la-la land, fantasizing about him.

"I don't know how you do it, but I commend you." I clapped for her. "I love sex too much to abstain. Not to mention my man definitely puts in work in the bedroom." I smiled. Now I was the one in la-la land thinking about what me and Dom would do later tonight.

"It's easy! My mother always told me men won't buy the cow when they get the milk for free," she explained.

"Child, please! I believe in trying it before buying it. Hell, if your man's sex game ain't tight, you don't want that nigga buying your milk anyway." Trina was on a roll, and once again I agreed with her.

"Anyway, Chanel, how is the wedding planning going?" Noel changed the subject, something she often did when the conversation became uncomfortable.

"It's coming along. We're down to thirteen months, and I can't wait." I pushed my plate aside.

"Do you love Dominic unconditionally?" she asked as Trina took the dishes into the kitchen.

I paused for a minute to let her question sink in. "What do you mean?" I knew what she meant, but I needed to buy some time to think about my answer.

"I mean will you love him when the grass ain't so green? Will you love him if his looks change or his chips go down?" she explained.

"Yeah, I guess so." I sipped from my wineglass. I didn't know why, but Noel's question had caught me off guard. When I thought of me and Dom, I always pictured us at the top. I never one time thought of that "for better or worse, richer or poorer" nonsense.

"Chanel, I know you love him, but if we are being honest, you love him with limits," Trina added as she sat back down to join us.

"I don't know about limits, but I do have expectations," I defended myself. "Decades from now I want my husband to be the same person I fell in love with, appearance and portfolio included. The same way he obtained me, he should try his damnedest to maintain me."

"What if something beyond his control happens?" Noel asked. "Like an accident or something and he gets disfigured, or the loss of a job?"

"Look, y'all are killing my buzz. I'll figure that shit out if it happens. Until then, stop speaking negativity on us." Quiet as it's kept though, I prayed right then and there that those things wouldn't happen, because if they did, our relationship might just be in trouble. I wasn't mentally prepared to deal with anything major right now. I just wanted to stay in the honeymoon phase as long as possible.

The remainder of the evening went off without an issue. We drank wine and talked shit until almost eleven o'clock that night. Though my day had not gone as planned, I had to admit, it still was special. I got some pretty nice gifts, and it was good seeing my sister, niece, and friends.

When I got home that night, Dom was fast asleep. I wanted to wake him up for some birthday sex, but then I decided not to bother him. Instead I showered, then crawled in bed beside him and was asleep in no time.

Chapter Six

Our days always started off hectic, with breakfast on the go, a kiss at the door, and us racing out of the two-car garage, waving to each other as we drove in opposite directions. Today was no different, but I was glad it was Thursday. Tomorrow my mother would be here, and I had big plans. Dominic also had another birthday surprise for me, and I couldn't wait to find out what it was.

Pulling into the parking lot at work, I tossed my phone inside my purse and grabbed my leather briefcase. I didn't need it, but it did make me look more professional. Therefore, I never went to work without it. I believed in looking the part at all times.

"Hey, Chanel," Rodney, the lead teller, called from the front door as I sashayed across the parking lot.

"Good morning, Rodney." I stood still as he held the door open for me like always. I couldn't tell if Rodney was a true gentleman or just sucking up to the boss. Nevertheless, I didn't mind it one bit.

I walked into the branch with my head held high, like I owned the joint. My black hair was pinned up into a neat French roll. I rocked a sapphire silk blouse, a Michael Kors pencil skirt, and blue Manolo Blahniks. I was the shit and everyone knew it. I'd learned early how to play the game. Although I was only a senior banker at Greensway, a mere $3 or $4 higher in pay than the tellers, I believed wholeheartedly I would one day move on to investment banking. That was where the big bucks

were, and the fact that an entry-level position was about
to become available at our sister company had me giddy
like a schoolgirl. For eight years, I'd given my all to this
company. I'd stayed late, done the work others passed
over, and my numbers outdid the other senior bankers in
the region.

"Good morning, Ms. Franklin," Rosa greeted me from
behind the counter with a bright smile.

"Rosa, call me Chanel." I patted her back as I passed
on my way to my office. She was a 65-year-old Hispanic
woman with short, curly hair, sunken eyes, and a wonderful smile. Off the record, she was my favorite employee. I
admired her work ethic. She was the first person through
the door and, nine times out of ten, the last person to
leave.

Rosa came out of retirement from her florist business
to provide for her grandson. He was dropped off by his
mom and dad one night on their way to see a movie, but
they never returned. It was date night for them but prom
night for their killer, who had been drinking and driving.
They were hit head-on and, upon impact, died instantly.
Rosa barely had time to mourn her daughter before she
walked in here looking for a job. She was dedicated to
giving her grandson the life his parents would've wanted
for him and had been here for almost four years.

"Okay, Ms. Franklin, will do." She smiled and I shook
my head. No matter how many times I insisted she call
me Chanel, she refused. I often felt bad that I didn't
call her Mrs. Lopez out of respect for her age, but when I
tried, she adamantly refused. "No, no, no. Call me Rosa
because 'Mrs. Lopez' makes me feel too old," she would
say, and I did as I was told.

Walking past Rosa and the other three teller stations,
I noticed someone pacing back and forth in my office.
I glanced down at my watch and noted that the bank

wouldn't open for another hour. Whoever was in there had to work for the company. Maybe it was a higher-up coming to interview me for the position I'd submitted an application for. I proceeded to my office.

When I opened the door, there were two sets of eyes staring at me. One set belonged to Frank Tompkins, our district manager, and the other set was unfamiliar. "Good morning, gentlemen," I greeted them.

"Marcus, this is Chanel Franklin, our senior banker. Chanel, this is Marcus Thatcher, the head of the organized crime division here in Ohio."

Frank's introductions caused me to frown. "I'm sorry, Frank, but did you just say organized crime?" I wanted clarification.

"Yes, he did, Mrs. . . . ." He let his word hang out there to see if I would take the bait and correct him with a, "Ms.," which would indicate if I was married or single. Choosing to keep him guessing, I shot him a look.

"Chanel will do," I said flatly. I wasn't interested in flirting, but I did need to know why he was here and what business he had with me.

"Chanel, I'm not sure if you know this, but there has been a string of bank robberies throughout Ohio." Marcus looked serious now.

"Really?" I looked over at Frank. "I haven't heard about any." I walked around them and placed my briefcase down onto my leather chair.

"For the most part, these robberies have been committed outside Cincinnati, but we have reason to believe they're headed this way," Marcus announced.

"And what makes you think that?" I replied with my hand on my hip.

"It's quite simple." He paused—for dramatic effect, I was sure. "They don't have anywhere else to rob. They've hit a string of banks in Lima, Toledo, Akron, Columbus,

Sandusky, Cleveland, and a few more places. Unless they're planning to strike out of state, Cincinnati is basically the only place untouched," Marcus stated matter-of-factly.

I didn't say anything for a moment to let his words sink in. I was from Detroit, where shit happened all the time, so this potential bank robbery wasn't too farfetched. However, I'd lived in Ohio for a while now, and never had I heard of such a large-scale crime being committed here. I'm not saying a bank robbery hadn't happened here or there, but a string of robberies was beyond me.

"I want to be prepared, Chanel," Frank intervened. "I'm calling for a mandatory staff meeting this weekend."

I almost fainted when he announced the meeting. I had plans. "Frank, we already have a plan of action. Do you really think a meeting is going to make a big difference in a real case of emergency?" I pleaded. Honestly the meeting didn't bother me, but the fact that it would be over the weekend was an entirely different story. I had plans to chill with my man for some uninterrupted us time, as well as spend time with my mother.

"Our plan of action is so old that I don't even remember it," Frank contested. He was right. The plan of action hadn't been revised since 2001, and with new technology at the fingertips of criminals, we did need a new strategy. But damn, couldn't we go over this on Monday?

"If I might add, most plans go astray when you're looking down the barrel of a gun," Marcus chimed in.

"Right!" I snapped. "So if most plans don't work under pressure anyway, what's the point of this meeting?"

"The point is I'm not going to unload a bunch of bullshit on you and your staff. I don't want to waste your time or mine. There have been several bank staff members wounded during these robberies. These criminals don't play, and I can't take a chance of someone losing their life because they didn't want to give up a weekend to learn something that could ultimately save their ass!" The vein in his forehead bulged, and his jaw muscle flexed.

"Chanel—" Frank interjected.

I raised my hand to stop him. "Look, I understand the seriousness of the situation, and once it's put to you the way Marcus just gave it to me, I'm game. I do see the mandatory meeting as necessary, but I don't see why it has to take place this weekend." I sighed.

"Saturday we're only open four hours, and we're closed on Sundays. The weekend is our only opportunity to conduct this meeting without affecting our service hours," Frank answered.

"Why can't we do two separate meetings during the week? Half the staff can attend the meeting while the other half mans the floor?"

"I'm out of town next week," Marcus answered, and before I could recommend another week, Frank chimed in.

"My schedule is booked solid after this weekend, so it will have to do."

I was pissed because these motherfuckers couldn't change their plans, but I had to. Grudgingly, I nodded my understanding, half smiled, and told them I'd see them Saturday at noon.

After coming to grips with my new weekend plans, the rest of the day flew by, and I was home before I knew it. "Dom, I'm home."

"There's my girl," Dominic called from our sunken family room as I entered.

After removing my shoes, I walked down the two steps and sat beside him on the couch. He was a huge LSU fan and in the Omega Psi Phi Fraternity, so everything in the family room was purple and gold. Reaching for the remote, I turned the sixty-inch television off. Dom had been watching ESPN, but I could tell something was bothering him by the way he sounded and the look on his face.

"Hey, baby, what's wrong?" Kissing him on the lips, I lay back into his arms.

"Chanel, I don't want you to worry," he said, which immediately caused me to worry.

"Dom, just tell me." It had been a long day. I wasn't in the mood to dance around any issues.

"I was let go today," he sighed and took a swig of the Miller High Life bottle resting at his side.

"Let go? As in fired?" I panicked.

"Not fired. Laid off." He nodded.

"Laid off, fired, same damn thing when you no longer have a job!" I didn't mean to snap. It just came out that way.

"Damn! You could at least pretend to be concerned before you jump down a nigga's throat," Dom yelled back.

"I am concerned and you know that." I sat up and rubbed my temples.

"Yeah, concerned about your damn self. You couldn't care less about what I'm going through." He looked at me then downed another swig of beer. My man was hurting, and I didn't know what to do or say to comfort him. The only thing running through my mind was the stupid conversation I'd had yesterday with Trina and Noel. "Damn, Chanel, at least say something," he barked and slammed his beer bottle down onto the marble coffee table.

"Dom, don't lash out at me." I stood from the couch. "I know you're angry, but we will work this out."

"Baby, I don't mean to take this out on you. It's not your fault those pricks let me go. I'm just frustrated, that's all." Dom stood and kissed the side of my neck. "I'll figure everything out, but right now, I need to know you've got my back."

"You know I've got your back." I kissed his lips, and my reassuring wink sealed the deal.

"That's why I love you."

"I love you too, baby, and I can't wait to be your wife." As I wrapped my arms around Dominic's neck, I noticed his facial expression change. "What's wrong?"

"Well, baby, you know we have to reanalyze the wedding budget and cut back on a few things."

"Cut back? No, we can't!" I turned my nose up. I was sorry if it sounded selfish of me, but I'd been waiting for the big day ever since he'd popped the question. I'd also planned everything down to table linens and light fixtures. Dominic was not about to throw my dream down the drain just because he got laid off.

"Chanel!" he protested. "I can't believe you sometimes."

"You act like you're broke! You have savings, money market accounts, IRAs, a 401K, and one hell of an investment portfolio." I whipped my neck side to side until it hurt.

"You've got to be kidding me. Is your ass really that spoiled?" Dom was up out of his seat and in my face.

"You act like I'm being unreasonable." I stared him down.

"Do you hear yourself?"

"Yeah! I hear myself loud and clear. The question should be, do you hear me?" I pointed at him.

"I hear you, but I'm done listening." He brushed past me in a rage.

I should've handled things differently, but it was too late and I wasn't into apologizing, so oh, well. Chanel Franklin was not about to chase after no man. When Dom cooled down and came to his senses, I'd be right here to talk about it with a cooler head. For now, though,

I went into the bedroom and began pulling out my clothes for tomorrow.

Good thing for Dom it only took him thirty minutes to get over it, because I was about to go to bed when he walked into our Victorian suite. I stood in front of the mirror and slipped on a lace nightgown. I usually slept naked. The pajamas were to indicate to him that no sex would be happening tonight until his attitude was adjusted.

"My fault for earlier," he apologized dryly.

"It's all good. You're upset, and I don't blame you, but it's not the end of the world." Greasing my feet with Vaseline, I never looked up at him.

"In this economy it may take me a minute to find a decent job." He sat down on the gray chaise.

"Can't you collect unemployment?" I sat up on the bed to face him.

"Yeah, but it won't be nearly what my salary was." He frowned and I did too. Although I was a bit disturbed by that info, I bit my lip and pressed forward.

"That's okay! At least it's something." Standing from the bed, I sat down beside him and wrapped my arms around him, cuddling him like a baby. "I'm here for you, and we will work this out, okay?"

He nodded as if a huge weight had been lifted off of him with my words. "You deserve the finer things in life, and I'm afraid that if I can't provide that for you, you'll leave me." He looked as if he was about to cry.

"We've been together too long to throw it away because you lost a job." I was telling the whole truth and nothing but the truth. I wouldn't dare leave him in his time of need, but you better believe I wouldn't hesitate to call in a temporary replacement if shit got too tough.

"I promise, baby, I'll find another job, and we will be okay."

I looked into his eyes and prayed that this dark cloud would pass over us quick, fast, and in a hurry.

That night we made love as usual. Dominic swooped me up in one swift motion, and before I knew it, his pants were down and I was on top straddling him hard. We made love for the better part of an hour. Although he put it down as usual, something with me was off. This was the first time I didn't experience a mind-blowing orgasm and had to fake it. I didn't know all of what was going on, but the issue of money was part of it. That was just the way my body worked.

Chapter Seven

Saturday morning had rolled around, and I was upset. For one thing, I was on my way to that damn mandatory meeting that was so unnecessary in my opinion. I also had to ask Kristian to come over to my house and keep Porscha company for the day in my absence, which neither of them was happy about. I promised to make it up as soon as I was done with the meeting, but that didn't make leaving any easier.

"Ms. Franklin, it's about time you showed up," Thatcher called over the railing from the upstairs conference room.

"You're lucky I even showed up." I rolled my eyes and headed up the carpeted stairwell. Stepping into the small room, I took a seat behind Rosa, who was putting the smash on a bagel with cream cheese. I was handed a pamphlet and told to turn to page three.

"Before we continue, are there any questions?" Marcus asked from the front of the room. I couldn't resist the opportunity to be a smart-ass, so I raised my hand. "Yes?"

"What time will we be out of here?" Everyone burst into laughter except Marcus.

"You're laughing now, but it won't be funny when a gun is pointed at your head," he warned, and I flexed my Cartier wristwatch to add emphasis to my statement.

After he chastised us like school-aged children, we settled down and he continued with the lesson plan. For several hours, he spoke about safety tips, new protocols, new procedures, and the new feature installed on our safe. "If the bank robber demands you open the safe, please do not hesitate!" Marcus paced the floor. "Stalling will only irritate your assailant and could possibly turn the situation deadly. With the new security feature, all you have to do is punch in the code 911, and it will open. This will not only please the perp, it will silently alert authorities that there is a robbery in progress."

I was only halfway listening to him ramble on and on because my mind was elsewhere. I thought I was doing a good job until I was cold busted when Marcus called out to me. "Chanel, please come up and demonstrate for the group."

"Why me?" I sat up in my seat and tried to remember what the hell he had been talking about for the last few minutes.

"Because as the senior banker, you set the example your employees follow." He took a swig of water. "Now please, if you don't mind, show us how the new feature works."

Damn! I cursed silently as I approached a mock safe that was identical to the real piece of steel downstairs. My palms were sweating as I tried to remember the code.

"Ten seconds, Chanel, or I will kill you!" Marcus yelled as if he were an actual robber.

Shit, what did he say again?

"Six seconds."

Um, 411. No, that's not it.

"Three seconds." Raising his hand, this time he aimed his real gun at me. "Two."

Suddenly I remembered the code and pressed it in right before my last second had expired.

"Damn, girl, you almost got yourself killed." He shook his head and sipped from the bottle again. "See what happens when you don't pay attention?" he asked the group. "Anyway, thank you for sharing your valuable time with us today. You all have a great weekend."

The group stood as Marcus closed the meeting. "On your way out, I want to leave you with this. It's easy to complain about giving up a few hours on a Saturday, but what you don't realize is these classes are in place for a reason. These tips are lifesaving, and the life you save just might be your own."

"Famous last words." I couldn't help myself from being a smart-ass.

"See you later, Chanel." He waved.

Without a word, I grabbed my purse off the back of my chair and headed to the door. Once outside, I peeled out of the parking lot like I was being chased and made my way to see my mother in no time.

Chapter Eight

Pulling up to my house, I noticed three cars in the driveway, which let me know Dom, Kris, and her bitch-ass husband were inside. "Hey, Mama!" I stepped through the door and squeezed her super tight. She was sitting on the couch, playing a game on her phone.

"About time you showed up." She smiled and moved aside to let me sit down.

"I was stuck in that damn mandatory meeting all day." Slipping my shoes off, I spoke with my head down.

"You need to find you a real man so you can stop all the working." My mother didn't mind speaking her thoughts, no matter whose feelings would be hurt.

"Shhh! I don't want Dom to hear you talking like that." I didn't know where he was in the house, but I didn't want any drama between them.

"It's not a secret, so there's no need to whisper. I have nothing against Dominic, but he can definitely do better." She stood her ground, and I laughed lightly. My mama was a mess.

"Porscha, what is wrong with you?" Kristian snapped from the living room. She was sitting on the floor, playing with the baby.

"What do you mean what's wrong with me?" Porscha snapped back.

"You got some nerve to come up in this man's house and talk down on him like that." Kristian was getting red in the face.

"First of all, nobody was talking to you! Second of all, I'm grown as hell. I can say what I want, when I want, and to whom I want to say it. There ain't a damn thing you or nobody else can do about it." Porscha turned back to me after putting my sister in her place.

"Where is Dom anyway?" I questioned as I picked up my shoes and carried them to the closet to put them back into their place.

"Child, I think he got tired of me and left. He said he had to make a run, but I think he went to his friend's house next door. The fool never moved the car from the driveway." She followed me into the room.

"Mama, what did you say to him?" I braced myself for whatever abrasive comment she made.

"I didn't say nothing out of the way if that's what you're worried about."

"Whew." I blew out an audible breath that came just a tad too soon.

"I only said what was necessary." Leaning up against the wall, Porscha folded her arms. The tailored peach Yves Saint Laurent blazer and white skinny jeans with gold accessories looked great on her.

"What exactly did you say?"

"I told him that keeping you happy meant keeping a j-o-b. You are not some hood rat from the projects, Chanel! You don't have to settle for this." Porscha took a seat at my vanity.

"Settle for what, Ma? Dom has only been unemployed for two days. We ain't in the poor house yet." I laughed but she frowned.

"As long as you have that moneymaker between your legs, you shouldn't be anywhere near a damn poor house period!" she hissed.

"You want me to become a prostitute now?" I laughed again and slipped into a Victoria's Secret Pink spandex outfit.

"No, that's not what I'm saying." She laughed. "What I mean is, God gave a woman everything she needs with the slit between her legs."

"Pussy shouldn't be sold! It should be given to someone you love, with no monetary value behind it." Kristian stepped into the room and closed the door. She was now rocking baby Deona, who was fast asleep.

"Bitch, please!" Porscha snapped. "Men pay for everything else in life, why not pay for my good-good?"

"Porscha, I'm no one's bitch. Let's get that straight first. Second, you're too damn old to be talking about good-good anyway."

Kristian had her with that one, so I burst out laughing, and eventually everyone caught on and began to join me.

"Old? Child, ain't no expiration date on this." Porscha rose from the seat and walked out of the room, strutting like a peacock. I looked at Kristian and shook my head.

Walking back into the family room, I asked my sister where her man was while I dialed my man's cell. She told me he was out in my neighborhood passing out flyers for their businesses, just as Dom answered. "Hey, baby."

"Hey, you. Where are you?" I stretched out on the couch.

"Next door with Tone." He sounded tired.

"When are you coming back?"

"When your mother leaves." He wasn't serious, but I could tell that he was already ready for her to go.

"Baby, come back. I miss you," I purred.

"Look, Chanel, I ain't for being disrespected in my crib, so you better get her in check," he warned.

"I got you," I agreed, although I had no plans to go up against my mother. But I did ask her to leave him alone.

Dominic walked into the house about five minutes after I gave my mother the speech. She swore she'd be on her best behavior, but I wasn't too sure. I greeted him with a kiss as he and my mother stared at each other. "Everyone, play nice," I said to mend the fence. Just as I was about to ask what everyone wanted me to order for dinner, Dominic spoke up.

"Ms. Porscha, I love and respect you as Chanel's mother, but I won't be disrespected in my home." Dominic took a deep breath. "I am the man of this house, and I will be treated as such." He stood up for himself, and I was proud. Going up against my mother was a tough thing to do, so I admired him.

"Dominic, what's your definition of a man?" Porscha asked with a straight face, and I knew it was about to get ugly.

"I know what a man is because I am one!" Dom raised his voice a tad too loud for Porscha.

"Slow your roll, son." Porscha stood. "See, my definition of a man is one who provides for his family. He puts his woman on a pedestal, and she wants for nothing." She pointed a freshly manicured finger.

"Chanel is my world, and she doesn't need for anything." Dominic looked at me for support, but this was his battle.

"I didn't say 'need.' I know all her needs are taken care of." She rolled her eyes. "I'm talking about her wants. Hell, right now you couldn't afford to buy her a pair of Giuseppes on sale if she desired them." My mother laughed wickedly and I winced. Even I knew that was a jab below the gut. I dared not speak up because, once again, this was his battle.

"Ms. P, you're acting like I'm a broke nigga!" I watched as Dom's chest moved erratically with his breathing.

"If the truth fits, accept it!" She let her smug remark hang in the air. Dominic looked as if he could've taken her head off at that moment.

"Porscha!" Kristian snapped loudly, which caused baby Deona to cry out.

"You old bitch!" Dominic spat at my mother, which caused me to jump in between them. "You didn't have a problem with me when I was making almost six figures and buying you expensive gifts and shit! You didn't have a problem with me when I paid the note on that condo, and you didn't have a problem with me last month when I loaned your broke ass a few stacks to pay your credit card bill." Dom was seething.

"Dominic, that's my mother! You better check yourself." I gritted my teeth. Earlier I said this was his battle and I didn't want to get involved, but I wouldn't stand here while he disrespected my mother.

"And I'm your man!" was his comeback. "When are you going to have my back for a change?"

I didn't have an answer for him, so I stood in silence as he walked around me and into our bedroom. My mother was smiling at a marvelous victory, and Kristian was packing up the diaper bag.

"Why are you leaving?" I asked.

"You two crazy broads deserve each other!" was her reply as she stormed out the front door.

The remainder of the evening went to shit. Dom didn't say another word to me. He wouldn't even come out of the room to eat when the pizza I eventually ordered was delivered. I should've handled things differently, but I was a sucker for my mom. I knew he would get over it, so I decided to enjoy the rest of the night with my mom and deal with him when things calmed down.

Chapter Nine

My mother had been back in Detroit for two weeks now, and Dominic still hadn't uttered a word to me. Aside from him handing me the newspaper in the morning after he'd taken the classified section to job hunt, there was no interaction. After time to think about what happened, I did feel extremely bad. On one hand, I felt where he was coming from, but on the other hand, he was in the wrong for addressing my mother that way. I was done waiting for him to apologize, and he was a fool if he thought I was going to apologize, so fuck it.

It was Saturday afternoon, and I was not about to let him put a damper on my weekend. I called my girls for an emergency shopping trip and was headed out the door when he stopped me. "Where you going?"

"I know you ain't talking to me," I snapped, releasing the attitude that had been building.

"Who else could I be talking to?" He walked over to the kitchen bar with the newspaper and a cup of coffee. I snuck a peek at his toned bare chest and the print in his Polo pajama pants. He'd been spending all his time at the twenty-four-hour gym around the corner, and his body told it all. At first, I was upset when I was asked to take over the membership because he couldn't afford to. Now I saw that the money had gone to good use.

"Do you hear me?" He waved his hand in my face.

"What did you say?"

"I said I think it's time we talk about what happened when your mom was here."

"Now you want to talk?" I smacked my MAC-covered lips. "Where has all that conversation been the last fourteen days?" I was over this nigga and just about done with this conversation.

"Shut the fuck up sometime, damn!" he yelled, and I blinked rapidly because he had never talked to me like this. "First off, I wanted to apologize for popping off at your mom like that, but"—he paused—"I was only reacting to the way she came on me."

"You know how Porscha is."

"That don't matter and it's no excuse. Your mother was dead wrong, and you should've had my back." He sipped from his mug.

"That wasn't my battle." I raised my hand in protest.

"Oh, but it became your battle when I stepped out of line? You didn't hesitate to check me." Dominic shook his head.

"Dom, that's different and you know it is." I shifted my weight to one side.

"She's your mom but I'm your fiancé! You should've had my back. You let her flat-out dog me, and you didn't say a word."

I thought I caught a glimpse of a tear in Dominic's eye, but I wasn't sure. He continued, "I don't have a mother or a father, and my only siblings are my frat brothers. Do you think it feels good to know that the one person in the world I thought was in my corner is really playing for the other team?"

I was caught off guard and didn't know what to say. Instead of talking, I embraced him in the tight hug I knew he was in need of.

"Baby, I need to know it's me and you against the world." He spoke softly.

"Dominic, I got you, but there's only so much I can do. Eventually more bills will come, the wedding is around the corner, and I'm one person. You know what you need to do."

He didn't say a word as he looked away from me. A few days ago, I had Trina's brother, Mack, call Dominic out of the blue with an offer of joining his team. He was in need of another location and wanted to set up shop down here in the Nati. Mack wasn't the Bill Gates of the drug industry, but money was money, and right now we needed a few stacks to stay afloat. I could've dipped into my personal stash to help out more, but I felt as though I shouldn't have to when Dom was able to hustle.

"I ain't selling no drugs!" Dominic pushed away from me.

"Why not? You sold cocaine to get out of Lima," I reminded him.

"I'm not that nigga no more." He went to stand by the sink and stared out the window. "I did that shit to get me out of the hood." He hit the granite countertop, which caused me to jump.

"Sometimes desperate times call for desperate measures." I folded my arms. Dude was starting to tick me off again.

"Well, I ain't desperate yet! Even if I were, I will never sell another rock, vial, sack, or nickel or dime bag. I have two degrees, and I'm not throwing my accomplishments away for nobody, not even you." He gritted his teeth, and I went ham.

"So you saying I'm not worth it?" I screamed. "Do you see this?" I did a slow spin in place to show him what I was working with. "I know plenty of men ready and willing to take care of me for life. All I asked you to do is hustle for a minute, just to cover the wedding, and you can't even do that!" I spat. "You are a worthless-ass nigga, and I can do broke all by myself!" I was done with this shit, so I grabbed my keys and stormed away.

"Worthless? Worthless?" I heard Dom yell as I headed for the door. He stood on the porch yelling at me, but I paid him no mind as I hopped into my car, turned up the music, and peeled from the driveway.

Fuck him!

Chapter Ten

"I can't believe that shit!" Trina exclaimed as I told her about what just transpired.

"I know, right?" I sipped on the pink Moscato and picked at my food. After the whole ordeal, I cancelled shopping because I was no longer in the mood. Instead, I needed comfort food, so we headed downtown to our favorite spot, the Mixx Ultra Lounge. It wasn't the 40/40 Club, but it was just what you needed after a long day. The decor was simple yet sexy with black walls, white furniture, and neon pink lighting. The chandeliers and marble floors also gave the place a nice touch. The drinks weren't watered down like some of the other places I'd been to, and the food was outright banging.

"Okay, am I the only one who heard the whole story?" Noel asked through a mouthful of chicken. "It doesn't sound like Dominic was wrong to me."

"Bitch, whose side are you on?" I asked and downed the last of my third drink. The more this chick talked, the more I was beginning to dislike her. Lately she'd been adding too much of her input into my business, and I wasn't feeling it.

"I'm for what's right, and I think you were wrong." She licked the signature sauce from her lips.

"What's so wrong about what I said?" I folded my arms.

"For starters, why should he have to sell drugs when he's getting unemployment and you're bringing home an income too?" She popped a loaded French fry into her mouth.

"Because." I smacked my lips, so annoyed. "His un-employment can barely cover the house payment, his car payment, and mine, let alone the monthly bills. We still owe twenty thousand on our wedding." I was highly irritated that I had to break shit down to her, and I was rethinking her invitation to lunch.

"Wait, hold up." She damn near choked. "He's paying the mortgage, cars, and bills?" She looked at me side-ways. "What are you doing with your paycheck?"

"Stacking my shit for a rainy day," I snapped.

"You can't be serious." She was looking like a fool with her mouth wide open.

"When Dominic asked me to live with him and marry him, he promised to take care of me. I've never paid a bill as long as we've been together, so why should I start now?" I glanced over at Trina, who was cracking up.

"Because he is your man and that's what people in a relationship do! You hold one another down and weather the storm together."

"My mama didn't raise no fool! When the storm comes, I won't be nowhere in sight. You know why?" I paused. "'Cause I'm using my stack to buy a lifeboat and get me the fuck up out of there." I laughed as the waitress placed fresh drinks down on the black tablecloth. By now I was tipsy, and Noel was too, because she burst out laughing.

"I love your gold-digging ass, Chanel." She sipped her red velvet wine.

"Call me what you want, but you can't call me broke." I raised my plastic cup.

"I'll drink to that!" Trina sipped her Jack and Coke, and we all laughed.

Noel eventually backed off, and things for the rest of the afternoon and into the evening were all good. "I wasn't going to tell you until it was time to leave, but . . ." She paused for dramatic effect.

"But what?" I could smell a surprise brewing.

"We're going to take you back home to Detroit to turn up next weekend," Trina blurted out before Noel had the chance.

"Aww, guys, that is so sweet. Thank you." I was excited for the late birthday celebration for two reasons. For one, I was always game to go back home and party. For two, I desperately needed to put Ohio and Dom in my rearview for a few days. I believed the time apart would be great for us. Maybe he would come to his senses and decide to take Mack up on his offer by the time I got back.

Chapter Eleven

The remainder of week flew by in no time, and I was in Detroit before I knew it. The four-hour ride was nothing because we talked and laughed all the way. Noel had been to Detroit with me and Trina several times before. Nonetheless, she acted like a tourist every time. "What's the name of that beautiful bridge that connects you guys to Canada?" She pointed as we passed the Ambassador Bridge.

Trina answered her question as I sat up in my seat and pulled down the visor. The sight of my city always boosted my adrenaline. It was usually during this point in the trip that I began reapplying makeup and fixing my hair. I never knew who I would run into. Therefore, I had to make sure I was presentable at all times.

After a quick stop at the liquor store to grab a bottle of Cîroc for the room, we grabbed a bite to eat at Erica's Place, a local soul food joint. Trina got a rib tip dinner, Noel got a BBQ lasagna, and I opted for a small Caesar salad. These bitches could grub all they wanted. I, on the other hand, wanted to look as slim as possible all weekend.

Just like old times, after eating and showering we were dressed to the nines and ready to party. It was about 10:40 p.m., and we were on our way to the MGM casino. I decided to wear a beige halter top with ruffles. My gold metallic leggings looked as if they were painted on, and my beige and gold chunky Michael Kors wedge pumps were to die for. Trina looked fierce in a pink snakeskin dress with the matching shoes and jewelry. Noel was sexy yet modest in a black catsuit with parachute legs that gathered at the ankles.

We pulled up to valet parking, bumping Moneybagg Yo. After handing over the keys, we walked inside and ventured around the casino until we found some machines that called our names. Within thirty minutes, the $20 I initially played was up to $180. Things were going great until Trina said she was ready to go to the club. Noel was losing her money, so she was ready to quit too. Reluctantly I grabbed my ticket and cashed out.

As we made our way to the club inside the casino, all eyes were on us, and we were enjoying every minute of it. "Wassup, Chanel!"

I turned to see my boy Rock from back in the day. Everybody in the city knew me. "What's up, big homie?" I embraced him into a tight hug. He and I went to high school together, and he used to date my sister.

"You're what's up. What's good, my baby? Can I get you and your girls a drink?"

"Yeah, you can get us a bottle of Möet Rosé." I wasted no time because I knew Rock was and would forever be a hustler, unlike Dom. His paper game was never anorexic, and I was glad he was my friend.

"Damn, a whole bottle, huh?" He smirked.

"You know how I roll, and besides, it's my post-birthday celebration!" I flashed a smile and he nodded.

While he placed the order at the bar, I signaled for my girls to follow me. I pressed through the thick crowd to find a seat near the dance floor. Everybody was out tonight, and I was loving it. For some reason, the casinos were the hot spot in Detroit. They were always packed, and tonight was no different.

"Girl, there are some fine-ass niggas up in here," Trina said as she sat down next to me.

"I see them, but a fine nigga can't do shit for me. Remember, it's the ballers I'm after." I scanned the crowd and added up the sum total of what people were rocking, to weed out the real niggas with money from the ones pretending.

"Engaged people shouldn't be looking at all," Noel interjected.

"I know, but Chanel can be single for the night. I mean, damn, it is her post-birthday!" Trina responded, and Noel rolled her eyes. She was definitely a party pooper, and I was beginning to question why she'd come in the first place.

"You can't be engaged and single. Birthday or not, it's unfair to Dominic," she added.

"OMG, would you freaking relax? I know I'm engaged, but it's my post-birthday celebration, and I'm going to have fun. I can look. I'm not dead," I said, and that was that. I was a grown-ass woman. I knew what I could and couldn't do. I'd been handling myself for twenty-seven years without her help, and today was no different.

Just then a light-skinned dude walked up and dropped game. "You three are the finest ladies in the building tonight," he said and sat on the arm of Trina's chair. He was fine and all, but I wasn't really attracted to light-skinned men, so I was glad he was all up in Trina's face.

"Thank you," she said, and they continued to hold small talk. Rock spotted us in the dim lighting and brought over the champagne bottle and three glasses.

"Thanks, Rock!" I said and wasted no time pouring my drink.

"For sho', Chanel. You know it's always like that for you." He stood and observed the club through his triple-black stunner shades. I never understood why people wore sunglasses in the club, but to each his own.

"You're so sweet, and I'll make sure to tell Kristian hello for you." Winking, I reached for the bottle and poured a drink for Trina and Noel. We participated in small talk and caught up for about five minutes before Rock said he would be right back. I began to search the crowd for someone else from my youth I might recognize who would buy us another bottle.

After a few moments or so of straining my eyes in the dim light, I gave up on my search. My girls and I bobbed our heads and swayed to a few songs while sipping our drinks. More people had entered the club, and the air became so hot and muggy, sweat was gathering on my nose. I reached into my bag for a tissue to wipe my face when I saw my phone light up. It was Dominic and I groaned inwardly. Honestly, I didn't know why I was so frustrated with him. It wasn't like he chose to be unemployed. Nonetheless, I was very irritated when I answered the call. "Yes, Dom."

"Hey, baby, are you having fun?" He spoke lovingly to me, and I didn't know why, but I rolled my eyes. I wanted to tell him I'd have more fun if he quit calling, but I didn't want to piss him off.

"Yeah, baby, I'm having a blast!"

"That's good. I'm not gon' hold you. I just wanted to wish you a happy anniversary," he said, and I stared at the phone.

"Dom, have you been drinking?" I didn't wait for a response. "It's May thirtieth. Our anniversary is next month," I reminded him in the slow tone one might use for a mentally challenged person.

"I know what today is, but obviously you don't. Today is the anniversary of the day we met in Sociology 101. I remember shit like that, but I guess you don't." Now he was irritated with me. "Anyway, I was thinking about you and just wanted to make you feel special. Talk to you later. Have fun and be safe," he added.

I felt dumb and bad for hurting his feelings with my sarcasm. I was about to call him back and smooth things over when someone tapped my shoulder. Turning to see who was touching me, I was caught off guard by the handsome stranger.

"Wassup, gorgeous." He smiled a perfect smile. "I'm Rico, and you are?"

"Hey, Rico, I'm Chanel," I replied while straining to hear him.

"Are you here with anybody?"

"Yeah, my girls." I nodded to my crew. Trina was still flirting with light-skinned, and Noel was nursing her champagne glass while giving me the evil eye.

"Okay, okay." He rubbed his goatee. "I see y'all looking fly and shit. What's the special occasion?"

"It's my birthday," I lied. I could tell Rico had a little dough and he was willing to share some with the birthday girl. There was no need to tell the truth. Hell, I wanted to see how generous he was.

"Aw shit!" He smiled, exposing a platinum grill. I knew then that he wasn't originally from the D, because we don't rock grills, but his was still hot. "How old are you?" he asked.

"I'm legal." I threw the catchy comeback out there, and Rico smiled again, exposing the dimples on his chocolate face.

"Do you and your girls want to kick it with me and my niggas up in VIP?" He nodded his waved head toward an area in the back.

"Yeah, that's cool." I smiled but was cut off just as my favorite Beyoncé song came on. This boy and his VIP offer would have to wait, because it was time to do my thang. Trina looked at me and was up out of her seat in a flash. I grabbed Noel, and we hit the dance floor like three women on a mission.

We worked it out on the floor as B sang, *Getting bodied, getting bodied, a little sweat ain't never hurt nobody*

It must have lasted forever, because by the time it ended and we got back to our seats, I saw Rico and a few of his dudes approaching us. They were being followed by a few waitresses carrying bottles of champagne with sparklers sparkling everywhere. "Happy birthday, baby girl," he said and gave me a hug like he knew me.

"Thank you," I said and grabbed a napkin off the table to wipe the sweat off my forehead. I was sure by now the natural curl in my hair was returning and the straightness from the flat iron was wearing off, but I didn't care.

"Follow me," he said. We followed him and his guys to a VIP area that was set up like a cabana.

"This is what's up," Trina exclaimed.

"Yeah, this is pretty fly," Noel added. I was glad she was starting to loosen up and have fun.

"I know, right?" I said back.

"Y'all were working it on the dance floor." Rico took a seat on the black leather sofa. He looked good as hell in his tan linen 'fit and matching Mauri gators.

"Y'all look like y'all came together with those matching 'fits," Trina pointed out, and I agreed.

"Great minds think alike, I guess," Rico admitted while pouring everyone drinks. He introduced his crew, and I introduced my girls.

After several rounds of shots, we partied so hard that I hadn't realized that it was almost two o'clock in the morning. We all were faded, and the pictures we'd snapped on our cell phones showed it. I went to the bathroom and splashed a little cold water on my face to prepare for the ride home to sober up. When I returned, I saw Rico over at the DJ booth.

"On the count of three, I want you all to wish Ms. Chanel a happy birthday."

"Aw, you requested a shout-out for my birthday." I gave Rico a hug when he returned.

"I just wanted to make the evening more special." He shrugged. "So what's next? Where we headed?"

"I'm a little hungry. Do you want to grab something to eat?" As I asked the question, I spotted a girl staring so hard in our direction that I could actually feel it. Knowing this girl had to know Rico or someone up in this cabana booth, I nudged him and put him up on game to her appearance.

"Damn!" he cursed, which let me know the two definitely knew each other.

"Go ahead and handle yours, baby." I played it cool because I knew the deal. I'd played this position several times in my younger days. He looked relieved that I wasn't pressing him or trying to start shit with his girl. Hell, I had gotten what I wanted, and I was content. Rico and his friends showed me a damn good time on my special day, and they were gentlemen about it. For that I was grateful. He stood and kissed me on my cheek, sliding some money in my bra.

"Take a cab, baby. You're bent," he said, referring to how drunk we were.

"Don't worry, Rico. I got this. You just go and handle your girl," I said, and he walked away. "Are y'all ready?" I asked my girls.

"Yeah, if you are," Noel answered. Trina was so wasted she didn't say anything.

"Let's roll." I grabbed my bag, then we proceeded to exit the club. I walked right past Rico like I didn't know him, and I could tell he appreciated it. The girl was still staring at me, but she didn't say anything.

As we found our way to the car, I fumbled through my purse to find the keys. "Chanel, you sure you're straight?" Noel asked.

"I'm cool, girl. You know I wouldn't drive if I thought I would fuck something up." I smirked, pretending to be cooler than I felt.

"You better get us home in one piece," Trina said and got in.

"I had so much fun, girls. Thanks for the good time." I was elated. The little time away from Dominic had done me some good. My friends knew I was going through something and went out of their way to make my day special, and I appreciated that.

"You know you're my bitch until the world blows up," Noel, who rarely cursed, said, and we pulled off laughing all the way back to the hotel.

Chapter Twelve

We pulled up at the light and proceeded to pull off when it turned green. Out of nowhere, an SUV slammed right into us, causing us to spin out of control and hit a light pole. Instantly, I sobered up and jumped out of the car to see who had just hit us. I looked back to see if Trina was okay, and she was, because she had jumped out of the car too. Next I glanced at Noel, who was holding her head. She might've been in a daze for a second, but she too was okay. We all approached the SUV mad as hell, ready to fight.

"My bad, baby," was what I heard from some guy as he emerged from what I now recognized as a Yukon Denali.

"Your bad? Nigga, is that all you gon' say? Look at my shit!" I pointed to the smashed-in passenger side and crunched-up hood. Not to mention the fact that my car was up against the light pole.

"Ladies, are you okay?" another guy asked as he slid out of the back seat.

"Nigga, do we look okay?" Trina asked with a busted nose.

"Do you need me to call an ambulance?" the backseat rider asked.

"No! I need somebody to teach this dumb ass to drive, and while they're at it, they need to teach his ass how to write a check for my shit!" I placed my hand to my mouth to catch the blood from where I'd bitten my lip.

"Chill, ma, accidents happen. You'll be taken care of."

I couldn't believe this nigga had the nerve to say that accidents happen. "Well, of course they do when muthafuckas like him run red lights!" I spat and pointed to the driver.

"I'm about to call Mack. He will take care of this," Trina added, referring to her brother.

"Ain't no need to call nobody. I'm going to take care of this," the backseat passenger said and went to the back of the SUV. He returned seconds later with a duffle bag and handed it to me.

"What the fuck is this?" I questioned.

"Little mama, calm down and look in the bag." He looked straight at me. I looked over at Trina, and she shrugged her shoulders. I unzipped the bag and almost lost my breath when I saw the huge quantity of money it contained.

"Shit, how much is this?" I wanted to know. Noel walked up beside me and looked inside at the contents, then shook her head.

"I ain't sure. I just picked it up from the spot, but whatever it is, it's yours," he said confidently.

Staring into his beautiful eyes, I finally noticed how damn fine he was, and I could smell his paper trail from a mile away. He looked just like Tank, body and all!

I must've looked dumbfounded, so he continued, "I told you I got you. Take whatever is in the bag. Treat you and your girls to a massage or something tomorrow. Then go shopping on me. After all, it was my driver's fault." He flashed his pearly whites, and my vagina pulsated. Did this nigga say "driver"? I was mesmerized by his ass, and the fact that he had bank really got my panties wet.

"What about my car?" I whined. "What if this ain't enough to fix it?" I held up the heavy bag.

"Sweetheart, I will buy you another one!" he said in a chill tone like it was nothing.

"Damn, you got it like that?" Trina asked, not skipping a beat.

"As a matter of fact, I do," was his answer.

"Well, damn!" Noel yelled from where she was sitting on the curb still holding her head.

"All right. In that case, when can we go shopping for my new whip?" I was not one to miss an opportunity to come up on a new whip.

"First thing tomorrow!" He didn't even blink. "Put your name and number in this phone." He handed me his iPhone. I did as I was told, and he laughed when I gave it back to him.

"What's funny?" I asked.

"Ms. Franklin, huh? Sweetheart, what's your first name?"

"Chanel."

"Chanel, I'm Cashus, but everybody calls me Cash." He put the phone back into the phone holster that was clipped to his Gucci belt.

"Can we take y'all anywhere?" the bad driver asked.

"Oh, shit! I forgot just that quick that we don't have a way back to the hotel." I looked over at Trina.

"I'll call Mack. It's the weekend. I'm sure he's down here partying at someone's club. He'll take us to the hotel." She pulled out her phone and called her brother.

"Cool. While you do that, I'm going to call my uncle Tee so he can come and tow my car to his junkyard." I pulled out my phone and called my uncle to handle the removal of my car.

Chapter Thirteen

We sat on the curb forever as we waited for the cavalry to arrive. The men who had plowed into us had offered for us to sit in their vehicle, but we declined. Just as my body began to ache, Uncle Tee finally showed up and loaded my car onto the back on his tow truck. Watching my baby take its last ride through the city of Detroit kind of brought tears to my eyes, but I blinked rapidly to keep them from falling.

Looking at the time on my cell, I turned and asked Trina where Mack was.

"He said he would be here in an hour," she said with the same tired and irritated look on her face that I wore on mine.

"He said that an hour ago." Noel smacked her lips. After the four-hour drive to Detroit, partying at the casino, and being in a car accident, we were beat.

"Ladies, we can drop you off. This Denali is still drivable," Cash said from the passenger seat. He refused to leave us until our ride came. I guessed he felt bad about what happened.

"Is that nigga driving?" I pointed to the driver and let out a laugh. Though nothing was funny, I had to find a way to ease the tension.

"Don't do my man Caesar like that." He chuckled. "If it makes you feel safe, I'll drive."

I looked at my girls, who were just as tired of waiting for Mack as I was.

"Okay cool, but your ass had better drive the speed limit all the way," I warned, and with that they changed seats. I gave him the name of our hotel, and we were on our way.

The entire drive to the hotel was silent. No one spoke. It was late and everyone was tired. Cashus pulled up to the Marriott and put the SUV in park.

"Good night," I said while collecting my things and easing out of the whip. I hadn't even closed the door good before Trina got started.

"That nigga was fine as hell, Chanel!"

"Girl, you know I peeped it." I closed the door, then walked over to the wall, leaned against it, and removed my shoes.

"Sorry about that. Y'all have a safe night." Cashus tossed his apology out the window.

"He was all right," Noel commented, ignoring him, and I threw my purse at her.

"Girl, you must be blind to not see how gorgeous baby was." I walked into the hotel.

"I'm not blind. He just wasn't my type."

"So exactly what is your type, Ms. Goody Two-shoes?" Trina jumped in.

"Well, first of all," Noel said, trying to get fly, "my guy doesn't have to be drop-dead gorgeous, he doesn't have to be wealthy, and he doesn't have to be hard-core. You girls expect too much from these men, especially when y'all aren't perfect your damn selves." She shrugged.

"Girl, bye!" Trina smacked her lips.

"Noel, if you don't require any of those qualities, why aren't you with someone? Hell, there are a bunch of ugly-ass, poor-ass, punk-ass men out there in the world. Go nuts!" I slapped fives with Trina, who was hysterical.

"Just because they don't have to possess those specific qualities doesn't mean I don't have any requirements. My man must be God-fearing, respectful, and hardworking." She smiled and I frowned.

"Boring!" I shouted as we reached the elevator.

"Hey, to each her own." She waved me off. "I like what I like, and you like what you like. I don't have time to be chasing behind some thug and his hoes. Nor do I have time to be writing letters and visiting prison."

I thought about what she was saying and took it as real talk. Noel was right. To each her own. She didn't have time for thugs, and I didn't have time for lames. Back in high school, my girl Gucci used to tell me that she could do broke all by herself, and so could I. I didn't need to struggle when there was another motherfucker capable and able to get out and make money. My love wasn't free. You had to pay to play in this kitty cat, and that was on my mama.

"Anyway, enough about this bitch and her saved, sanctified, and ugly, broke man." Trina rolled her eyes at Noel. "Let's get back to Cash. You bet' not let that nigga slip through the cracks, girl." She walked into the hotel suite, dropped her shoes, then headed over to the sofa and plopped down.

"Trust me, I'm on it! I will definitely friend request that nigga on Facebook." I laughed. "Dom better step his game up, because Cash might end up being my damn husband," I said, and we slapped five again. Noel, of course, added her two cents as usual.

"Women kill me! We always complain there are no good men around, but when you have one, he's never good enough." Shaking her head, she sat down beside Trina, and I took the La-Z-Boy chair.

"I know what Dom was and what he is capable of, but right now the truth of the matter is he's just another nigga without a job." I rolled my eyes. Honestly, after being in the presence of Cash, I was once again over Dom and this unemployment situation. Shit needed to get straightened out and fast!

"I wonder if he felt that way when you were unemployed a few years ago," Noel snapped.

"That doesn't count. We were in college then!" I blew her off. I looked over at Trina, who was doing the same.

"It doesn't matter though. Dom had your back then, and you should do a better job of having his now." Noel tried to school me like she was my mama, but she was a far cry from Porscha.

"News flash: that's what a man is supposed to do." This bougie broad was starting to irritate me.

"But he wasn't your husband, and he didn't have to," she had the nerve to say.

"Well, currently I'm not his wife. I guess I don't have to either then, huh?"

"I'm just saying you have a great man! I would hate for you to lose him for this thug."

"Look, I know my man is a good catch, but everybody has their faults. Not being a true hustler is Dom's weakness. Most dudes I'm used to won't ever go broke because of their hustler mentality." I sighed. "I wish Dominic had more thug in him. We wouldn't be in this position if he got out there and hustled. I told him to take Mack up on his offer, but he refused and called me crazy."

"Do you blame him?" Noel looked at me sideways.

"Not everybody's made for the streets, Chanel," Trina added.

"He didn't have a problem selling cocaine to get out of Lima. He didn't mind pushing weed and pills in college to make ends meet. Now we have a mortgage, bills, and two vehicle payments. Not to mention the wedding that probably won't be happening anytime soon." Exhaling, I shot up from my seat. I totally forgot about the bag Cash had given me. Trina and Noel sat up too and watched me grab the bag.

We all stared nervously yet eagerly, anticipating the exact amount of the bag's contents. I unzipped it and poured the money out on the wooden coffee table. Trina raked it her way and began to count it aloud. I closed my eyes, held my breath, and leaned back against the couch cushion, daydreaming. I was silently praying it was a lot of money and tomorrow we would be able to tear the mall up.

After nearly forty minutes of silence, I sat up to see why she'd gotten quiet. I looked over to see her silently counting.

"Girl, you won't believe this!"

Her tone was concerning. "He didn't play me, did he?" I hoped that I hadn't fallen for game. If there wasn't a lot of money in the bag, I was screwed. I had failed to get his insurance information and his fucking number because he had me gone. I hoped it was at least enough to get me a new car that could get me back to Ohio.

"Girl, there is twenty-two thousand dollars in this bag!" Trina exclaimed with a high-pitched squeal.

My mouth fell wide open in shock. I thought she might've messed up, so I recounted, and sure enough there was $22,000 in cold, hard cash lying in neat stacks on the table. For once today, Noel was speechless and didn't offer her opinion.

"What are you going to do with all that money?" Trina asked after the initial shock wore off.

Without a word, I counted out $8,000. I slid half of it to Trina and the other half to Noel. I kept $4,000 out for me and put $10,000 back in the bag just in case he didn't show up tomorrow. At least I could get another somewhat decent car. "Y'all are my girls! If I hit a lick, we all hit a lick."

"I know that's right," they said in unison while slapping five. I typically wasn't that generous, but tonight there was more than enough to share.

"I wonder if he knows he gave you all that money," Noel said as we made our way to our individual rooms inside of the executive suite to turn in for the night.

"Oh, well. It's mine now!"

"I know that's right!" Trina agreed. Simultaneously they both turned and thanked me for the money. I told them in all fairness they were entitled to something because they were in my car with me. I also knew that they would've done the same for me.

After saying our good nights, we all headed to bed. I was sure my friends didn't have any trouble drifting off considering how eventful the day had been. I, on the other hand, could barely contain myself thinking about the money I'd been given, as well as what could possibly be hiding on the other side of Cashus's rainbow. He was something special. I could feel it.

Morning came, and I awoke to my cell phone vibrating on the nightstand. I reached over and looked at the caller

ID. I started not to answer because I didn't recognize the number, but then I quickly answered as I remembered my Prince Charming was going to call me. "Hello," I said in my sexiest morning voice.

"Hello, is this Chanel?"

"It is."

"Hey, it's Caesar, Cash's homey from last night."

"The guy who hit me, right?" I asked with a small chuckle. I could laugh at the situation now knowing I was a few thousand dollars richer and on my way to get a new car. This guy wouldn't have called if he were shady.

"Yeah, that's me," he said, kind of annoyed.

"What's up?"

"Cash doesn't have time to go to the dealership with you, so—"

I cut his ass off. "Don't tell me that nigga is trying to play me!" I sat straight up in bed.

"Damn, shorty, let me finish! He ain't have time to go to the dealership, so he had the car sent over to your hotel about an hour ago. It should be in front of your building already. He left instructions with the manager."

"He picked out a car for me?" I asked, a little confused.

"Yeah. He said if it ain't your style, just let him know and he'll handle it. I'll holla at you later." With that he ended our call.

I was so excited that I threw on a jogging suit and made my way into the living room to put on my Nikes. Hearing the noise, Trina, who had been asleep in the next room, opened her door and asked what was going on.

"Girl, get up. We need to go downstairs. Cash didn't have time to go to the dealership, so he picked a car out and had it sent over," I whispered so as not to wake up Noel.

"For real?" She started jumping up and down. "I'm going in this." She pointed at her pajamas.

"Fuck it. Come on." I was too excited to care how ghetto we looked.

After she put on her shoes, we were out the door, practically running down the hall. "Come on." I hit the button for the fifth time. It was taking the elevator too damn long in my opinion. Finally, it came just as I was about to suggest taking the stairs.

"What kind of car do you think it is?" Trina was just as excited as I was.

"I don't know, but for it to have been delivered, it has to be something nice." I shrugged. The anticipation was killing me.

Seconds later we stepped off the elevator and made our way through the lobby. I had to admit my stomach was flipping at the expectation of what I wanted to be waiting for me.

"Ms. Franklin, wait up a second," James, the concierge, yelled as he practically had to sprint to catch up with me. "Here." He handed me a card. "This was left for you along with a very nice surprise."

I thanked him and headed out the door.

No one could've prepared me for what I saw next. Right outside the door, front and center was a black 2020 Mercedes-Benz E 550 coupe with chrome trimming. "Oh, my God!" I yelled with tears in my eyes.

"This bitch is bad as hell!" Trina added. Though I agreed with her completely, I stood there in awe as I took in the fact that I would be pushing a Benz back home to Ohio. My heart raced at the thought of taking this luxury car back home. I worried about what I would tell Dominic, but I didn't have time to dwell on it right now because I was too excited.

"Open the card," Trina insisted.

"Shit, I forgot about the card." With shaking hands, I
tore it open and began to read.

> *Chanel,*
> *Let me start by apologizing for the accident and*
> *asking that all be forgiven. I hope the money you*
> *got last night was enough to treat yourself to some-*
> *thing as beautiful as you are. I also hope the Benz*
> *is to your liking. If not, don't hesitate to let me*
> *know, and I will definitely make other arrange-*
> *ments for you. I would also like to invite you out*
> *tonight for dinner. If you want to pass, I'll under-*
> *stand. However, I would love to see your sexy ass*
> *again.*
> *Until next time,*
> *Cash*

Chapter Fourteen

Trina and I stayed outside admiring the new ride and test-driving it for almost two hours. We drove around the whole city just to flex. I couldn't believe such a good thing had happened to me. It was like a fairy tale.

"The million-dollar question is, are you going to dinner with Cash tonight?" Trina asked as we pulled back up to the hotel. Our trip was supposed to end today, and we were scheduled to hit the road by 2:00 p.m. in order to get home and prepared for the coming workweek.

"Life is about taking risks. I think I'm going to stay and go to dinner. I have to see what Cash is about." I was so open for this nigga that he could've driven a Mack truck up my nostrils.

"I'm not even mad at you. This is a real once-in-a-lifetime encounter. Hell, if you don't call the nigga and accept the date, I sure will!"

"Bitch!" I punched her arm.

"I was just playing."

"Yeah, okay." I looked at her sideways. "Hey, let me have a few minutes of alone time to call Dom. I'll be up to the room as soon as I'm done."

"You better sound believable," she coached before stepping out of the car and leaving me alone.

Lying to Dominic was as easy as 1-2-3. I told him I needed to extend my trip for an extra day because of the car accident. After swearing to him I was okay and uninjured, I told him I loved him and would see him to-morrow. I failed to mention the new car because I didn't feel like doing all that explaining. My plan was to show up with the car and a fabricated story. My lie included a wealthy white lady who paid for the car outright. I would say that she didn't want her husband to see an insurance claim or police report for drunk driving. It sounded believable to me, so that was my story and I was sticking to it.

Even with my lie to Dom covered, I was still nervous. All day I pondered calling Cash and actually accepting his date invitation, or declining. On one hand, he was the very man I'd prayed to meet my whole life. On the other hand, I feared what spending more time with him would do to my relationship. I was so attracted to him that it would be hard to disconnect from him and return to my regular life.

After a little more thought and persuasion from Trina, I decided to go. Of course, Noel was out of the loop on this one. Trina created a diversion by taking her sightsee-ing to get her out of my hair for a while. Right now, they were probably at the Motown Historical Museum, which was the old Motown recording studio. Of all the times Noel had visited the D, she'd never been. Therefore, the plan was perfect, and she was none the wiser.

As I paced back and forth in the hotel suite, my mind kept telling me to call Cash and cancel, but after glancing at the nightstand clock, I changed my mind. He would be arriving in a few minutes, which meant it was too late to back out. Besides, I had been cooped up in the house with Dom for too long with tension thick enough to cut. A chance to hang out in good company was just what the doctor ordered.

Everything about what I was doing was wrong. I didn't know what it was about Cash that had me going against my better judgment. Truth be told, dude had me gone. Maybe it was his style, his money, or his good looks, but whatever it was, I was fiending hard. Looking myself over in the mirror, I blew my signature kiss and took in the beautiful sight before me. I had on a red strapless Yves Saint Laurent sundress with gold accessories and gold wedge sandals. I air-dried my hair, causing it to curl even tighter than it already was. A little oil sheen and curl activator put the finishing touch on my Marilyn Monroe look. Just as I grabbed the gold LV bag Trina had given me for my birthday, my cell phone rang.

"Hello," I said in a sexy tone because I knew it was Cash.

"What's up, Chanel? I'm downstairs," he said in the most masculine voice I'd heard in a while.

"Be there in a sec."

"All right. Don't keep a nigga waiting with your sexy ass."

If I'd had on any panties, they would've been wet behind that statement. Without another word, I ended the call and headed out the door.

I smiled wide when I saw the money green Range Rover parked outside. Cash's boy Caesar jumped out and opened my door. As I stepped inside, the smell of some serious Kush filled the air. "Damn, y'all are smoking good!" I sat back on the leather seat, then clicked on my seat belt.

"Only the best," Cash replied as Caesar pulled off, bumping Plies's "In Love With Money."

"That's my favorite song!" I said, rapping along to the words.

"Mine too! My favorite part is when he says, 'Talk to a broke nigga, I bet his life rough, talk to a rich nigga, I bet he cheer you up.'"

I smiled and nodded because that was also one of my favorite parts.

"Where to, boss?" Caesar asked.

"Stop in Highland Park really quick. We need to talk to that nigga Dino about that count coming back wrong."

Caesar nodded and continued driving.

"You don't mind, do you, ma? Can we make a quick stop?" he asked, looking at me with dreamy eyes that I had just noticed for the first time.

"Not at all. Handle your business," I said with a wave of my hand. Truthfully, I didn't give a damn where we went as long as I was with him.

As we pulled up in front of a run-down, seemingly abandoned house on Eason, Caesar turned down the music and pulled his cell phone out. "What up doe, where is Dino? Send that nigga outside!" he demanded before getting out of the whip to open Cash's door.

A young male about 18 or 19 walked from the side of the house, and I noticed a look of pure evil come across Cash's face as he got out of the SUV. His grimace reminded me of one a cutthroat killer might wear. It kind of scared the shit out of me, but it also turned me on at the same time.

"Where the fuck is my motherfucking money?" Cash asked with saliva flying from his mouth.

I could tell the young boy was scared out of his mind as he replied, "Cash, um, Moe told me, um . . ." he stuttered.

"What the fuck are you trying to say, little nigga?"

"Um, Moe said that he would collect the money last night, and he let me go home early," he said with what looked like tears in his eyes.

"Did I give you that order personally?" Cash's question was rhetorical. "No, the fuck I didn't, so I'm holding you responsible for my shit coming up short!" In one swift motion he backhanded Dino so hard his nose and lip busted at the same time. The action scared me so bad it caused me to leap from my seat. Dino bent down instantly and grabbed his face just as Cash punched him so hard in the stomach he threw up all over the sidewalk. I turned my head because I had a weak stomach, and I didn't want to ruin my dress by throwing up too. I was unable to look away for long, however, so I turned back to the scene. Poor Dino was now laid out cold. Caesar bent down, picked up his arms, and dragged him to the back of the house. Cash reached into his back pocket and retrieved a black leather glove as he walked behind the two men. Seconds later I saw two bright flashes and heard two gunshots.

"Oh, hell no!" Was all I could say before Caesar and Cash were back at the car. Right then and there I wanted to jump the fuck out and pretend I never met either of them, but fear kept me planted in my seat.

"Sorry about the detour." Cash got back into the SUV just as calm as he'd been when he picked me up. "Let's ride." He tapped the back of Caesar's seat, and we pulled off.

Chapter Fifteen

I couldn't believe what had just happened, and my facial expression told it all. I barely talked on the way to wherever we were going. After about a good twenty minutes into the drive, Cash leaned over and whispered in my ear, "Don't sweat it. That nigga fucked up my money, baby. It had to be done." He shrugged.

"But did it have to be done in front of me?" Right now, I was concerned about being charged as an accessory to the crime. I wasn't about this life.

"This is how I roll. You have to learn not to take shit like this personal if you want to fuck with a nigga like me." He looked me square in the face. "If it's too much for you to handle, Caesar can take you home, no hard feelings." He winked.

"Do you do this all the time?" I really didn't want to know, but I had to ask.

"If I have to, then I will, believe that, but please don't let this mess up our date. I'm really feeling you, and I can't lie, I want you bad as hell, but you are kind of blowing my high, sitting there acting all antisocial and shit." He laughed.

Hearing the nigga say he wanted me bad cheered me right up. I did feel bad for Dino, but I didn't know the boy personally, so what did it matter?

We pulled up to a beautiful house on Santa Barbara, and I began to wonder if he'd brought me to his house just to hit it. I wasn't that easy, which he would quickly find out if he tried me. Cash got out and came around to my side to open my door. I stepped out and followed him to the front door of the brick home and then inside. Caesar blew the horn and backed out of the driveway.

"I thought he was coming in with us," I said after Cash closed the door.

"Nah, he ain't done working," he said and then asked me to remove my shoes because of the white carpet. I looked around and noticed that everything was white: the walls, the furniture, the window treatments, and all.

"Someone loves white," I announced and followed him into the kitchen then down some stairs that led into the basement.

"This is my sister's crib, and she has a crazy fascination with white." He cut the light on and revealed a simple little area with a white sectional and a seventy-inch flat-screen television mounted to the wall with a fireplace beneath it. There was an air hockey table off to the side and a small bathroom next to it. Cash took a seat on the couch, and I joined him.

"I have to admit this isn't what I had in mind for a date." I was a little disappointed. He didn't think enough of me to treat me to at least dinner and a movie before trying to get into my panties.

"What's wrong with this?" He frowned.

"Well, I thought when you asked me out on a date you were actually going to take me somewhere," I said in all honesty and was beginning to rethink why I'd called him in the first place. If I was going to step out on Dom, it would be with someone with more class.

Cash looked at me and smiled a seductive smile. "Baby girl, I wanted you all to myself! Yo' ass is fine. I don't want to be in public so all them other niggas can be staring and shit. My sister, Yoyo, owns a restaurant, and I asked her to bring us something home. Is that okay?" he asked with sincerity, which softened my feelings toward him.

"Yeah, that's cool." I immediately changed my tone from pissed off to perky. "What's the name of her restaurant?" I asked, turning sideways to face him.

"It's called Yolanda's House, on Woodward. She opened it about two years ago."

"Oh, that's nice! I've never heard of it. Is it soul food?" I asked, knowing that most black people could throw down on some soul food.

"Soul food with a little Caribbean flavor. I'm surprised you haven't heard of her. She's well-known for her cooking. I know you'll love it. Plus, I need to thicken you up," he said, rubbing my thigh, and I felt the heat rise. I was already thick enough, so he was a fool if he thought I would let him talk me into gaining weight. My size nine told it all.

Cash got up and walked over to a mini-refrigerator on the floor next to the pool table. Retrieving a drink for himself, he also handed me a personal-sized bottle of Kai. I admired the way the bottle resembled a perfume bottle. We made a toast to our meeting and each took a sip.

After talking for a while, I must admit, I did enjoy his conversation. He was smooth and I liked it. He told me he and his sister were raised by their grandparents. Their dad was in jail their whole lives and, in fact, recently died there. Their mom died of an overdose while they were practically still babies. He and his sister were only eighteen months apart, and she was his world. He said even though he was the youngest, he always acted like the oldest.

Ever since he was a young child he ran with the big boys and broke all the rules. After his grandfather died, he really stepped up and took care of the family by doing anything necessary to put food on the table. Of course, his grandmother didn't approve. It wasn't until after the bank threatened to take the house she and her husband had broken their backs to pay off that she had a change of heart. She was a few months behind on the taxes and told him to do what he had to do. With that being said, he hustled hard and never looked back. I didn't ask him what his hustle was, because I figured it was drugs.

"Wow, that's deep," I said, feeling a small buzz from the Kai.

"Yeah, as long as I had permission from my old girl, wasn't shit gon' stop me."

"Where is your grandma now?" I asked, hoping to meet her eventually. He looked off, then told me she'd passed away a few weeks ago from cancer. Before he had time to get sad, we heard the alarm indicate that the side door was open.

"Cash, I'm here," someone yelled, and I assumed it was Yoyo.

"Come on, baby girl. Let me go introduce you."

We walked upstairs, and I wasn't the least bit nervous. I wasn't some high school girl trying to fit in.

As we reached the top of the stairs, the aroma of some good, home-cooked food crept into my nostrils. "Yoyo, I told yo' ass to start using the front door instead of the side door," he said in a low but serious tone.

"Nigga, the side door is closer. Plus, I had bags in my hands," she said, lifting two big bags up in the air. Yolanda looked nothing like Cash, but you could tell they were related by those dreamy eyes. She was about five feet five inches tall, cocoa brown, maybe a size six, and really busty with no ass at all.

"Hello," I said as we made eye contact.

"How you doing? I'm Yoyo," she said and extended her hand as Cash removed the bags.

"I'm Chanel."

"What you bring us?" Cash asked as he pulled out plates from the cabinet.

"Jerk beef brisket, collard greens, candied yams, corn muffins, and some banana pudding for dessert."

"See? And you were worried about going out. We got the hookup right here," Cash said, then removed the food from the containers and placed it onto plates. I smiled and thanked Yoyo for the food, then Cash and I retreated to the basement, where we ate in silence until I had to say something.

"This food is good as hell!" I licked my fingers to catch the sauce that was dripping down.

"I told you she was the truth!" Cash slid his plate to the side and popped the lid on his pudding, then placed his spoon inches from my mouth. I was so stuffed that I couldn't even attempt to taste it. Waving my hand, I stood and grabbed his plate. As I turned to head upstairs to place them in the dishwasher, Cash stopped me. "Leave them there. I'll get them. Come over here and show a nigga some love."

I put them down and sat back on the couch. He grabbed my hand and placed it on his erect dick. *Oh, my God,* I wanted to shout as he slid it out of his boxers. It was beautiful and had a curve, so I knew that he could work it.

"Baby, I want you," he whispered.

"Cash, not on the first date. I just met you yesterday, remember?" I let out a nervous laugh, but Cash wasn't laughing at all. Truth be told, I would've jumped his bones right then and there, but I was engaged, and Dom's face was in the back of my mind.

"Damn, Chanel, I thought I was fucking with a woman who was about her shit, not a scared little girl!" he snapped. "People don't wait anymore to have sex. They just do it if they're feeling each other. I'm feeling you. How do you feel about me?" he said, still slouched back with his dick hanging out of his red Dior jeans.

"I am a grown woman," I clarified. "I'm feeling you too, but—"

He cut me off before I could tell him my situation. "Shit, I could call a bitch right now to come suck my dick while another bitch eats her pussy if I wanted to. But I don't want that, Chanel. I want you."

Looking into his piercing eyes, I asked, "Why do you want me? You don't even know me."

"I knew the minute I laid eyes on you I wanted to make you mine." Licking his lips, he continued. "I like your style, and I love the way you look. Plus, I know that pussy gon' be fire."

He got up and leaned over me, causing me to lean back. He slid his finger right up my dress and into my vagina. He gave a look of shock because I'd chosen not to wear panties. I smirked as he continued to rub my clit in circular motions. Unexpectantly, he dropped down onto his knees and began feasting on me like he hadn't just eaten. I moaned so loud that I was sure Yoyo heard me, but I didn't care. Dominic was king between the sheets, but his head game was close to nonexistent. I hadn't been with a man who knew how to work his tongue in so long, and the sensation was indescribable.

"Damn, you got that Aquafina flow." Cash looked up at me with my juices on his mouth. He pulled his shirt off, then his wife beater, and came back to the couch, pulling down the top of my dress to reveal my very aroused nipples. As he positioned his body to enter me, I asked if he had a condom.

"Look at me. I'm good." He flashed a smile. "I'm the healthiest Negro I know, so what do we need a condom for?"

"Are you sure?" I was scared to death but at the same time horny as hell. What I was doing was wrong, but it felt so damn good. I prayed this boy was being honest, because I would hate to take something home to Dom.

"Yes, Chanel. Are you clean?"

"Yeah." I nodded, and we made music that night for two hours straight. He gave me the best dick I had ever had. Earlier I'd thought Dom was the king. Well, he had just been dethroned.

Cash went to the bathroom upstairs to wash off as I did the same in the basement bathroom. I was too embarrassed to go up there and face his sister. As I sat back on the couch and fixed my dress, I couldn't help but reflect on what I'd just done. It was very irresponsible to sleep with Cash raw, but I was feeling him. I knew he was feeling me too, although I didn't know what he'd think after I told him about my fiancé. I wasn't too worried though. It seemed like his ass was already whipped, and I was loving it. As long as Cash stayed in Detroit and Dominic stayed in Ohio, I could have my cake and eat it, too. Chanel Franklin was about to be rolling in dough, and I also knew the haters would be lurking soon!

Chapter Sixteen

Shortly after we finished fucking, Caesar was back to pick us up. He was engrossed in a conversation on his cell phone during the ride, paying us no attention.

"When can I see you again? I have tickets to the Tigers game tomorrow, and I would love to take you," Cash said as we sat in back of the Range Rover, holding hands.

My stomach did backflips as I pondered how to tell this man my situation. At first, I'd planned to play it cool. I could lie and tell him my job kept me on the road traveling, but that was too messy. It would be hard to keep that up after a while, so I decided to tell the truth. Not only did I have a man at home, but my home was in another state. I hoped he would understand, because I didn't want to lose him.

"Cash, I have something to tell you," I whispered.

"What's the matter?"

"Well . . ." I stalled. "I haven't been completely honest." He looked at me intently, and I looked away like the scared coward I was. "As much as I like you and would love to continue seeing you, I can't." I frowned like a sad puppy dog.

"Why not?"

"I don't live here in Michigan. I live in Ohio." I saw no need to be more specific and name the city I lived in, so I kept on talking. "And I'm in a little situation right now."

"By situation you mean in a relationship?" His eyebrow raised.

"Yes. I'm so sorry I didn't tell you sooner, but I didn't know how. I saw you last night and thought God had answered my prayers. You are everything I've always wanted, but I understand if you want to pull off and never call me again." I held my breath.

"Baby girl, I'm glad you decided to be honest, and I respect you for it. I already knew both things about you. I just wanted to see how long it would take you to tell me." He laughed.

"How did you know?" I was confused.

"For starters, last night you had an engagement ring on that's nowhere to be seen today." He pointed to my left hand. I looked down at the tan line on my finger and smirked because he was right. I'd taken the ring off before I came downstairs for our date.

"I also knew you were from Ohio because of the plates on your car."

"Damn, you're observant!" I sat back in the seat and stared at him. "So you knew those things and you still wanted to kick it with me?"

"See, I'm a nigga who goes after what he wants. It doesn't matter to me if you have someone at home, because obviously he ain't important. I mean, if he were, you wouldn't be here with me."

His comment was bold and made me feel bad. It also made me question my love and loyalty to Dominic. My man was important to me, but until he got back on his feet, I had to do me. I couldn't go from spending sprees to balling on a budget. I just wasn't cut that way, and it didn't work for me.

Since Cash obviously was okay with my situation, I would continue to use him to my advantage. I could stay and play the good wife to Dominic in Ohio and occasionally come back to Detroit from time to time. I'd be able to satisfy the need between Cash's legs and my pockets at the same time. I never shitted where I slept, so what Dom didn't know wouldn't hurt him. He'd only been to Detroit once, so the chance of him knowing Cash was slim to none.

"Like I said earlier, when will I see you again?" Cash chimed in.

"I go home in the morning, and I have a hectic work schedule for the next few weeks." I sighed. "I can come back here next month for a long weekend."

"Girl, I'm not trying to wait thirty days to see you again," he said. "I was thinking more like sometime this week."

"I live four hours away. I can't come back this week." I shook my head.

"If you were observant like I am, you would've noticed my license plate is from Ohio too," he said, and I almost pissed on myself.

"What?" I became nauseated.

"Yeah, I live in Cincinnati." He smiled deviously. I felt weak. "We can see each other a whole lot now. I can teach your man how to treat and keep a lady."

He winked and my panties moistened. There was something about the way he threw caution to the wind that intrigued me. For years I'd been caught up in the corporate world. Maybe it was time I tried a thug.

"I'll see your fine ass next week." He pulled me in for a kiss and rubbed my ass like he couldn't get enough. Luckily, we'd pulled up to the hotel before things could escalate.

"I guess it's a date then." I tossed the words over my shoulder and headed into the hotel.

Unbeknownst to me at the time, Noel was out on the balcony, watching the whole exchange.

Chapter Seventeen

Upon my entrance into the hotel suite, Noel charged in my direction. "For real, Chanel?"

"What's the matter with you?" I frowned and brushed past her.

"Don't tell me you did what I think you did!" she snapped as Trina emerged from the bathroom with rollers in her hair.

"What did I do?" I shrugged and looked at her sideways. I was innocent until proven guilty.

"You slept with that dude from last night, didn't you?" she accused.

"I suggest you stay out of my business." I was trying to give her a pass before I had to get belligerent.

"You are dead wrong for that shit, and you know it. You got a good man at home waiting for you, and this is what you do?" She squared up to me like she wanted some.

"Bitch, I'm going to ask your ass one more time to back off! You don't know shit about what I got going on." I pulled off my earrings, ready to go old school.

"Why are you so uptight and concerned anyway?" Trina wanted to know.

"Look, you and Dominic are both good friends of mine. I don't want to see either of you get played. Especially when he doesn't deserve it." She folded her arms and glared at me.

"Ain't nobody getting played." I brushed her off and prepared to walk away.

"Then explain why that thug-ass nigga just said he would see you this week!"

"Girl, in case you didn't know, I don't explain shit to nobody! Like I said before, mind your fucking business, because you don't want none of this." I was about to whoop her ass, friend or not.

"You might not want to explain it to me, but you will explain this to Dom." The bitch actually pulled her cell phone out and started dialing. Out of nowhere, Trina reached out and popped that ho right in the face. To my surprise, Noel swung back. She missed Trina but caught me in the bottom lip.

"You bitch!" I screamed and went in for her hair.

"Stop, you gold-digging bitch," she screamed just as her phone flew out of her hand and to the ground. During the scuffle she must've turned on the speakerphone, because Dominic kept saying hello. "Tell him, Chanel," she called out just as Trina wrapped her hand around Noel's thin neck.

"Hello? What the hell is going on over there?" Dom asked.

"Baby, I'll call you back." I couldn't get to the phone because Noel now had a death grip on my hair.

"Tell him," she gagged as I tried to break free.

"Tell me what?"

"I will call you back, hang up!" I demanded as there was a knock on the room door.

"Security!" someone said, and instantly the mayhem stopped. Trina let Noel go, who in turn let me go, and I made a dash to the phone. Instead of answering it, I stepped on it repeatedly and crushed it into pieces, then straightened my hair and went to the door.

After we assured the security guard there was no need to call the police, we were asked to leave the premises ASAP. Typically, I would have asked to speak to the manager and make a fuss, but it was time to go and get as far away from Noel as possible.

Once our belongings were packed, we took to the road. Noel may have thought it was over, but boy was she wrong. I couldn't believe she'd broken girl code like this.

"What in the fuck is wrong with you?" Trina asked Noel as we pulled up at the Marathon station for gas. My girl was a pit bull in a skirt, and I was glad she was riding on my team.

"Look, I ain't for the bullshit. I may be a preppy, spoiled rich girl, but I don't play either," Noel warned from the back seat.

"Damn, Noel, you were my girl. Why you have to call Dom?"

"I may have been your girl, but I'm not your yes-man! Like I said, Dom is a good man, and he is my friend. He doesn't deserve the bullshit you do behind his back. God don't like ugly. You will reap what you sow," she hissed.

"Sounds like you got feelings for Dom." Trina turned to face her.

I was waiting for Noel to say yeah, and I would have gone ham.

"He's like my brother." She shook her head.

"Bitch, I know about that play-brother shit," Trina replied, and I nodded. I'd been in this game too long not to notice when another chick was coming for my spot. Needless to say, I was fuming as we pulled out of the Marathon station. I needed to put a handle on this bitch, and I decided what better time than now to do so.

"Ay, Noel, since you on some grimy shit, consider this friendship through." I didn't look back as I spoke to her.

"What are you saying?"

"I'm saying it's been real!" I pulled over on the service drive and stopped the car.

"What?" She was confused.

"Get the fuck out, bitch!" Trina yelled, catching my drift. "You can't be serious!" She sat back in the seat.

"As a heart attack. Now get out before I put you out myself." The look I gave her was deadly, but it was real. I would fuck this bitch up in a Detroit minute and wouldn't think twice about it.

"Bitch, you got me tripping!" Noel looked at me like she thought I was playing.

Reaching into my glove box, I pulled out the pink gun I always rode with in case of emergency. It was only a Taser, but she didn't know that.

"Chanel, are you serious?" she asked while removing her seat belt. "How am I going to get home?" With a little pep in her step, she reached for the door handle and exited the car.

"The best way you know how. Now close my fucking door." As soon as it was closed, I pulled off like a bat out of hell and let that bitch eat my dust.

In all honesty, I knew what I'd just done was all the way wrong, but like I always said, there was no need to cry over spilled milk. Probably shaken by the gun, Noel had inadvertently gotten out of the car without her suitcase or cell phone. I also noticed her dumb ass had left her purse on the back seat. My first thought was to turn around and at least take her purse back so she wouldn't be out here without money, but oh, well. The sooner she learned not to fuck with me, the better off she'd be.

Chapter Eighteen

Days turned into weeks, and soon two months had passed. Noel still hadn't shown her ugly face on my doorstep, and I was thankful. I heard through the grapevine that she'd hitchhiked her way home and was seething mad at me, but as long as she kept her distance, we were good. Dominic was none the wiser, and my affair with Cash was better than ever. With awesome sex sessions and numerous shopping sprees, a girl would be a fool not to enjoy every minute of such risqué behavior.

Honestly, I'd even become more pleasant to Dom on the strength of what Cash was breaking me off with during our time together. I also hadn't asked him about hustling or finding a job lately. Every day I left him on the couch playing Xbox, and that was exactly where I found him when I got home. Dom was so caught up in his new, carefree world that he barely noticed that my feelings toward him were changing, or so I thought.

"Chanel, let me talk to you about something," he called from the bedroom one day.

I was in the bathroom shaving my pubic hair for an upcoming rendezvous with Cash, so I peeped my head out the door into the hallway. "What's up?" I was nonchalant.

"I don't like this thing going on between us." He looked at me with worry lines on his forehead.

"Dom, what are you talking about?" Walking back over to the sink, I dipped the razor into the hot, soapy water.

"Something isn't right with me and you, and I don't like it."

"What do you think isn't right?" I sighed. When he didn't respond, I smacked my lips and continued. "I'm not a mind reader, so you need to be clear." This nigga was holding me up. Cash was meeting me in forty minutes with a surprise that he'd been promising me all week, and Dom was making me late.

"Are you fucking with another man?" This time he walked up to the bathroom door, and it startled me.

"Huh?" was all I could say, completely caught off guard.

"You hardly look at me the way you used to. You got new shit in the closet, a new pep in your step, and your pussy don't feel the same." He rubbed a hand down his face. I could tell he was stressed.

"Dominic, stop being foolish." I tried to dismiss him, but it only provoked him.

"No, I'm serious. Ever since you came home with that Benz, you've been different. You used to constantly call me with wedding plans all day, every day, and now you barely wear your ring." Now Dom was pacing back and forth.

"Why talk about a wedding that's not happening anytime soon?" I snapped, my tone matching his. "Why wear a ring that don't mean shit!" Oh, yeah, I was tripping with that one, but your girl was feeling herself.

"Are you saying the ring I bought you don't mean shit?" He turned to face me with anger apparent on his face.

I didn't care that I'd hurt his feelings. *Hell, he wants to talk, so let's talk.* "Don't mean shit! As in never going to happen as long as you sit your lazy ass on the couch and do nothing." Sliding into a denim one-shoulder halter dress, I stood my ground. Things were moving so fast with Cash, I'd be kicking Dom to the curb soon anyway. I was only keeping him around out of pity until he got on his feet. Now, though, he was cramping my style.

"Wow!" was all he could say. "I don't know who you think I am, but 'lazy' isn't a word that would ever be used to describe me. I've applied for jobs daily, but either they don't call me back, I am overqualified, or they decide to go a different route. You know, the 'white route.'" He made air quotes with his fingers.

"Boo fucking hoo." I pretended to wipe my eyes. "Spare me the sob story."

"What happened to sticking by my side, Chanel? Are you really ready to bail at the first sign of trouble?"

"Look, I have somewhere to be. We'll finish this later." I stepped into my Polo boat shoes, grabbed my purse, and headed for the door. Dominic aggressively grabbed my arm and swung me around. "Get your goddamn hands off me!"

"I'm sorry. My bad." He raised his hands in the air, signaling his surrender. "Please don't walk out that door, Chanel," he begged, and I kind of felt sorry for his pathetic ass, but the money was calling.

"Don't wait up!" With that, I walked out the door and got into the G-ride, as I called it.

After bending a few corners and putting that interaction with Dom behind me, I pulled into the parking lot of a small grocery store and waited for my boo. Just as I received a text message letting me know Cash was about to pull up, there was a tap at my door.

"What's up, girl?" Tone said, and my stomach sank.

"What up, Tone. What are you doing here?" I asked nervously. He was obviously still on duty. The uniform and squad car were dead giveaways.

"My shift is almost over. I figured I'd grab some groceries while wasting their gas, you feel me?" He tried to dap my fists, but the money green Range Rover pulling up nearby had my attention.

"Shouldn't you be out protecting and serving on company time, Officer?" I said with my eyes still focused on Cash. I didn't have much of a relationship with the Lord, but I was praying Cash waited for Tone to pull off before approaching me.

"I'm protecting this grocery store right now and serving my hunger pains." He laughed again but I didn't. My cell phone began to ring. I didn't have to look at it to know who was calling.

"Ay, my man, what business you got over here?" Cash stormed up to us like he was the police officer.

"Say what?" Tone turned around like a trained vet with his hand on his pistol.

"Are you good, Chanel?" Cash placed his hand beneath his shirt to show he was packing too, completely unbothered by what Tone was saying.

"Yes, I'm good. This is my neighbor." I cringed because Tone was sure to tell Dom about this run-in.

"Now that my identity has been validated, who the fuck is you?" Tone squared up although Cash was much bigger, taller, and more intimidating than he.

"I'm that nigga, boy! Now are you ready to go, Chanel?" Cash blew him off like a breeze. I was trapped and didn't know what to say, so I didn't say anything. Turning off my engine, I grabbed my purse and stepped from my vehicle.

"Chanel, where are you going?" Tone's mouth dropped. I was sure his head was spinning as he tried to figure out what was happening.

"She doesn't need to explain nothing to you, fam." Cash escorted me to his SUV.

"You do know she got a man, right?" Tone hollered, but at this point I was already clicking my seat belt.

Cash rolled down the window on his side. "Well, tell her man I'm boyfriend number two."

Chapter Nineteen

"Oh, my God, I can't believe you just said that." I laughed, and though problems were sure to come behind this, I was turned on by his brazenness.

"It's true, ain't it? So fuck him." Cash lit a blunt like he hadn't a care in the world. "If that nigga were getting the job done, you wouldn't be here. So fuck it."

"True." I nodded. "So what's the surprise?"

"Damn, baby girl, just relax and ride." He blew Kush into my face and turned the music up.

As we rode, I tried hard to relax, although my phone blew up nonstop. I didn't want to think about the drama waiting for me back home and was glad I didn't have to. Being with Cash made me feel safe and secure. My problems didn't matter when I was with him, and for that I was thankful.

Just as I opened my mouth to again ask what the surprise was, we pulled up to the airport. My eyes lit up as we rode around to the back and pulled into a vacant lot. "Cash, where are we going?"

"I'm taking you to Jamaica." He leaned in for a kiss, and my heart skipped two beats.

"Are you serious? I don't have any clothes, shoes, panties—" I was cut off by a "shh" sound.

"Baby, when we vacation, we buy it all. Brand new socks and drawers." He laughed and led me to a small jet.

A woman in a red and black dress met us at the bottom of the stairwell. "Welcome aboard the *Horizon*. My name is Olivia. I'll be your stewardess. Would you like a tequila sunrise?" She was holding a silver tray with two perfectly made drinks.

"Thank you." With a smile I took a drink and headed up the stairs like Mrs. Obama or somebody important. "Oh, my God! Cash, this is beautiful." Like a person who was used to nothing, I lost my mind over the beige leather and wood-grain furniture. There was even a mirrored ceiling.

"It's not the Rolls-Royce of jets, but it'll definitely do." Cash took a seat on one of the chairs and got comfortable. I did the same.

"I don't have a passport. Don't I need one to go to Jamaica?" Instantly I was worried that the trip would be ruined.

"Relax, you're good." Reaching into his pocket, he handed me a passport. There was no way the document was official, but it was a damn good fake.

"You always be coming through, baby. Thank you."

"As long as you do right by me, I always got you, believe that."

Seconds after takeoff, the flight attendant came from the back with a fresh bottle of champagne, a bowl of fruit, and a can of Reddi-wip. "Just as you requested in your pre-flight confirmation email, sir." She placed the items down with a smile and walked away.

"Thanks." Cash nodded deviously, then smiled at me.

"I understand the champagne, but what's the fruit and whipped cream for?" I was confused but Cash grinned.

"Take your clothes off," he demanded.

"What?"

"Take that shit off," he barked, and I did so without any more questions. "Now lie down on the floor."

"Hell no," I said, reaching for my dress.

"Chanel, do what I said!" His tone indicated that this was not up for debate.

"What if the lady comes back?" I was not trying to get caught with my panties off thousands of miles above the ground.

"She seen a pussy before. Stop acting like a baby." He began to undress, and within seconds, out popped that dick I loved so much. "Now lay your fine ass down before I get mad."

"Okay, okay." Lying down on the plush tan carpet, I watched as he placed pieces of fruit over my nipples and then on my vagina. Next, he sprayed whipped cream down my stomach and went to work like it was his last meal. I can't explain how he made my body feel with his fingers and tongue, but I was on cloud nine, literally. Just as he entered me, I came all over his piece. The foreplay alone was so intriguing and mind-blowing, I didn't need the sex to climax, but it too was a welcomed pleasure.

Afterward, I went into the bathroom and cleaned off, then returned to the cabin to finish enjoying my first jet ride. In a matter of a few hours, we arrived at our destination. I was thrilled! Believe it or not, the thrill was not with Jamaica, although it was a beauty. The thrill was to be with a man who was capable of flying me to an island on a private jet. For regular dudes, this was the equivalent of taking their woman on a trip out of state for the weekend. Cash was the best man I'd ever been with.

"Welcome to Jamaica, mon. No worries." Our personal driver greeted us at the pickup stand in front of the airport. "We are headed to the Inia Estates, right?"

"Yes, but the lady has never been here before, so take the scenic route." Cash reached into his pocket and pulled out a few bills. He counted out $200, then handed it to him.

Though we hadn't yet made it too far away from the airport, the tropical sight was amazing. I loved seeing all of my people. There were women and children standing on the side of the road selling handmade items and flowers. The men hustled tribal art and jewelry under cabanas made from the trees.

As the cabbie took us on a mini tour through the rain forest, I began to admire the way of life there. Unlike America, there was no welfare, no handouts, and you had to grind hard to get paper. Even the kids had hustles. About thirty minutes later, we pulled into a gated community. Riding up the stone driveway, I noticed a lady and a man standing outside to greet us.

"Welcome to Jamaica. No worries here, mon." A heavy-set older lady handed me a drink. "Ta rum punch make you feel good, mon." She winked and I sipped.

"Cash, this is amazing! Thank you so much for bringing me here," I cooed. The stone home was something from a commercial. There were high ceilings with exposed beams. The floor was cold against my bare feet and appeared to be made of marble. Various art pieces were displayed around the home in various fashions. Some were paintings, others were statues, and a few were handmade clay creations.

"Only the best for my lady." He kissed my neck.

"Am I your lady?" I teased.

"Whenever you're ready to drop old boy and get with a real nigga, you can be my lady for real." He smiled before we ventured off to admire the rest of the house.

I didn't know what it was with him, but whatever he put on me had me whipped. I barely thought of my fiancé as I lay with my boo thang that night. Something about

Cash had shaken me to the core. I'd never been with a man of his caliber. Yet I knew I was the perfect complement to his game. All a man with money, good looks, and a big piece needed was a bad bitch by his side. I was all of that and then some.

For the remainder of the trip, we spent our days shopping, drinking all types of tropical drinks, and sightseeing. Our nights consisted of business meetings with his connects or walking along the beach holding hands. I was so caught up with this vacation that I hadn't thought about my job, Dominic, Tone, or anything else for that matter.

"I have one more surprise for you before we head back tomorrow." Cash spoke to me while texting someone on his cell phone.

"Baby, I can't take any more surprises. You are too good to me." My mind instantly wondered at the possibilities.

"You might not think so after this one." He pointed out the window as the vehicle stopped.

"Mondo's boat tours," the driver announced. I looked out the window to see a small boat and a man with a captain's hat waving at us.

"Come on, Chanel." Cash grabbed my hand and helped me from the ride.

"I don't do water like that." My stomach was in knots.

"Do you trust me?" His eyes pierced my soul as he waited for a response.

"Of course," I replied before thinking too hard about the question.

"Then let's slide." Leading me onto the small white and blue boat, Cash introduced us to the captain. A member of the crew presented us with two drinks called hummingbirds and told us to take a seat and prepare for the ride out into the ocean. The floor of the sitting area was completely see-through. It was amazing to see all the colorful little fish in the sea. I knew the farther out we went, the bigger the fish would become.

For a total of two hours we lounged on the boat, enamored with the tropical environment we were currently in. This was by far the most romantic thing I'd done in a very long time. Cash was that nigga, and I wanted to be that bitch on his arm, even if it meant giving up Dom. Sometimes in life you have to know when to fold, and I was ready to throw in my cards.

Chapter Twenty

Before I knew it, my weekend getaway was over and I was kissing my new man goodbye as we pulled up to the store where, thankfully, my car was still parked. Paradise was all of that and then some! A girl could definitely get accustomed to the lifestyle Cash could provide. I once had my sights set on becoming an investment banker, but with Cashus in my life, the job title and the pay increase were no longer important. I thought my degree would land me a wealthy corporate dude, but I guessed for now a corporate thug was all I needed.

Without going home for a shower or to take my new items and put them in the closet, I headed to work. I wasn't in the mood to see Dom or hear his shit. I was too relaxed to have my vibe killed, so I walked into the bank that Monday morning with no worries. After speaking with my coworkers shortly, I headed to my office, and that was when my phone began vibrating in my purse. I knew it was Dom, so I ignored it. On cue, the office phone started ringing. A quick check of the caller ID told me it was Dom. Again, I ignored it.

Barely two seconds went by before my cell phone started buzzing again. This back-and-forth went on for almost an hour before I finally answered. "Yes, Dom?" This was the nineteenth call this morning.

"For real, you just gon' do me like that?" he barked.

"Look." I smacked my lips and rolled my eyes as if he could see them. "I told you to man up and go make some money. Those measly unemployment checks ain't cutting it for me no more. After you pay for that house, your car, and the bills, I can't even get my nails done." I rolled my eyes again.

"That house?" he mimicked me. "That's the same fucking house you just had to have two years ago, and I bent over backward to give it to you. Now you want to act all stuck-up and bougie like you're too good for me." He was breathing hard. "Fuck you and that faggot motherfucker you're fucking behind my back."

When he said that, I gasped. I knew he would eventually find out, but I honestly didn't believe Tone would sell me out so fast.

"Dominic, grow up!" I didn't have any other comeback, so that one would have to do. My employees were starting to stare at me through the glass window, so I had to end this conversation.

"Chanel, you grow the fuck up! I'm sick of you and your bullshit! You ain't no real woman, and you can't handle a man like me," he announced as a matter of fact.

"A man handles business. A man provides for his family. So I guess you're disqualified," I whispered into my Android on my way to close the blinds.

"Fuck you, Chanel. Don't come back home. I'm done with you, bitch!" Dominic hung up on me, and I was in shock. He had never called me the B-word, so I knew he was livid, but I didn't care. All he had to do was get out there and hustle until he found a job, but he was too much of a pussy to do that. I was over him.

Shaking my head, I sat down, logged into my computer, and called Cash.

"What's up, sweetheart?" he answered on the third ring.

"Hey, baby, I just called to say that I miss you," I cooed, instantly forgetting the drama with me and Dom.

"I miss you too. Are you sneaking out tonight?"

"Nope, no more sneaking for me. I'm done with that lame." I didn't know why I said that, but dissing Dom in that moment felt good.

"Word?" Cash replied flatly. I didn't know if he was happy or couldn't care less.

"Word."

"I guess your two-day getaway didn't sit right with old boy, huh?"

"I guess not."

"Okay, cool then. I'll see you later at the spot." With no goodbye, he hung up, signaling the end of our conversation.

I was about to call Trina when my phone rang. "Hey, you must have ESP." I smiled as I read through my emails.

"Girl, I don't know what that means, but tell me about your weekend in paradise!"

"Oh, my gosh, T. Jamaica was wonderful. I could live there forever!" I squealed. "I drank hummingbirds and tequila sunrises, shopped to death, and we even took a glass-bottom boat out into the ocean." Sinking down into my chair, I reminisced on paradise.

"You lucky bitch!" she laughed. "I wish Giorgio would take me some damn where."

"Yes, I must I admit I'm lucky. Cash is the one, and I'm head over heels," I admitted.

"You sound pretty serious. What are you going to do about Dom?"

"Fuck him!" I spat and swiveled around in my chair. "That nigga just put me out, so I guess the fat lady has sung." I laughed because he thought he was hurting me. Honestly, he had helped me out, and I was thankful. No more sneaking around and lying. No more hiding clothes, shoes, and jewelry. I was free to do me now and not feel bad about it.

"So are y'all through for real? What about the wedding?" She was flabbergasted.

"Girl, forget Dom and that wedding. That low-budget shit is beneath me now," I stated, and Trina cracked up at my antics. "My wedding with Cash is going to be budget-less!" I began to fantasize.

"I hear you, boo. You're a mess but I love you. Tell Cash to hook me up with one of his boys."

"Don't worry, I got you. Now let me get off this phone and do some work."

Chapter Twenty-one

Today we were shorthanded because three people called off. It was summertime and everyone wanted to extend their weekends with an extra day. I couldn't say that I blamed them. Had my future position not been on the line, I might have called off too. I would've done anything to stay wrapped up in Cash's massive arms a little bit longer, but duty called and I had to answer.

"Greensway Bank, this is Chanel," I answered the phone.

"Ms. Franklin, this is Rosa. It's time for my lunch break, but the line is too long out here," she said with irritation.

I walked over to the door and peeked out. There were at least twelve people waiting to be served. "Okay, Rosa, here I come." Rolling up my sleeves, I prepared to take on her line.

"Don't forget I'm taking an hour lunch today. Remember I asked you last week?" she reminded me as she logged out of her computer and I logged on to the one next to hers.

"Yes, I remember. It's your grandson's first swim meet, right?" I punched in my user name and password then waited for the teller screen to pop up.

"Yes, and I'm so excited." She was giddy, and I smiled because her smile was contagious.

"Don't worry about coming back. Go enjoy the rest of your afternoon with your grandson." I winked and waved the next customer over to the counter.

"Oh, thank you, Ms. Franklin." She smiled harder before disappearing to the back room to retrieve her purse. I was glad I could make her day, but I needed to get these impatient people out of my line.

Turning my attention to the young African American customer, I smiled and asked how I could help him today. He smiled politely and adjusted his bow tie, cleared his throat, and slipped a withdrawal slip my way. I glanced down at the incomplete slip and back at the gentleman. This wasn't anything unusual. People left these blank all the time, so it was no biggie. They would get up to the counter, give us their social security number, and we would fill it out. Although this happened frequently, for some reason this time it felt different. I couldn't see his eyes through the dark shades, but I got a chill just looking at him. He looked like he was trouble.

"Turn it over," he demanded coldly.

With my hand trembling, I contemplated what to do. My gut told me this wasn't a real customer and things were about to get ugly. I glanced around the small bank, trying to make eye contact with Mick, the makeshift security guard. His back was to me because he was glancing out the window. The man noticed my hesitation and frowned, but he didn't say anything, just stared. I didn't want to piss him off further, so I reached for the bank slip and turned it over. My left hand stayed under the counter as I contemplated pushing the emergency button to alert authorities. I didn't want to push the button, and this wasn't an emergency yet, but I wanted to have my finger ready just in case.

Flipping the slip over, I held my breath and exhaled loudly when I noticed the bank account information I needed was written on the back. Raising my left hand, I wiped my forehead, which was beginning to perspire. "Why didn't you just fill in the information on the front?"

I said with an attitude. He didn't know how close I'd been to pushing that button and calling the police.

"Because I'm making a deposit for my dad, and this is what he gave me." He shrugged his shoulders, and I rolled my eyes. This bastard almost gave me a heart attack acting all suspicious and shit. Keying in the information and taking the $300 to deposit, I told the customer to have a good day and waved my next customer over.

"Hello, young lady." An older Caucasian woman with gray hair and yellow teeth smiled.

"Hello. How can I help you today?" I smiled back.

"I wanted to get these pennies wrapped." She placed ten pennies down on the counter, and I looked at her.

"Ma'am, the penny rolls hold one hundred pennies. You only have ten here. Do you have any more?"

"Why sure." She nodded while clutching her wooden purse for dear life. "Come here, Cecil," she called behind her, and my mouth dropped. Up walked a young teenager sliding two large Spring Mountain water jugs toward the counter. There had to be at least $200 in pennies. I would definitely have to use the coin machine in the back to roll these.

"Ma'am, if you don't mind, please have a seat. As soon as I get this line finished, I'll get those pennies wrapped for you, okay?" I smiled. She was obviously not happy, but she told Cecil to slide the pennies back over to the waiting area. At that same moment, Rodney finished helping a customer with a loan application and stepped behind the counter to assist me. I was grateful for the help, and within minutes we had cut the line in half.

Waving my next customer over, I held up my index finger, signaling to the penny lady it would be just a few more minutes. "Rodney, can you take those pennies to the back and wrap them for me?" There were only five more customers in line, and I knew Rodney wouldn't mind the break. He would use the downtime to step out the back door for a smoke break, and I would pretend not to notice as always.

"Yeah, no problem, Chanel. With all those pennies, I'll be gone at least fifteen minutes. Are you sure you're good?" he asked, concerned yet anxious for a smoke break.

"I'm good. Just don't get locked out like last time." I winked and he smiled. He then went to retrieve the pennies. "How can I help you today?" I asked the gentleman now standing before me. He was in a hurry. I could tell by the way he kept checking his watch. I figured he was on the clock because he was in full construction gear: a blue jumpsuit, black steel-toe boots, tan construction gloves, gray plastic goggles, and an orange hard hat that said COUNTY.

"I'm going to need all the money in that register to be placed into this here bag." He threw me a black sack. I looked over at him and then back for Rodney, who was already out of sight. I scanned the place for Mick, who was outside talking to a pedestrian on the sidewalk. Instantly, I went to hit the panic button when he reached across the counter and hit me with the butt of the gun.

"Bitch, don't be stupid!" he yelled as I grabbed my head, which was now a bloody mess. I felt dizzy and a little nauseated, but I had to focus. I needed to remember his face and what his voice sounded like just like Marcus Thatcher taught us at the meeting.

"Damn, cuz, tell the bitch to hurry the fuck up!" someone called from behind him. I looked over to see another man in the same construction getup pointing a gun at the penny lady and her grandson. The customers who had been in line were now on the ground. Mick was being hemmed up in a full nelson by another makeshift construction worker as he entered through the front door.

"Do I need to hit you again?" My assailant raised his gun, and I flinched.

"No, please don't!" I screamed, which caused my head to throb tremendously. Reaching for the bag, I began to empty my register. Swiftly I moved over to the next register and did the same thing. Once I'd finished all four registers, I handed him the bag back.

"Nah." He mugged me. "Hit the safe."

"Man, hurry up! This bank ain't got no blinds and shit. Motherfuckers can see straight through here," one of the robbers called out.

"Seven minutes," the other one yelled.

My assailant grabbed me by the arm and walked me toward the back of the bank. Once we reached the vault, he pushed me forward. "Hurry up and crack that thing open."

I closed my eyes and tried to remember procedure. All the time I wasted complaining about giving up my weekend to the attend the training, I should've actually paid attention.

"I don't know the code," I cried.

"You better try something before my gun goes off." He aimed his pistol for my head, and I shrieked. At this point I knew I was dead because I honestly couldn't remember the damn code. I didn't know if it was nervousness or my headache, but as hard as I tried to remember, I just kept coming up blank.

"Four minutes!" we heard in the distance.

"Stop fucking playing around!" the irate gunman yelled at me, and I cried. Reaching up to the safe, I began to punch in numbers frantically, but nothing worked. Instantly, I remembered the new feature on our vault that was also talked about in our meeting. I reached up and pressed in the code that would open the vault but also alert authorities to the robbery.

"Yo! It's time to go, man. Fuck that safe," someone said from the doorway.

Just then Rodney must've come back inside through the back door, because I heard him yell out, "What the fuck is going on in here?"

There were three shots and the thud of his body falling as it slumped against the wall.

"No!" I cried as the gunman grabbed my ponytail and wrapped my hair around his hand for a tight grip. I closed my eyes and prepared for him to end my life.

"Not her! We got orders, remember?" the other robber called out.

Instead of blowing my brains out, my assailant sent several blows to my head with his massive fists. The pain was excruciating, but I took it all in silence. I wanted to make him think I was dead. Inwardly I felt nauseated and dizzy. Though my eyes were closed, the room felt as if it were spinning before my ears started ringing. I felt myself losing consciousness as he finally landed one last punch and then dropped me to the floor in a pile of Rodney's warm blood.

Chapter Twenty-two

"Chanel, the medics said you're fine. I know you can hear me. It's Marcus." Detective Thatcher stood there with a pissed-off look on his face. As I came to, I tried to blink a few times to get a clear picture, but it was useless. My left eye was swollen shut, and the image in my right eye was black and white. I didn't know how long I had been in their presence because my brain was in slow motion.

"Where am I?"

"You're still here at the bank." Frank patted my shoulder.

"Where are the robbers?" I tried to look around, but we were in my office with the door shut.

"The robbery is over." Marcus stood there with his arms folded.

"Where is Rodney?" Now my heart was in full-fledged panic mode.

Both men looked at each other then back at me. "Rodney is no longer with us." Frank bowed his head, and I shook mine vigorously.

"What are you talking about?"

"He is deceased!" Marcus snapped, and I jumped. "What in the hell happened to the procedure?" I didn't answer him fast enough, so he continued. "Because of you and your actions—or lack thereof—a man is dead!"

"I . . . I didn't do it on purpose." My voice shook and I began to cry.

"Chanel, we know you didn't." Frank tried to console me, but Marcus wasn't having it.

"Listen! All I know is you went against the grain on this whole thing from day one!"

"What exactly are you trying to say?" I sat straight up in my seat.

"Of all days, why did you blow policy and procedure today?" Marcus asked.

"What do you mean?" I was confused.

Frank looked at me with his brow furrowed. "You were already short-handed today, so why did you let an employee go home early? And you also let Rodney go to the back to smoke while there were still customers in line. The procedure is to have at least three of you working your stations at all times, and you knew that," Frank scolded me.

"I let Rosa go home because it was her grandson's swim meet. She works hard and never asks me for anything. The one time she did ask, how could I tell her no when other people called off today?"

"We spoke with Rosa, who told us she only asked for an hour off, but you gave her the remainder of the day. Isn't that right?" Marcus asked.

"It doesn't matter if it was an hour, the whole day or the week. The robbery happened only thirty minutes after she left anyway." I was beginning to get pissed off.

"Well, what about Rodney?" Frank asked. "It wasn't his break time, yet you let him go outside."

"First of all, I didn't let him do anything!" I was up on my feet now. "I sent him to the back to roll pennies for a customer. I can't be blamed if he snuck outside to smoke," I stated because I knew for a fact that our video system had no sound. There was no way they heard me tell Rodney not to get locked out like last time, and dead men don't talk, so my secret was safe.

"You may be right, but tell me why, out of everyone in here, you were the only one left alive?" Marcus's question left me speechless for a second.

"What happened to Mick and the other customers?"

"They were all killed execution style!" Marcus answered.

"Are you serious?" I reached for my heart. It felt like I was having a heart attack.

"I wish I weren't, but everybody was killed. Even the old lady and her twelve-year-old grandson." Frank dabbed at his tears as I allowed mine to slip down my cheeks freely.

I wondered why my life had not been taken, though more than anything I thanked God it was spared. "Am I done?" I asked Marcus through my tears.

"For now, but don't skip town!" he warned. As I grabbed my purse and cell phone, the door to my office opened.

"Here's the box you asked for." A lady cop handed Marcus a packing box, and he placed it on my desk.

"What's this?" I asked Frank, who was staring at the floor.

"Chanel, you're a good employee, but it's in the best interest of the bank that you be terminated until this investigation is over."

"What?"

"Please don't make a scene on your way out." Frank stood from his seat and started placing my items into the box.

"Don't make a scene? I've worked at this bank for years. I've never been late and never had a register come up short. Today I was held against my will at gunpoint and all you got for me is a pink slip?" I wiped the tears pouring down my face. Frank didn't say anything for a moment because he knew I was telling the truth.

"Chanel—"

"No, Frank, don't 'Chanel' me. You're firing me because I didn't get killed along with everyone else, and that's some bullshit!" I snapped. "Where's your evidence that I was in on this? I thought I'm supposed to be innocent until proven guilty." I stepped toward the door. "I guess it don't work that way no more, huh?"

"You're forgetting your things," Frank called out, but I kept walking. He, the box, and the bank could suck a fat one for all I cared.

As I walked through the lobby, I cried a little more. The bodies covered in white sheets grabbed my attention. I was shaken up because I came close to being one of them. Today could've ended very different for me. Instead of being fired, I could be dead. With that consolation, I chalked up the loss and peeled out of the parking lot using what little vision I had left to get home.

Chapter Twenty-three

Pulling up to the home I once shared with Dominic, I winced. My clothes and belongings were tossed all over the lawn. My panties were in the bushes and my bras were hanging from the tree out front. I moved slowly because of the pain in my face, but piece by piece I gathered my shit. An older couple out walking their dog stopped and asked if I was okay. I guessed they figured I'd been abused because of the bruises and the display of clothing that had been tossed out onto the street. *What a mess!*

"I'm good, thank you." I smiled as best I could, and they eventually went on. Leaning down to grab my last pair of shoes, I noticed a police car in my peripheral vision. I groaned because I didn't need another run-in with the law today, but then I sighed with relief when Tone walked up.

"Damn, what the fuck happened over here?"

"It's nothing."

"Chanel, look at your face. Did D do this?" He looked at me and back toward the house.

"Would you be surprised, snitch?" I mean-mugged him.

"Snitch?" He looked confused.

"You told on me and that's cool. I thought we were cool, but you're his frat brother, so you don't owe me any loyalty." I wasn't really mad at him. How could I be?

"On the frat I didn't say nothing to D." Tone made the fraternity symbol with his arms and hand. "I couldn't break my dude's heart like that, and I wouldn't. Even though you ain't shit, D loves the ground you walk on, and I wouldn't dare throw salt on that." Tone was telling the truth. I could see it in his eyes.

"So who told on me I wonder?" I said more to myself than to him.

"My guess is that plain-looking girl you used to hang out with. She was over here the other day."

"Noel?"

"I guess that's her name." Tone shrugged. "Anyway, back to your face. Did that nigga from the other day do this?"

"No, I was robbed at work today." I sat down on the steps.

"Damn, that was your bank? I heard about that shit earlier. You okay?"

"Yeah, I'm good." I leaned forward to remove my heels because my feet were aching.

"Why are you out here? Let me get you inside." He reached over to help me up, but I waved him off.

"I can't go in there. Me and Dom are through. He put me out." As I informed Tone of the tea, his expression wasn't that of a shocked person just finding this out. Therefore, I knew he had already been put on game.

"Damn," was as all he said.

I smacked my lips. "Don't act brand new. You probably knew he was putting me out before he even told me."

"Look, I ain't gon' lie. He told me y'all was having problems. He also told me you were cheating on him with a nigga from Detroit. He asked me to look into it, and I did, but I never got a chance to tell him what I found out. I guess your girl got to him first."

"That bitch!" I laughed lightly. What else could I do?

"Let me ask you something. Why did you do it? You used to call Dominic the man of your dreams, but the minute his chips fell, you bounced."

"I don't know." I shrugged my shoulders. "I guess my addiction to money outweighs my love for Dominic. I need to be with someone who can make my dreams come true, Tone."

"I mean, look at this house. Eventually Dom will get back on track, and y'all would've gotten married and had beautiful babies. What woman doesn't dream of this life?" He waved his hand, gesturing to the manicured lawn, upscale neighborhood, and picture-perfect scenery.

"You know I'm different. I've never dreamt of picket fences, kids, a dog, and playing the Stepford wife. My dreams consist of being rich, living in the lap of luxury, shit like that," I replied honestly.

"Why is having money that important to you?" Tone leaned back on the step.

"I can't really explain it. You know how some people are addicted to drugs, sex, or food? Well, I'm addicted to money. I just have to have it because I love the way it feels. I like pushing the lavish whips, wearing the latest gear, and flossing expensive jewelry. I do stupid things like toss money over a balcony in a club or go into a store and spend a grip just because I can. I like the power and the respect it gives me."

"Wow, that's deep," was all he said.

"I tried to hang in there as best I could, but Cash came along, and my common sense flew out the window." I laughed to lighten the mood.

"Speaking of Cashus, do you know he is a convicted felon? That dude ain't no joke, Chanel."

"What exactly did you find out about him during your investigation? I don't know about all his dealings, but I know he is into something with drugs."

"He is into a whole lot of something other than drugs. Robbery for one. Abduction, money laundering, and running a criminal enterprise."

Tone ran down the list, but the one thing sticking out was robbery.

"Dude manages to beat the system every time. There are more cases being built against him as we speak, so we will catch him eventually. I advise you to stay away from him, but if I know you, I know you won't." He shook his head and stood when I didn't respond. "Chanel, you take care, and please call me if you need me." Tone left me sitting there.

I waited another hour to see if Dominic would come home, but he didn't. I wanted to apologize in person for the way things turned out but had to write a letter instead.

Dominic,

I know you don't want to hear anything I've got to say, and I don't blame you. If I were you, I'd hate me too. I just wanted you to know my disloyalty had nothing to do with you. You are a great man and will make a great husband someday. I'm just sorry you won't be mine. Here's your ring back. This should help on a few bills.

Chanel

Chapter Twenty-four

I didn't know what forced me to leave Dominic my ring, but it felt like the right thing to do. I wasn't a horrible person, and I knew that, without my income, he'd be extremely strapped for cash. For nearly an hour I sat in my car and contemplated what to do. I wanted desperately to take a bubble bath and fall asleep in Cashus's arms, but I would die before letting him see my face this way. With no other options, I headed to Trina's place.

As soon as I pulled into the parking lot, I noticed her car was gone. "Shit!" I hit the steering wheel.

Thinking fast, I called and reserved a room at a nearby Marriott. After making the reservation, I headed there, checked in, and went to my room. It wasn't a palace, but it would do. Silently I slipped off my clothes and took an hour-long shower. No matter how hard I scrubbed, it seemed like the day would not wash off. Once the water got cold, I stepped out, grabbed the plush white robe from the closet, and got into bed. I was drained and about to call it a night when my phone rang. It was Cash.

"Hey, baby," I answered.

"What's up, baby? Where are you?" He sounded like he was with a crowd. I could hear a few different men's voices.

"I'm at the Marriott." I spoke low. My head was still pounding.

"Can I come see you?"

"Not this time. I need a few days."

"A few days? You must be trying to work things out with that sucker-ass nigga," Cash hissed.

"Nothing like that. My bank got robbed today. One of the robbers beat me up pretty bad. I don't want you to see me like this, but in a few days, I should at least be able to cover it with makeup."

"Are you okay?" His tone was flat, not at all as concerned as I thought it should be, but he was like that.

"I lost my job, but I'll be fine."

"Well, you could always move in with me and let me take care of you."

"Are you serious?" I smiled.

"Of course." He paused. "Take a few days, get yourself together, and when you're ready, big daddy will be here waiting for you with open arms."

Needless to say, after that conversation I decided to take Cash up on his offer.

About three months had passed since Cash and I became an official item with no strings attached, and I was loving it. From the week after the robbery forward, I'd lived with him in his custom-built home, which sat on two acres. He made me move in and promised to take care of me. He said I never had to worry about another bill in my life, and I was happy but cautious. I stacked a few dollars here and there just in case he wanted to get stupid and put me out like Dom. My mama always told me to never let your right hand know what your left hand was doing. Speaking of my mother, she absolutely adored him and invited herself out to our house constantly! Hell, I saw her more now than I did when we lived in the same city.

"Hello," I answered the phone.

"Hey, Chanel, where is my son-in-law?"

"Who, Deon?" I teased.

"Child, please, you know I'm talking about Cash. I wanted to thank him for those new Louboutin boots he sent me. Also, I wanted to ask if the matching leather jacket I asked for was on back order, because it hasn't gotten here yet."

"Damn, don't be pimping my man."

She ignored me. "Ask him where my jacket is."

"He's still asleep, ma. I'll have him call you later, okay?" We had just come back from Las Vegas not more than six hours ago, and we were jet-lagged.

"Make sure he does," she said, and we hung up. I placed my phone back over on the nightstand and turned to get out of bed.

"Where are you going?" Cash asked, and I nearly jumped out of my skin.

"To use the bathroom, baby," I said and headed to the en suite bathroom.

"Keep the door open," he mumbled. I thought it was a strange request, but I ignored it. Over the past few weeks, I'd learned he was a little bipolar at times. Even though he hadn't lashed out at me personally, I didn't want to test the water to see if he would.

"Okay," I said and went on with my business. When I returned, he was sitting up in bed on the phone. I put on my black satin robe and went downstairs to start his breakfast. Every day, he wanted two slices of turkey bacon, two scrambled eggs with cheese grits, and wheat toast. I loved that he was mostly only home for breakfast, because that was really the only thing I knew how to cook. Every day, he left the house at about noon and didn't return until some odd time in the morning. I didn't like that part, but I wasn't dumb enough to make an issue out of it. He kept me laced with top-notch designer things and money in my purse, so why make a scene and fuck that up?

"Chanel," he called from upstairs.

"Yeah," I shouted back. He came down the stairs in a white and red beater, red basketball shorts, white socks, and his Nike flip-flops.

"Ay, baby girl, I'm going to take breakfast to go. I got to go check up on some shit, and it needs to be handled now," he said as he walked up behind me at the stove, kissing me on the neck.

"That's okay, baby. Just give me few minutes and this should be done," I said with a smile. I was trying to have this wifey thing down pat because I definitely wanted to marry this nigga. He went to the other side of the kitchen to the breakfast nook and sat at the table with a bag of weed and swisher papers. After moving in, I learned that he was an avid smoker.

"Okay, it's finished. Here you go." I went to the pantry and retrieved a plastic bag to place the food container in. Then I walked over to the refrigerator and took out the orange juice to pour into his plastic bottle.

"Cool," he said and stood, then ran up the stairs. He was back in five minutes, having changed into a brown and orange Balenciaga button-up shirt, brown pants, and his brown Gucci loafers. "Chanel, what do you have up for the day?"

"Um, maybe I'll go shopping with Trina. Why, what's up?" I asked and handed him the bag, the orange juice, and his keys all in one motion.

"I don't want you out after eight o'clock tonight, do you understand?" he said like he was my daddy.

Just like a kid in fear of being punished, I shook my head rapidly.

"Here, take this for shopping, and while you're out, pick me up a baby gift for Yoyo's friend Hazel. I'm the goddaddy, and I think it's a boy. Don't get no cheap shit.

Make me look good." Handing me a stack of money, he leaned down to kiss my cheek and was out the door.

As I heard his truck rev up, I unfolded the stack of bills to see what he gave me to work with. It was $5,000 and I was geeked.

I called Trina and told her to come over so we could head out to do damage. I slipped on a pair of Seven7 jeans and a pink Ralph Lauren fall sweater with my pink Michael Kors gym shoes. I unwrapped my hair, sprayed a little oil sheen, put on my lip gloss, and blew my routine kiss. Next, I grabbed my cell phone and made my way downstairs. I decided to grab the keys to the Black Cadillac Escalade that Cash stored in the garage. I figured my car was too small to take shopping and get a decent-size baby gift.

Just as I set the alarm and stepped out the side door that connected to the garage, I heard Trina's transportation service blow. I got in the truck and hit the remote to open the garage door. After backing out, I hit the button again to close it.

"What up? How was Vegas?" she said, hopping into the passenger seat.

"Girl, we had too much fun. Me and you need to do a girls' weekend up there soon."

"I can't wait. Just let me know when," she said, pulling down her visor to block the sun, and I did the same.

"What's been going on in the D that I missed?" While I was in Vegas, Trina had been back in Detroit for a weekend visit.

"Shit, same ol' same!" she said as she pulled out a blunt and extended it to me. I waved it away. "He would have my ass if I smoked that," I said.

"What that nigga don't know won't hurt him!"

"Nah, I'm good." I hadn't smoked since college because of my job at the bank, but it used to be my thing.

As we made our way to Appleton Mall in Indiana, we used the ninety-minute drive to talk about the latest gossip as well as her relationship with Giorgio.

"I stepped out on him," she admitted.

"What?" I was amazed. "With who?"

"I don't want to hear your mouth, so I'm not telling you," she said and started laughing.

"Bitch, you better tell me. Is it that bad?" I asked.

"Girl, promise you won't talk shit."

"I promise," I said as we pulled up and found a parking spot. She hesitated, then blurted, "Caesar."

"Caesar who works with Cash?" I asked in disbelief. I was at a loss for words, because the many times they'd been around each other, they never said more than two words to each other. Not to mention Caesar was a ho and never wanted to settle down.

"I don't know how it happened, but it did!"

"OMG!"

"I know, right? I didn't think I would ever leave Giorgio, but I'm tired of playing in the background. I deserve better, and so does my son," she snapped.

"I feel you." We slapped five.

"I didn't tell you this, but he gave me his number a while ago, and we've talked a few times. While you were in Vegas, we hooked up."

"How much did he give you for shopping?" I asked straight to the point, just to see what Caesar was working with. If it was a few hundred, that nigga was fronting and just wanted some pussy. If it was a few thousand, then I had to give props, and maybe he was feeling her.

"Two thousand dollars," she said like it was nothing.

"Well, damn, I guess it's all good then. I ain't mad at you." I slapped her another five. She smiled and popped her collar.

We walked the mall for hours and finally took a break at the Grand Pointe Café to grab a bite to eat. Periodically during the day, Caesar called Trina to say he missed her or was thinking about her. It made me take notice of the fact that Cash only called once to remind me to be home on time. I was a little jealous but blew it off because my man was worth way more.

As we got ready to leave, we ran right into Yoyo. "Hey, girl, what's up?" I said and gave her a hug and an air kiss. "What are you doing here?"

"I'm just doing a little shopping for my girl's baby shower. Then I'm off to help her get prepared for the event," she said, looking down at her bags.

"I'm glad you said that, because Cash gave me some money to get your friend a gift too. I better make my way over to that baby store before I forget," I said, thinking that I needed to take the eight bags I already had to the car before I could buy one more thing.

"He told you about the baby shower?" she asked with a confused look on her face.

"Yeah, why wouldn't he? He is the godfather, right?" I looked at her with my own confused look.

"Oh, yeah. Right. My bad. I'm slipping, girl. It's been a long day. Y'all take care, and I will see you soon, Chanel." She walked off.

I turned to Trina, who was on her phone, and mouthed that we had one more stop before we could leave.

Lucky for me, Neiman Marcus was filled with all kinds of baby stuff. After grabbing a Louis Vuitton diaper bag, and a few little outfits and shoes, we headed back to the truck. As we rode home, I had to admit that my run-in with Yoyo had me mystified. Why was she acting like it was a secret that her friend was having a baby and Cash was her baby's godfather?

I shook it off as we hit traffic a few exits from the house. I noticed the clock on the console in the truck said 7:49 p.m. "Shit!" I said.

"What's wrong?" Trina looked up from her iPhone.

Not wanting to tell her the whole truth, I said, "Cash wanted me to record a show for him that starts at eight, and if I don't make it there in time, he will be pissed."

"What time is he coming home?"

"Later tonight."

"Well, just catch the rerun. You know they replay them shows all day." She went back to texting.

Once we were able to come up on our exit, I flew to the house. My heart dropped to my stomach when we pulled up. Cash and Caesar were sitting on the front porch. I glanced at the clock and knew I was done for. It was 8:38 p.m.

"Hey, baby. What's up, Caesar?" I said nervously as I hopped from the truck like it was on fire.

"What up doe?" Caesar nodded.

Cash looked at his watch but didn't say a word to me.

"Hey, y'all," Trina said, walking up behind me.

"What up?" they both replied, Cash being the loudest. He even stood up to hug her. I gave him the evil eye and watched him squeeze all on her.

"How much damage you do?" He finally looked over at me, but I ignored him.

"A lot of damage was done. You know your girl should be a professional shopper, right?" Trina joked. I didn't say anything. Instead I went to the trunk and began to unload the bags.

Walking past them, I entered the house and ran upstairs to drop the bags in the second bedroom. I had begged Cash to turn it into a walk-in closet. It was almost the exact replica of the one I had at my old house but a lot bigger. This custom home had five bedrooms. One was ours, the second was my closet, the third and fourth were guest rooms. The fifth room was Cash's office, and I never went in there, although I hadn't been warned not to. Truthfully, as nosy as I was, I didn't want to know anything that could get my ass incriminated if he ever went down.

I walked back downstairs for round two, and this time Trina followed to help. "Girl, this place is nice." She looked around at the custom decor as this was her first time seeing it.

I wish I could've taken credit for the design, but it was already like this when I moved in with Cash. There were Italian floors, furniture pieces from France, and custom paint that was flown in from Germany. Cash definitely had expensive taste, and I was loving it. Trina ran her hand up and down the wall as I laughed.

"It feels like actual leather, doesn't it?" I laughed again because the look on her face was priceless. She was so amazed and rightfully so. Honestly, that's some shit you don't see every day. I too was in awe the first time I felt the paint texture.

"Damn, you hit the jackpot with this nigga."

"Thanks, girl!" I said as we entered the kitchen. "If you think that paint was something, wait until you see this." I pulled on what appeared to be part of the cabinetry and revealed the custom refrigerator. Trina's mouth dropped as I grabbed two bottles of water for us.

"Damn, this is some state-of-the-art shit! I'm looking for a new place now, but it damn sure won't be nothing like this." She sipped.

"Are you serious?" I asked in shock. She must've been feeling strong about Caesar to give up her cushion with Giorgio.

"I'm not doing this for him." She pointed toward the door. "I'm doing it for me." She took another drink.

"Yeah, okay." I looked at her sideways.

"I'm for real." She was about to argue her case but was cut off.

"Come on, baby. You ready?" Caesar called into the house.

"All right, girl. I'm out. We have late dinner plans," she explained and gave me a hug. I walked her to the door and teased the new lovebirds on their way out.

Chapter Twenty-five

Minutes later, I damn near jumped from my skin as Cash entered the house and slammed the door so hard the walls shook. "What time did I ask you to be home?" he asked calmly although I knew he was pissed.

"Baby, there was traffic just as we got two exits from the house. There was a major accident, and somebody must've been hurt really bad. The cops blocked all the lanes on the freeway so that a helicopter could land," I answered quickly.

"That's not what I asked you!" he yelled. "What time were you to be back?"

"Eight."

"And what time did you get here?"

"Eight thirty-eight," I answered.

"Since you don't like following rules, don't fucking leave this house for the next three days!" he said sternly.

Trying to calm him down, I asked in a sexy tone, "Am I on punishment, daddy?"

"Right now, just get the fuck out of my face!" He looked at me and patiently waited for me to move, so I did. I went into the bedroom and began to cry.

My feelings were super hurt. I couldn't believe he was tripping like this. Damn, I was only thirty-eight fucking minutes late. I dried my tears and went into the bathroom to run a bubble bath.

"Chanel," he called out.

I didn't bother to respond. I just walked into the hall to see what he wanted.

"Next time answer me! Shit! I know you ain't mad," he said.

"I'm not mad, just upset that's all." I folded my arms.

"I'm upset too! All I did was ask you to be home by eight. Rules are necessary when dealing with me. I set these rules for a reason, and I expect them to be followed. I'm out in these streets tough, and I got enemies! I don't ever want to put you in harm's way. My rules are meant to keep you safe, Chanel. I want you to be my wife one day, and I need to be sure you can follow simple directions so that in the event you are given a major task to do, I know you will be okay." He walked up and kissed my lips.

Damn, when he put it that way, I felt bad. However, I still knew it wasn't that serious and he didn't have to go off like that.

"I'm sorry," I heard myself saying even though he should've been the one to apologize.

"It's cool, baby. Just make sure it doesn't happen again, okay?"

I nodded my understanding and walked back into the bathroom to turn the water off.

"Do you want to go with me to make a few runs?" he stepped into the bathroom and asked.

"Not really," I answered honestly. I began to undress and saw that he was aroused. I grabbed his piece through his pants and stood on my tiptoes to kiss him. "Don't you want to stay here and make love for the rest of the night?"

"As tempting as that sounds, I have business to handle and a party to go to."

"A party?" I stopped kissing him and stepped into the bathwater.

"Yeah. One of my boys is throwing a going-away party. You sure you don't want to go?"

"Where is he going?" I asked from the Jacuzzi tub.

"He's about to do a bid with the Feds," Cash explained.

"No, I'm good. I'll stay here. Have fun, baby." I had no interest to be in the presence of criminals. Plus, my bathwater was so warm and relaxing and just what I needed to unwind. If Cash wanted to go, he could go right ahead, because I was staying right here. He nodded and left me to my bath.

"Ay, does this go?" he asked just as I began to drift off. I looked up to see him wearing a black Versace button-up with a pair of red jeans and a pair of black-and-white Nikes.

"Um, yeah, it goes, but I think you should change shoes." I began to wash up, then I dried off and was into my pajamas in no time.

"What did you get from the mall?" He went back into the closet and came back, then laced up his black, silver, and white Louboutin shoes.

"Oh, yeah, I forgot to show you," I said, going over to my closet and bringing the bags to the bed. I laid out a few handbags, lingerie sets, gold thigh-high boots, and a Gucci set for him. Next, I laid out all the stuff for the baby. I also gave him the receipts for the crib, bassinet, rocking chair, and changing table that were going to be delivered to the baby shower.

"Damn, you hooked me up. Thanks, bae."

"No problem, sweetie. Have fun." I climbed into bed and grabbed one of the books I purchased from the bookstore today. It was called *The Real Hoodwives of Detroit*.

"What you gon' do tonight?" Cash inquired as he placed his wallet and cell phone into his pocket.

"I'm going to bed after reading a few chapters." I waved the book for him to see.

"Okay, good night."

"Good night," I replied and listened as he left the house and pulled off.

Chapter Twenty-six

It was 5:00 in the morning, and Cash was still not back, so I called his cell phone. It rang twice, and I was sent to voicemail. I called Trina because I knew at some point during the night Caesar had probably hooked up with Cash.

"Hello," she said kind of groggily.

"Hey, is Cash over there with Caesar?"

"No, they're still out partying I guess." She blew it off, but I was pissed.

"Okay," I said and hung up before she got in my mix. I debated calling Cash's sister but decided against it. She was probably at the party too, but I didn't know her like that, and if she hadn't gone to the party, I would feel bad if I woke her up.

I got up from the bed and walked downstairs just as I heard his key turn the locks. "Where have you been?" I asked as rage overtook me.

He looked at me like I had no right to ask. "I know you ain't checking me." He pointed toward himself.

"I'm not checking you. I'm just asking you a question," I said in my defense.

Cash stepped up the stairs to where I was standing, and he got right in my face. "Bitch, you don't pay no bills around here, so you can't ask me shit!"

I was nervous as hell, but the thought of him with another bitch charged me up. Usually, I sat back and kept quiet about things. However, I'd found my voice tonight.

"I'm your fucking woman. I can ask you whatever the fuck I want to!"

He backhanded me so hard I thought I'd lost a tooth. Immediately I grabbed my face and began to cry.

"What are you crying for now, huh? You were big shit a minute ago. What happened?" he asked and waited for a reply.

I was in too much pain to speak, so I continued to cry. I thought he would leave me alone, but I quickly learned how wrong I was.

Cash put his big hand around my neck and lifted me off the ground. I was fighting for air, and his grip only got tighter. "You think you're the shit, don't you? But you ain't! Bitches like you come a dime a dozen, and I keep me a handful. If you fuck up, there is always someone waiting to replace you, you hear me?" he screamed. Just as I felt myself losing consciousness, Caesar walked into the house.

"Hey, man, you left your keys in the door. What the fuck? Cash, let her go. You're about to kill her," Caesar yelled.

As if somebody turned the lights on for Cash, he let me go. I was dropped to the edge of the stairs good and hard on my butt. I was so hurt and embarrassed that as soon as I caught my breath, I ran up the stairs and locked myself in the bathroom.

After about thirty minutes of crying, I began to wash my face and look at the damage that was done to my mouth. It wasn't much except a puffy, bleeding lip. I couldn't believe he'd hit me, and if Caesar hadn't come in, he would've surely killed my ass. I knew right then and there that I had to get out of here because this shit wasn't for me. Damn, I'd dealt with some fucked-up people, but nobody had ever put their hands on me. I made my mind up. I was about to walk right out the door and never look back.

Just as I put my hand on the door, it shook hard as if someone were trying to break the knob off. I almost had a heart attack when the beating and banging started. Grabbing my chest, I tried to control my breathing.

"Open up, baby. I'm sorry. Please open the door," Cash said in a tone that I couldn't read. There was no sincerity in his voice, yet he didn't sound upset with me, so there was no way to tell which mood he was in.

"Please leave me alone," I yelled, searching the bathroom for something that I could use for my defense if he busted the door down.

"Please come out and let's talk." He sighed. "I swear I won't hurt you. I don't know what happened. It's like the liquor took over. Baby, you know I don't act like that," he continued, but I rolled my eyes. True, he didn't usually act that way with me, but I'd seen him act like a maniac on more than a few occasions with other people in his circle. I'd also seen Cash send people to the hospital, and I was scared to death.

After a few minutes of silence passed, my nerves calmed a bit. I took a seat on the toilet. Laying my head down on the cold ivory sink, I began to sob. My situation was fucked up, and I knew it. On one hand, my brain told me to bounce and never look back. However, on the other hand, I loved the life I'd been provided. In all honesty, even if I left today, eventually I would be back. Everything about Cash was wrong, but in some strange way, he felt right for me. Someone once told me that to whom much is given, much is required. I guessed in some twisted way the old saying legitimized my mistreatment. I was provided a lifestyle envied by many, and I guessed enduring Cash's abuse was a requirement.

After some thought, I decided to lick my wounds and keep on trucking. The good in my relationship far outweighed the bad. Therefore, I decided to stay. My mother always said that there was no need to get everybody up in your business when something like this happened, especially if you knew you'd be back. So at that very moment, I decided what happened tonight would stay between me, Cash, and Caesar.

I stood and opened the bathroom door. Cash was posted right there with a huge grin on his face and open arms. Like a fool, I fell right into them and wrapped my arms around him.

"I'm sorry." I wasn't the least bit sorry. I had no need to be sorry. Yet and still, I said it like I meant it.

"Me too. Let's go to bed."

Chapter Twenty-seven

Three days went by, and before I knew it, my punishment was over. I didn't know if Cash was actually serious about the restriction, but I damn sure didn't want to take any chances. Trina called a few times to see if I was up for shopping, but I declined. I told her I was cramping and to go without me.

Truth was, I didn't want anybody to see my swollen lip or the sensitive mood I was in anyway. My mind was all over the place, and I kept replaying the situation over and over. It was baffling to me that I wasn't able to throw Cash the deuces. Normally, I was always in control, but ever since the other night, I'd felt weak and helpless. It was so easy to see people in abusive situations and talk shit about how weak they were or how I would act differently. However, when I was placed in that same situation, I didn't know what to do.

Ring. Ring. My cell phone blared and grabbed my attention. "Hello."

"Hey, Chanel, I was wondering if you were busy," my sister said.

"No, what's up?" I hadn't spoken to her in a while, so I was shocked. She was upset about my moving in with Cash, but I guessed by now she was over it.

"Me and Deon wanted to catch a play at the Aronoff tonight, and I wanted to know if you could watch Deona?" Kristian asked in a hopeful tone.

"Yeah, I don't mind, what time?" I looked down at my gold-face Burberry watch. It was only three in the afternoon, and I wanted to make sure I still had time to make it to my nail appointment with Bre'.

"Around six. The play starts at eight, but we wanted to grab some dinner beforehand," she explained.

"Okay, no problem. I'll be there, K." I was actually happy to see my niece. She definitely knew how to put a smile on her aunt's face. "Make sure her little butt has been fed, bathed, and given something to make her sleepy." I laughed and she did too. It was a joke, but I wouldn't mind if Kristian did slip her a Mickey. Deona was a load of fun. However, she could go all night. I was only in the mood to play for two hours max.

"Fed and bathed yes, but no meds! Her aunt will have to actually play with her and make her sleepy."

"Yeah, yeah." My line clicked. It was my mom. "Hey, K, let me hit you back. This is Porscha." I listened to my sister grunt, and I clicked over. "Hey, you."

"Hey, you, my ass. Where you been?"

"Dang, ma! What happened to 'Good afternoon' or 'How is your day?' Just straight to the point, huh?" I rolled my eyes.

"You know that's the only way I roll. What are you doing today?" She sneezed in the background.

"Bless you. I've got an appointment to get my nails done, and then I have a date with Deona. Kristian and Deon are going to some play."

My mom smacked her lips as I grabbed my keys to lock up. Cash had been gone since six this morning, and I was happy. Although he'd been real calm since the other morning, I made sure not to trigger him, by staying out of his way. Even though he had been coming in much earlier, now it didn't matter. If his ass left home and didn't come back for a week, my ass still wasn't going to say shit.

"It would be nice if you treated your mama to a fill-in and a pedicure."

"I would if you were here," I lied. Today I needed some me time.

"Well, it's a good thing I'm in town this weekend, huh? So what time are you picking me up?" she asked.

I rolled my eyes, instantly regretting that I had even told her about my plans. Don't get me wrong, that was my ace, but I kind of was looking forward to relaxing by myself today. "Be ready in fifteen minutes," I said before hanging up. I knew she was staying at the Marriott nearby, like always.

After ending the call with my mom, I called Cash, who answered on the third ring.

"What's up, baby? Are you okay?"

Yeah, why wouldn't I be? was what I wanted to say. Instead, I just said, "I'm fine. I just wanted to let you know I'm going to get my nails done with my mom, and then I'm going to watch my niece for Kristian."

"Oh, okay, that's what's up. But I need you to take them baby gifts over to the baby shower today for me. I won't make it in time for the gift part."

Hell no! Why does it matter when the chick gets the gifts as long as it's before the baby is born? That was what I wanted to say, but again I just replied, "Okay."

Before I pulled out of the driveway, I went back into the house and retrieved the gift bags. I glanced at the clock and was glad that the shower location was only about eight minutes away. After picking up my mother, I would've been late to my appointment if it was any farther.

As I drove to the location on the GPS, my mind was in overdrive. Lately I'd become really nervous and anxious about everything. My confidence was still there, but my light had been dimmed. The zest I'd once had for life wasn't there anymore.

After pulling up to the location, I had to park a few houses down because the block was packed with cars. Grabbing the bags, I headed toward the sound of music, which was blasting from the backyard of a house in the middle of the block. The house was covered with storks, bottles, and teddy bear balloons. Streamers decorated the fence, and there was a sign on the lawn that tripped me out. It said WELCOME, BABY CASHUS.

"What the fuck?" I mumbled under my breath. *Why in the hell would she name the baby after my man and not her own baby daddy?* I asked myself. *Maybe because he is a bum,* I answered myself quickly. I reasoned that there was no need to curse a baby with a bum's name, so I guessed I didn't blame the poor girl.

The backyard was full of guests, and everyone got notably quiet upon my entrance into the yard. I scanned the crowd for Yoyo, who must've spotted me first, because she ran up to me. "Hey, girl, what brings you by?" She smiled awkwardly.

I held up the bags. "Cash can't make it, so he sent me." As I spoke, the woman I assumed was Hazel waddled over toward us, looking pissed off.

"That's right! Go handle that shit, Hazel!" a blond chick yelled from the back of the yard.

Handle what? I wondered to myself.

"What the hell are you doing here?" She looked like an overweight Robin Givens, gap, complexion, and all.

"Who in the hell are you talking to?" I really wanted to know. This bitch had me completely fucked up.

"I'm talking to you, bitch! You don't got no kind of respect coming up in here on my day. You just had to come and cause a scene, didn't you?"

Other guests were beginning to stare.

"You don't even know me, so I suggest you calm down. I'm bringing gifts from Cash. You know, your baby's godfather." I smacked my lips. Hormones had this chick bugging. I would hate to lay her pregnant ass out, but I would if she kept talking.

She looked like I said something wrong, and a few guests began to chuckle. I looked at Yoyo, who looked apologetic.

"Look, Chanel, I don't know why Cash would have you come here or lie about the baby, but this is his child." Yoyo pointed to Hazel's belly.

"What?" I needed clarification.

"Baby Cash is Cashus Jr., dummy!" Hazel spat.

"You know what?" I shook my head, completely pissed that this nigga would send me into the lion's den without warning. "Well, congrats anyway. Here are your gifts. I hope you have a healthy, happy baby." I dropped them to the ground and stormed out of the backyard toward my car.

I wasn't pissed that he lied about the baby. She was obviously pregnant before we got together, but why would he set me up? I went over there looking like a damn fool.

Chapter Twenty-eight

After leaving the baby shower, I flew off the block and merged onto I-75, then pulled out my cell phone.

"Hello," Tone answered.

I didn't know why I called him, but for some reason I was beginning to miss my old friend. Truth be told, I was starting to miss everything about my old life. I wasn't going to tell him that though.

"What's up, Tone?" I smiled and sniffed back my tears.

He paused, and I was sure he was trying to figure out who I was, because I blocked my number. I couldn't have him calling me back out of the blue when I was around Cash.

"Chanel, is this you?"

"Yes, it's me. What have you been up to?" I dabbed at my mascara with the back of my hand.

"Where in the hell you been? I called you a few times, but your number was disconnected. Hey, as a matter of fact, why are you calling private?" His voice sounded mad but relieved at the same time.

"I got a new number, and I can't give it to you. That's why I called private," I answered truthfully.

"It's like that now, huh?"

"Don't start, Tone, please."

"What's wrong? You sound sad. Are you okay? That nigga isn't hurting you, is he?" Antonio bombarded me with questions.

I wanted to tell the truth. *Hell yeah, he hurt me with his fist, and he hurt my heart by sending me into the lion's den with his baby mama and her family looking on.* "No, nothing like that," I lied. "I'm cool, just wanted to hear your voice and tell you that I honestly miss you, that's all."

"I knew you was feeling a nigga." He joked like he used to, which made me smile. "No, I'm kidding, but let's hook up for lunch or something."

"Um, not today. I'm taking Porscha to get our nails done. Then I have to watch my niece, but I will hit you back later in the week, okay?"

I was preparing to hang up, but he caught me off guard when he dropped a bomb on me. "D wants me to ask if you're happy."

Now how do I answer that? Yes, I have all the money in the world to blow. I have the best clothes in my closet and designer shoes on my feet, but I'm scared to death of pissing my man off for fear of a beatdown.

"Look, Tone, tell Dominic I've got to go." I ended the call, choosing not to answer at all.

I pulled up to Porscha standing on the curb smoking a Newport and talking to someone on the cell phone. She was dressed sexy in a pair of red capris with a matching one-strap halter top. Her bra had her boobs sitting up extra high, and Claudia sandals showed off her toned legs. Today her hair was styled in an asymmetric bob with tiny curls in the back. *I should have chosen something other than a plain denim BCBG baby doll dress and the silver goddess sandals with the small heel.* My hair was in a simple finger-swept ponytail that I immediately took down and let fall over my shoulders. I pulled out a spray bottle from my glove compartment as Porscha got in. I sprayed a mist of water over my hair and watched as it began to curl just a little.

"Damn, I thought you would never get here," she complained, and I didn't respond, just pulled off. "What's the matter with you?"

"Nothing, Ma." I waved her off because this was something I couldn't talk to her about.

"Well, anyway, I can't wait to get my nails done. This time I think I'm going to get some nail art and rhinestones. What you think?" She extended her hands.

"In my opinion, I don't think someone your age should be wearing nail art, but it's up to you." I shrugged.

She rolled her eyes. "What the hell you mean, someone my age? Girl, bye! Anyway, what's been up with my son-in-law? That man is the shit!" she exclaimed like a giddy schoolgirl. "Chanel, I knew you took after me, and I'm so proud of you! He is definitely a keeper." She went on and on, and I just rode in silence. "He is perfect, and I think it's time for y'all to move to the next step. You need him to marry you before somebody creep up on him."

"He is far from perfect," I snapped, and she looked over in my direction, smacking her lips. I couldn't believe she was throwing me down the aisle to Cash when my engagement to Dominic hadn't been off that long.

"He is rich, rich, fine, and rich. Need I say more?" she added, and I rolled my eyes. "So what he hit you? Big fucking deal!" she spat.

Her words caught me completely off guard, and I damn near sideswiped the car in the next lane. "Who told you that?" I asked, knowing my secret hadn't left my lips.

"I know when a woman has been hit, believe me. Even though the marks are gone, I can still see the hurt on your face. I've been there." She pointed to herself.

"Okay, well, if you've been there, why would you say it's no big deal when it is?" I pulled into the parking lot of the nail salon.

"Because there are plenty of women out in the world being beaten for less!" Porscha snapped. "At least you're getting paid for your troubles. Yeah, you got hit, but look at the house you live in or this car we riding in. Shit, look at the stack of money you've got in that purse of yours." She pointed to my Hermès bag. "Don't start complaining and fucking this up for us. Get over yourself, and try not to make him mad, all right? Now let's go."

She exited the car, and I was left in shock. My mom just gave me permission to be someone's punching bag as long as the pay was good.

"Hurry up," she yelled from the sidewalk, and I followed her.

The Candy Shop was packed. There was standing room only for walk-ins. I was glad I had an appointment. "Hey, Angel, is my girl here?"

"Yeah, she will be with you in a minute, but I don't have any open appointments for your mother. Everybody is booked. Tonight is the Beyoncé concert," Angel informed me.

"It's cool, sweetheart. My daughter is willing to pay extra if we take somebody else's spot," my mother chimed in, causing both Angel and me to frown.

"Mom, chill out and follow me," I said as Bre' motioned for me to come back toward her. "I'll just ask Bre' to try to fit us both in."

"Hey, Chanel. Hey, Ms. P."

"Hey, girl. I was going to get a fill-in and a pedicure, but I'll settle for a fill-in if you can fit my mom in for the pedicure."

"What about my nails?" Porscha pouted.

"You just gon' have to come back another day. I'm the one with the money, so you roll with it or don't get nothing done," I said, shutting her down quickly. Usually, I spoiled my mom, but today I wasn't in the mood.

As soon as Bre' was done with my nails, my cell phone rang, indicating a call from Cash. My stomach felt queasy, and I got nervous. I told Porscha and Bre' I'd be right back, and then I stepped outside and into my car. "Hey."

"Hey, yourself. Why did it take you so long to answer?" he questioned.

"Sorry, baby. I was inside the nail salon. It's kind of noisy in there, so I stepped out," I explained like a child to her father.

"Uh-huh. So did you take that gift over to the baby shower for me? Did Hazel like it?"

"I took the gift, but I didn't stick around long enough to find out if she liked it," I answered honestly.

"Why not? You were there on my behalf, so you should've stayed, Chanel."

"Well, after she told me that she was having your son, and my being there was ruining her day, I left." I held my breath for his reply. When a few moments went by in silence, I sighed into the phone. "You should've told me about the baby. I would've understood. I can't be mad at something that happened before me, Cash."

"You right. My bad. Me and Hazel got down a few times, but nothing serious, so you ain't got nothing to worry about."

"Okay, Cash, it's no big deal," I found myself saying although I was beyond pissed off. I wasn't mad about the baby, but I was mad as hell that he sent me over there knowing that I wasn't welcome. I decided to leave well enough alone and not mention it for fear that it would put him back into a sour mood.

"Baby, I want to make it up to you tonight. Be ready about eight, and wear something sexy, all right?" he said in a seductive tone.

"Sorry, I can't because I already promised Kristian I would watch my niece while she and her husband go out,"

I regretted to inform him again though I knew I'd already told him this earlier.

"Can't that little motherfucker stay with your mom?" he asked, and I wasn't sure if he was joking. I didn't like my niece being referred to as a motherfucker but decided to ignore the comment.

"You know my sister and my mom have issues. Besides I really want to hang out with her. That's my baby. If you want, you can come over there, and we can watch movies and order a pizza." I let the seat down to recline.

"I am nobody's babysitter! I can't believe you would rather hang with a baby over your man. This is some bullshit! I'm trying to spend time with you, and this is how you do me. Be for real, what other nigga you got coming over there?"

I rolled my eyes. "What? If I had another man coming over, I wouldn't have invited you over there." I let out a laugh but quickly stopped laughing when I noticed that Cash had hung up. "Fuck!" I hit the steering wheel to let off some steam.

After taking a few deep breaths to calm down, I called my sister.

"Hey, sis! What time will you be over here? I need you to help me get dressed." She sounded excited, and I regretted what I was about to do.

"K, about that . . ." I hesitated. "I will have to take a rain check on babysitting."

"Are you serious?"

"I'm sorry. When I made the agreement, I didn't know Cash already had plans for us," I lied.

"Chanel, I never ask you for anything. The one time I do ask, you play me." My sister was disappointed, and I couldn't blame her. I didn't want to cancel, but pleasing my man meant more to me than pleasing her.

"It's not like that, I swear. You may not have to cancel, because Mom is here, and she will do it."

"You know how I feel about her," Kristian said, sounding annoyed.

"Look, you need a sitter, and Mom needs to see her grandchild. I say we let bygones be that for tonight," I said, trying to mend fences.

"I guess so. Tell her to be here by six." She hung up. Just then, Porscha walked up to the car still wearing the foam slippers from the pedicure.

"All right, what's next? Let's go shopping," she demanded.

"Well, something came up. Cash wants to take me out, so Kristian needs a sitter." Before I could finish, she cut her eyes at me. "If you watch the baby, I'll pay you," I bribed.

"How much?"

"It'll be enough!"

"You need to name a figure before I agree." She crossed her arms. I frowned because it was ridiculous that I had to pay her for watching her only grandchild.

"One hundred dollars."

"Make it three hundred, a pack of Newports, and those new Cartier glasses that just came out, and we've got a deal."

Though I thought it was fucked up, I peeled off the money, and we shook on the rest.

Chapter Twenty-nine

Later that day I dropped my mom off at my sister's. "Kris, I am so very sorry," I hollered as soon as she opened the door.

"I cannot believe you are playing me of all people." She turned and walked away.

"I am not playing you, Kris, but I don't need Cash up my ass tonight. Please don't be mad." I really hated myself for bailing on my sister, but she would get over it. Cash, on the other hand, was a different story.

"I guess you have to do what you have to do." She shrugged. Though she wasn't completely happy with me, I knew she'd forgive me.

After that, I flew home to shower and dress for the evening with Cash. I wasn't extremely excited for the date because I was still mad about the baby shower, but it was what it was.

"How much do you love me?" Cash asked as we rode home from the Cheesecake Factory that night. He'd taken me shopping and spent over $12,000. For all the pain he caused, I walked away with a new wardrobe and a few pieces of jewelry. I guessed Mom was right: at least I got rewarded for my trouble.

"I asked, how much do you love me?" Cash broke my train of thought.

Despite the past few days, at this particular moment, I loved his ass a whole lot. "I love you this much." I stretched my arms as far as they would go with a huge grin on my face. In all honesty, our relationship had taken a turn for the worse, but I would say anything to make him happy.

"That's good to know." He leaned back in his seat and pulled out a Diane brush to smooth his hair. "I need you to do something for me."

"Like what?" I was curious to know.

"I'm short on runners, and I need you to step up to the plate," he said casually.

I didn't respond right away because I was pondering his words. On one hand, I wanted to do anything to keep him satisfied, but on the other hand, I wasn't into the street life. For goodness' sake, I wanted to be an investment banker, not a damn drug runner.

"Cash, are you serious?"

"As HIV!" He didn't even blink. "The way I figure it, you needed me to save you from that wack-ass life you were living. Now I need you to keep my ends coming in. I took you from living paycheck to paycheck, and now you got the Gucci store on speed dial," he reminded me, and I cringed. There was something about the way he said that he'd saved me that didn't sit well with me. "If you want to continue to live the way you live, you got to put in work! Simple as that."

"Baby, I don't know anything about drugs. That's not my thing," I tried to reason with him, but he didn't miss a beat.

"You're from Detroit. What you mean, you don't know about drugs!" he snarled. "In public schools you learn how to cook crack before you learn what two plus two equals." He laughed but I sat silent. I'm not saying what he mentioned wasn't the truth for some people, but it wasn't my truth. Even in Detroit, my mom kept me away from things of that nature, and I managed to live a somewhat sheltered life.

"Cash, let me think about it, okay?" I asked in a low tone.

"I need to know today. I don't got time to be playing games with you. I thought you would be the Bonnie I needed, but I guess not, and that's okay." He shrugged. "I'll find another woman to play your position. It's not a problem!" With that he pulled out his cell phone and proceeded to make a call. Placing the phone on speaker, he set it down on his lap so I could clearly hear what the other person was saying.

"Cash, is this you?" a seductive female said.

"The one and only, baby girl." He pulled a Cuban cigar out of the case and lit it. The smell was overwhelmingly strong, but I didn't want to roll down the window for fear of not being able to hear the conversation.

"What do you need, boo?" she purred, and I rolled my eyes. For one thing, I couldn't believe his audacity to call this chick in front of me.

"I got a little business I need to be handled out of town, and I knew you'd be woman enough to handle the job." He looked at me and blew out a smoke ring.

"Daddy, you know I have your back. No questions asked. Just tell me when and where I need to make this move, and I'm there. After that, tell me where I can meet you for some of that magic stick."

At this point, I was fuming. Cash was grinning like a fat rat in a cheese factory.

"Baby girl, you can't handle all this. Plus, I'm taken at the moment." He winked at me and melted my heart.

"Taken by who? Obviously, the bitch isn't doing something right. You're on my phone! Anyway, like I said, I have your back, and when I get the job done, you can come over and reward me." She sounded like a sex phone operator, and I'd had enough.

I snatched the phone off his lap and spoke into it. "Look, bitch, nobody is getting rewarded with no damn magic stick but me. Thanks for your time, but the position is no longer available!" Hanging up on her after my final words, I handed the phone back to Cash, who looked impressed.

"I guess that means you want the position?" he asked rhetorically.

I didn't respond. I just leaned in and kissed him passionately. I wasn't sure why I'd just agreed to do something I had no business taking part in, but I wanted so desperately to be his ride-or-die chick. I wanted to show him that he needed no other woman but me, and just like that, I was now a part of Cash's organization and headed out on my first drug run back to Detroit.

Chapter Thirty

The gray Ford Taurus had been taken apart and loaded back up with heroin, crack cocaine, marijuana, and ecstasy pills inside the fender, bumper, door panels, and headlights. To say I was nervous was a huge understatement, but here I was, riding dirty on I-75. My speed was a steady sixty-five, not one notch higher nor lower because I didn't want to get pulled over for nothing. My stomach was doing flips because inadvertently I'd added Trina to my trip. She invited herself, and I didn't want to travel alone, but she probably would've killed me if she knew what was really going down. "Why are we in this beat-up jalopy?" she asked.

"This is no jalopy." I cut on my left blinker to signal a lane change. "Cash has a cousin who needed an out-of-state car for his next run, so I'm dropping this one off. We will ride back much better, believe that," I reassured her.

"How does it feel being with a notorious drug dealer?"

"I guess it feels okay. I mean, how does it feel dating Caesar?" I didn't really know how to take her question.

"Caesar isn't really that deep into the game like Cash. He's basically the chauffer/assistant. Not the boss," she pointed out. There was something in her tone I didn't like. "Being the boss's chick has to be exciting, adventurous, and dangerous." She sounded as if she was fantasizing.

"You watch too much television." I laughed. "It's a little bit exciting and a little bit dangerous. Most of all I love the perks, like shopping and living life in the fab lane," I replied honestly without letting her know we were in the danger zone right now.

"He is a sexy mofo, too!" She licked her lips. "You better be glad he wanted you," she teased.

"Girl, you wouldn't have given up Giorgio for Cash, and you know it." I laughed.

"No, not back then, but now is a different story. You better be glad you're my girl, because I would've damn sure tried to have my cake and eat it, too without getting caught." She pulled the visor down to apply more lip gloss.

I glared at her. My instincts told me she was one to watch.

"I love Giorgio, but I can't have him the way I want, and that sucks. I need someone to go to bed with, wake up to, and all that good shit. Caesar will have to do."

"I feel you, T. Maybe you and Caesar will work out."

"Yeah, he is cool, but don't get it twisted. Your girl is still looking." She popped her imaginary collar. "Hey, have you heard anything else from Dominic?" she asked, totally switching subjects.

"Yeah, he called a few times. I had to make it clear that I've moved on and he should do the same." I didn't like talking too much about the Dom situation. It was still a sore spot, and I had regrets. In my heart I knew I did him wrong by leaving him during his time of need.

"I saw him the other day, and he was out on a date. I guess your pep talk worked." She laughed but I didn't.

"Are you sure it was a date?" I rolled my eyes.

"Well, most people who hold hands over a romantic candlelit dinner are usually on a date," Trina clarified.

"I'm glad he found someone who can afford to cover his broke ass." I tried to brush it off like it was nothing, but my ego was bruised a bit.

"Boo, you must not have heard." T wrinkled her nose and looked at me sideways.

"Heard what?"

"Dominic was called back to work and offered a partnership at his old company." She smiled and I forced one too.

"That's good news!" I pretended to be happy although I was kicking myself in the ass.

"Yeah, buddy, he is back on the block with a six-figure income. The night I saw him at the restaurant having dinner, he informed me of the good news, and he even bought me a drink." While Trina continued to go on about Dom, my mind drifted off. Not only was he employed again, but this motherfucker also made partner. If only I had hung in there awhile longer, I wouldn't have been in this car transporting drugs. *Damn!*

Anyway, there was no use crying over spilled milk, so I didn't. We made the trip to Detroit and dropped the car off. After spending a little time with Trina's brother, our trip was over, and we were headed back home in no time. Although this run wasn't as bad as I believed it would be, I didn't want to make this a habit. Eventually my good luck was sure to run out.

However, much to my dismay, Cash had enlisted my help on yet another journey no sooner than I returned from this one. Before long, this became a part of my weekly duties. Almost overnight he'd turned me into a professional drug runner.

Chapter Thirty-one

I was on the road again, but this time I was alone and headed to Chicago. This was about my fifteenth drug run, and I'd gotten just a tad loose and too comfortable. I was ready to get this trip over with, so my speed fluctuated as I pushed the gray Impala in and out of traffic. We always used gray cars because a study showed that cars with that color often went undetected. They blended in with the open road and weren't as noticeable as red or yellow would be.

I looked at the time. 3:45. If I played this right, I could be at the drop-off location within an hour and back on the way home in three. Just as I was about to pull out my cell phone to call Trina, I saw the boys in blue coming up behind me.

"Shoot!" I said aloud as the sirens got closer. The officer yelled over the loud speaker to pull my vehicle off to the shoulder. As instructed, I pulled the car over and waited for the officer to approach.

"Ma'am, do you know why I stopped you?" the Caucasian middle-aged man asked.

"No, sir, I don't." I needed to steady my voice, but I was too nervous.

"You were doing eighty-six in a sixty miles per hour zone. Did you see the sign at all?"

"No, sir. I'm sorry! My mom is sick, and I need to get back home," I lied.

"I'm sorry to hear that, but you don't want to put your life and other travelers' lives in jeopardy, do you?" His mirror-tint glasses blocked me from seeing his eyes, but I was sure he was kind and about to let me off.

"No, sir. I don't want to hurt anyone." I batted my long eyelashes.

"Okay, I believe you don't, but I am still going to need to check your license, insurance, and registration."

"Of course." Reaching into my bag, I handed the officer my documents. Minutes felt like hours as I waited for the cop to return. Though I knew I was clean, part of me panicked over what he was going to find. I started to call Cash but didn't want to alarm him if this was nothing.

I fumbled with the radio, trying to find a song I liked to calm my nerves, but it was useless. Finally, I looked in the rearview mirror and saw the officer return.

"Due to the circumstance, I'm going to issue you a warning. If you're caught speeding again, you'll receive a ticket." He wrote something down on a piece of paper and handed it to me.

"Thank you!"

"Not a problem. You have a good day, and tell your mom that Officer Dan is praying for her." Tipping his hat like a gentleman, he walked back to his car.

I was so thankful for Officer Dan I didn't know what to do. For the duration of the trip, I rode right at speed limit and stayed on my p's and q's. I didn't even answer my ringing phone or play any music. I stopped at a rest stop, used it, washed my hands, and calmed my nerves before pulling into town.

Finally, I arrived at the drop-off location about an hour and thirty-five minutes later. It was a small red and black garage called Petey's Auto Shop. I pulled around back as instructed. The pickup person was supposed to meet me, but no one was there. After blowing the horn for three minutes, I pulled out my phone and called Cash.

"Yo!" he answered.

"Hey, baby, I don't see anyone. Is this the right place to get my tune-up?" I spoke in code in case the conversation was being recorded.

Cash hesitated for a second, but loud and clear came back with, "Who is this?"

I looked down at my throwaway minute phone to make sure I dialed the right number. "Yo, little mama, I think you got the wrong number." Click!

"What the . . ." I said just as police officers came from everywhere, surrounding the garage.

"Freeze! Driver, turn off the engine, and drop the keys out the window," I heard and quickly did as I was told. There were at least ten officers who looked like they didn't play.

"Step out of the car with your hands up." Once I was out of my vehicle, I was bum-rushed to the ground and handcuffed. My sundress flew up. By now, everyone knew what color boy shorts I wore today.

"You have the right to remain silent. Anything you say or do can and will be used against you in a court of law. You have the right to obtain an attorney . . ." *Blah, blah, blah,* was what I heard after that. My life flashed before my eyes, and I knew I was going to jail.

Once at the smelly, musty police station, I sat waiting for my turn for almost two hours. The place was packed with people coming in off the streets, and no one working seemed to be in any rush. The woman who booked and photographed me was nice but nonchalant. During my time with her, she asked if I was thirsty or needed to use the restroom. After that process was over, I waited another thirty minutes before being taken to the interrogation room.

As I waited for the cops to come in, I contemplated what I was up against. I should've known something was up when Cash pretended not to know me, but what could I have done? At that point, it was too late. Here I was, stuck in Chicago with no one to bail me out and no lawyer to call. Cash knew I was in heat and wouldn't touch me with a ten-foot pole, so I was riding this one out by myself.

"Ms. Franklin, how are you today?" a bald female cop asked with a huge smile on her overdone face. Her eye shadow was green, and her eyebrows had been drawn on. The woman's foundation was a shade darker than necessary, and her lipstick was red, which made her coffee-stained teeth stick out like a sore thumb.

"I'm fine."

"Do you know why you're here?" she quizzed.

"No, I don't. Would you be able to help me out with that?" I smiled, trying to kill her with kindness.

Placing a manila folder down on the steel table, she laid out several pictures. "There is a major drug operation going on here in Chicago, and we have reason to believe you're involved in it."

"Me?" I played dumb.

"Yes, you. We received a tip about the auto shop drop-off. We were told the delivery would be about the same time you happened to pull up."

"That's a mere coincidence. I needed a tune-up, so I stopped there." I waved her off.

"Then it's a 'mere coincidence' that we were given your description, the make and model of the vehicle you were driving, as well as the time you'd be there? Not to mention the drugs in the hidden compartment." The cop had me stumped, but I wasn't going to sweat it.

"Look!" I snapped. "If you think I'm guilty, just take me to jail."

"Jail is no place for a pretty bitch like you. Are you sure Cash is worth it?" She turned the chair around and sat down.

"Cash? Cash who?" I bluffed.

"You dumb bitches are all the same!" She smacked the metal table. "You think you're something special? You think he loves you? Well, news flash: that nigga don't love nothing but money and his damn self."

I didn't blink as she continued to scream in my direction. I'm not saying I wasn't shaken by her words, but I knew better than to show it.

"I'm done talking until my lawyer gets here." I thought the word "lawyer" would shut her down, but to my surprise she kept going.

"Look, Chanel," she sighed, "I don't want to see you make the same mistake so many others before you have made. Cash is a bad dude, and you need to separate yourself before you get on his bad side," she warned.

I laughed on the inside because this woman had no idea what I'd been through. Hell, I'd already been on his bad side. "Look, cop, in case you haven't noticed, I'm a grown-ass woman. I don't need you or anyone else telling me what to do. I know what I'm doing. I know what I'm facing, and I know I'm not guilty. Now what I don't know is who the hell Cash is."

The look on the officer's face was sad. I didn't know if it was because she felt bad for me or because I wouldn't give up Cash to her.

"Since you don't know this man, I'll tell you who he is." She held out an eight-by-ten photo of Cash talking on his cell phone. "He is a killer, drug dealer, liar, manipulator, womanizer, and"—she paused—"the mastermind behind several bank robberies. Including the one that claimed the lives of everyone except you, Chanel."

I damn near fainted when she brought the robbery at my bank to my attention. I didn't want to believe it, but it was hard not to. A mixture of hurt, anger, frustration, and confusion ran through me, but I stayed cool. Even after her shocking revelation, I once again denied knowing Cash. Somehow, I felt if I admitted to knowing him, the mercy she was pretending to have for me would vanish along with any plea deals. They would find a way to pin the bank robbery on me, and I couldn't have that. I may have been a lot of things in my day, but a murderer wasn't one of them. I knew better than to claim anything until I at least spoke with an attorney.

After a few more hours of interrogation, I was taken to a holding cell. I was eventually turned over to the county jail, where I remained for fifteen days. Throughout my stay, I called everyone I could think of, including my mother, but no one answered my calls or came to my rescue. I was given a punk-ass public defender who couldn't remember my name nor the details surrounding my case if his life depended on it. I was doomed and I knew it.

However, one day a guard came and unlocked my cell gate. He told me I was free to go because they no longer had a case against me. I didn't ask any questions for fear they would change their minds. At the front gate, waiting for me were the public defender and Kristian. I damn near cried when I saw her. I wanted to keep her out of my business with Cash, but I was sure glad she was here.

"Ms. Franklin, I have your paperwork right here," stated the pimple-faced young man, handing me documents.

"It says here 'insufficient evidence,'" I read aloud.

"Yeah." He nodded. "They ripped that car to pieces and didn't find anything. I'm not sure how you did it, but it worked." He winked and I winced. This son of a bitch already pegged me for guilty. Good thing I no longer needed his representation, because he would've sent me up the creek without a paddle.

Chapter Thirty-two

"What the hell is wrong with you?" Kristian asked as we rode home along the same highway I'd traveled fifteen days ago. She'd embraced me in a tight hug at the county jail but refrained from speaking to me up until now.

"K, I'm not guilty," I lied.

"Stop it! Just stop it! I know you, and I know when you're lying." She sniffed, and I noticed she was crying.

"What's wrong?" I hated to see my sister cry. I didn't like it as a child, and I didn't like it now.

"I'm scared for you," she admitted.

"Why? Nothing is going to happen to me."

"Do you realize who you're dealing with? I read the reports on your boyfriend. He isn't a saint, that's for sure."

"K—"

She cut me off. "No, listen to me. I'm your big sister, and I don't want to see you get hurt out there." She sniffed again. "You mess with men, their money, and their feelings all the time, and I don't say shit. But this is different, Chanel. I'm afraid that man is going to hurt you."

"He's harmless," I lied and sniffed too, trying to conceal my tears. My sister was right, and I too was scared. Fifteen days with nothing to do gives you a whole lot to ponder. I had to leave him, but I didn't know how.

As if she read my thoughts, Kristian spoke out. "You need to stay with me for a while until we can figure something out. Maybe I'll put you on a one-way plane to somewhere far away for a little while. We have an aunt who lives in Calhoun City, Mississippi. Maybe you can lie low there for a while"

"That won't work." I shook my head adamantly.

"Why not? He thinks you're still locked up anyway." This reminded me of how she had even found out I was in jail in the first place.

"How did you know where I was?" I twisted the cap from the Evian water bottle she had waiting for me in the car, and I drank like it was going out of style. After being on lockdown, you really appreciate the small things in life.

"Your mother told me," was her reply.

"You mean that bitch knew where I was and didn't have the decency to answer my collect calls, let alone come and get me herself?" I was fuming because I truly thought my mother and I were better than that.

"Porscha is out for self. She always has been and always will be. I don't know why you don't understand that." Kristian shook her head. "Why do you think I don't fuck with her?"

Shrugging my shoulders, I said, "I don't know."

"When we were little, she would make me do things that I didn't like." She sighed and rubbed her neck.

"Like what?" I wanted to know.

"For starters, she would hide me under her bed when she had male company. Once they were into the nitty gritty, I was told to pick the men's pockets for extra cash and sometimes credit cards."

"Are you serious?" My mouth dropped.

"I would be under there anywhere from ten minutes to a few hours." She sighed. "One night, I was under the bed for so long I peed on myself. I tried to sneak out of the room but was caught red-handed with the money in hand and pissy pants."

"Oh, my goodness," I exclaimed.

"Porscha acted shocked when the man accused her of setting him up. To prove she didn't put me up to it, she whipped my ass in front of the stranger, and I never forgot that." She wiped a tear. "I knew then she was the type of bitch to shit on you in a minute if it meant saving her own ass."

My mouth fell open. I was in disbelief. "Where was I when all this went down?"

"In la-la land idolizing that bitch!"

Her words hurt me because they were true. I had looked up to my mother my entire life. I used to think she was glamorous and gorgeous, but now I saw it was a facade. Her selfish ass was just another gold digger. I couldn't wait to see her again, because I had a lot of shit to say that she probably wouldn't like.

Chapter Thirty-three

House arrest with Kristian was no fun at all. In two weeks, I hadn't left the house, not even to get the paper off the porch. I wasn't allowed any phone calls, texts, tweets, emails, or anything. All I did was eat, sleep, and play with the baby. I didn't have to worry about her husband bothering me, because she'd kicked him to the curb. Some time ago, he confessed to cheating on her with their 18-year-old babysitter. My sister was hurting, and I was glad we could be there for one another.

Kristian also supplied me with a few outfits from her resale shop to wear around the house. I was surprised to see the clothes weren't as hideous as I'd believed they would be. There were actually a few name-brand pieces in the bunch, and a few still had tags. All in all, I was just glad my sister was in my corner. Without her, I might've still been back in Chicago scraping up bus money to get back home.

As I lay on the bed, I couldn't believe no one had called to see if I was okay. Although I wasn't using my phone to talk, I did turn it on just to see who would call me, and no one did. Next, I flipped through my pictures and began to miss my girl Trina. I wondered why she hadn't called. I was sure by now she knew the deal, so this was unlike her.

"Chanel, I'll be right back. ADT called me because the alarm went off at my store," Kristian called from the door to her guest bedroom, which I was living in.

"Can I go with you?" I was desperate to do something and go anywhere at this point.

"You know it's too dangerous for you to be outside," she reminded me. "Keep an eye on Deona, and I'll be right back."

"Yes, Mother," I teased and followed her to go play with my niece.

Kristian hadn't been gone ten minutes when my cell phone made a noise indicating a message. I jumped at the sound. Not only had it excited me, but it also scared me because it was unexpected. I tapped on the screen to see a message from Cash.

For real, Chanel? You been out for two weeks and you don't holla at a nigga?

I was amazed that he knew I was out of jail. Instantly, I got nervous and checked the locks on the door. Next, I slipped up to the window and peeked out, trying to catch a glimpse of anything out of place. Everything seemed fine, so I relaxed and called Kristian.

"I've only been gone a few minutes. I know the baby hasn't got on your nerves already," she said.

"I just got a text from Cash." I read the text to her as the knocking on the door began. "Oh, shit! I bet that's him." I was scared.

"Don't open the door. Set the alarm, and take my baby upstairs. I'm on my way." I could hear panic in her tone.

Hanging up on my sister, I cut the television off and picked Deona up from her walker. As soon as I reached the third step, Cash called out to me.

"Open the fucking door, Chanel!"

That's when I noticed I hadn't armed the alarm. *Shoot!*

"I'm not playing. Open this door now," he yelled. There was a small sound around the doorknob, and like magic the door opened. Cash entered the house with a gun and silencer in hand. This crazy motherfucker had shot the locks off.

"What are you doing?" my sister called out as she ran up the porch stairs behind him.

"Coming to get what's mine," was his answer.

"The only way she's leaving is over my dead body." Kristian ran over and stood in front of me and the baby.

It was in that moment I realized that my sister would die for me. Call me crazy, but I never thought anyone loved me that much.

"Have it your way." He raised his gun, and I screamed loud enough to make the baby cry.

"No! Cash, don't shoot her, please," I cried.

"Well, give her the baby, and get in the car," he demanded.

"Chanel, he won't hurt me. He's bluffing." Kristian was scared, but her poker face was solid.

"The last bitch who tested my gangster didn't live to tell about it," Cash warned.

As Deona cried louder, I handed her over to Kristian. I couldn't have her blood on my hands, nor could I be responsible for making my niece a motherless child.

"Chanel," she called.

"I love you, K. I'll be all right," I promised as I was pulled out the door.

Right then and there, I knew my days with Cash were numbered. I needed to devise a plan to retrieve my private stash from the bank and blow this Popsicle stand. It was time to get away for real. I wasn't prepared to die, and he'd kill me if I didn't kill him first.

Chapter Thirty-four

"Bitch, if you ever pull some dumb shit like that again, I'll kill you." He popped me with the butt of his gun. Blood flew everywhere and poured down my face. "The tracker in your phone alerted me the minute you hit the bricks. So why in the fuck didn't you call me?" He grimaced.

The pain hurt like hell, but I wouldn't give him the satisfaction of seeing me sweat. Caesar watched in shame through the rearview mirror as he drove us home.

"I thought you couldn't care less about me, seeing as how you left me in jail for fifteen days." I don't know why I felt brave today, but I did.

"I left your ass there to teach you a lesson," he spat.

"What lesson was that?"

"Next time don't get caught!" he snapped and backhanded me for good measure. Though I wanted to cry, I wouldn't dare give him the satisfaction. Therefore, I sucked up the pain and held my shit together for the duration of the ride.

Pulling up to the oversized home I once loved, I gagged. This place was no longer the estate I adored. Slowly it had become one of the many things I hated about life with Cash. The gated property now resembled prison bars, and I felt like an inmate.

"Go upstairs and get cleaned up. There are a few dresses waiting for you. Be back down here for my party in less than an hour," Cash demanded, and I did as I was told.

Upstairs in the mirror, I hardly recognized myself. The unfamiliarity had nothing to do with the swollen lip but everything to do with how I'd sold my soul to the devil. I thought Cash and this lifestyle were for me, but they weren't. I no longer wanted to be that girl. I no longer wanted this life. I just wanted to go back to my old life.

As I glanced over my clothing choices, I frowned because I didn't find any of them to my liking. Price tags and labels no longer appealed to me because I had to work too hard for them. I felt like a dog that had to do tricks for a treat, and I was fed up.

"Chanel," someone called out, and my blood boiled because it was my mother.

"It's unlocked." As I answered her, I slipped into a pastel pink Chanel dress.

"I guess you came to your senses and finally came home." She walked into the room and closed the door behind her.

"This prison is no longer my home, and I didn't come back willingly!" I snapped and fastened the straps on my sandals. "I was forced."

"Whatever! I'm just glad you're back in time for Cash's big party."

"What's this party for anyway?" It wasn't his birthday, so I had no clue.

"I'm not sure, but fingers crossed he will propose tonight." She smiled.

"Don't get your hopes up, because I won't accept it." Reaching for my diamond bangle, I glanced at her reflection from my dresser mirror.

"To hell you won't!" She stomped her leopard-print red-bottom shoe down on the plush white carpet. "We've worked too hard to snag a man like him. I will not let you blow this and give those other groupies a chance."

"If they want him, they can have him, because he ain't worth the headache," I told her honestly.

"While you were gone, your so-called friend Trina was all up on Cash," Porscha informed me.

"Trina?" My head whipped around so fast it made my neck pop.

"You heard what I said."

"It isn't like that. She's with Caesar, and besides, she wouldn't cross me like that." I dismissed the ridiculous idea.

"Child, Caesar is nothing to write home about. Fuck what you heard. Every bitch wants the boss, not the employee."

"You're tripping. That's my girl." I placed diamond studs into my ears and sprayed some perfume. I was not in a party mood, but anything was better than the punishment I had coming. Cash wasn't about to let me off the hook with just a jab to the face. I was sure what I was facing was much more severe.

"How many times do I have to tell you not everybody smiling in your face is always happy for you." She shook her head. "How many times did that ho answer your call while you were locked up?"

"I'll deal with her later." I turned on my heels. "Speaking on calls, what happened to you answering my calls?"

"Cash instructed me not to reach out to you or take your calls because I might've been brought in for questioning about him. I'm too old for jails, so you had to do you." She laughed like shit was funny.

"Porscha, I just spent over two fucking weeks in jail!" I screamed. "Fuck Cash. I'm your daughter. You should've had my back." I was pissed. "Kristian was right. You are no real mother. You just a cool-ass bitch." I snorted in disgust.

"Look, I'm not gon' argue with you, because you're right," she admitted casually.

I damn near passed out at her honesty.

"Maybe if I had been grown instead of seventeen when I had you, things would be different. I don't know how to be a mother, Chanel, and I know that. When I had y'all, I was still a child myself. I've been on my own since the age of fifteen, and I never looked back. Kristian may hate me, but if I were the cold-hearted bitch she made me out to be, her ass wouldn't be here."

She sniffed. For the first time in my life, I saw my mother cry, and it touched me. "I was given two options by my mother when I told her I was pregnant. My first choice was an abortion, and my second choice was to get out, and that's what I did. You think you're the only one who's been through something?" She tapped my chest. "News flash: I been through it all! There is nothing you can tell me that I haven't experienced myself. I know what it's like to have your ass beat, and I also know what it's like to do things you aren't proud of, but I did what I had to do because it was necessary!"

After wiping her eyes, she stood up straight, swept her fingers through her hair, and looked back at me. "No sense ruining fresh makeup because you're having a pity party."

Chapter Thirty-five

My conversation with my mother was put on hold when Cash knocked on the door. "Come on, Chanel. The guests have arrived."

With a fake smile plastered on my face, I placed my hand in his and walked down the spiral staircase with him. I didn't know what the celebration was for because there were no decorations, music, food, cake, or anything to symbolize the occasion. I only saw people waiting at the bottom of the stairs in anticipation of our arrival. None of the faces were familiar except for Caesar and that bitch Trina. I didn't know if it was my imagination, but I could've sworn the trick had a sneaky grin on her face.

"Thank you all for coming." Cash started his speech as I tried to read more into Trina. "I called you all here for two reasons. Reason number one is Chanel did her first bid, and now she's back home."

The crowd cheered, all except my alleged friend, who actually looked disappointed.

"The second reason is because I wanted to teach all you snake motherfuckers a lesson." This time the crowd stood still and hung on to Cash's every word. "Baby, please take a seat right there." He gestured for me to sit down on the chair that had been placed in the middle of the floor for all to see. I caught a glimpse of Porscha, who gave the thumbs-up. I frowned. If he was about to propose, he had a strange way of going about it.

"Cash, what's going on? Who are these people?" I whispered as he walked away from me, ignoring my question.

My hands were wet with perspiration, and beads of sweat gathered on the tip of my nose. My heart pounded loudly with every step he took back toward me. I squinted to see if he had a box in his hand, then gasped when I noticed large black leather straps.

"See, while my baby was away, a little birdie informed me that she's been stealing my money." He laughed like a madman. "You all work for me, and everybody knows my motto is what?"

"Never bite the hand that feeds you!" the crowd replied.

"I'm no thief!" I shouted. The grin on Trina's face told me everything. Porscha was right. She was after Cash and used my rainy-day stash to turn him against me.

"You're telling me the thirty-two thousand dollars you stashed away at the bank around the corner was saved without a dime from me? You mean none of the money I gave you for shopping, hair, nails, trips, or whatever was used for your private stash?" He stroked his goatee. I contemplated my answer carefully. If I lied, he'd come down on me harder.

"Yes, I saved a few dollars here and there," I responded.

"I respect you for telling the truth, but I can't forgive your actions. If I give you two thousand for a shopping trip, that's what I expect it to be used for!" he barked. "I don't care if you spend $1,699. When you come home, I expect $301 refunded to me. Do you understand?"

"Yes," I cried as he struck me the first time, then another and another. I blocked my face as I received my beating. The lashes continued for what seemed like days, and no one came to my rescue, not even my mother. My beautiful dress was ripped to pieces in front of the stunned crowd, leaving me completely exposed. I lay on the bloodstained floor in my bra and panties like an exhibition for all to see.

I couldn't believe my life had been reduced to this. I couldn't believe my friend had sold me out, and I couldn't believe my mother stood and watched this nigga beat me like a runaway slave. Lying on the cold floor, I prayed like hell that he killed me. In my mind, death had to be better than this.

Chapter Thirty-six

I still got chills when I thought of that day, which took place a month ago. Ever since that fateful day, my health had been declining. My skin was pale, my hair was falling out, and my stomach was always in knots. All the stress I was dealing with made me realize how fast I needed to get out of this life and away from Cash. I never questioned Trina about her loyalty, because I quickly figured out players in this game had no loyalty. Instead, I counted the days until I could make my move and get the hell out of dodge.

Today was perfect! Cash was away on business, and the coast was clear. My plan was to drive as far as my whip would take me and let God take over from there. It's funny how people find a relationship with God when their back is against the wall, and I was no different from everyone else. When I didn't have a soul to talk to, I called on Him in the name of Jesus. I hadn't heard Him respond yet, but I knew He was listening. I heard somewhere that He was a forgiving God, and all I had to do was ask, so I did.

As I pulled out of the driveway, I said a quick prayer and backed out slowly. Cash had people watching me, but I didn't care. All they could do was call and tell him that I was leaving, but by then I'd be far, far away. I didn't have a dollar to my name, so I needed to hit up someone for at least a twenty. Yup, the same twenty I told you couldn't do shit for me in the beginning of this story was now my only hope for survival.

Easing down 275, my mind raced about where to go. The first person who came to mind was my sister, but I didn't want to get her deeper involved in my drama. My second thought was Dominic, but I dismissed that for fear of rejection. My last thought was Tone, so I drove to the precinct where he worked. As I pulled up into the small lot, I searched my purse to find my phone. Just as I put my hand on it, the ringing started.

"Hello," I said hesitantly.

"Chanel, I've been worried sick. Are you okay?" my sister asked with a shaky voice.

"I'm sorry, K." I coughed and instantly began to not feel so well. I felt faint and nauseated.

"Where are you? Why do you sound like that?" She drilled me with questions.

"I'm not feeling well." I coughed again and grabbed my stomach to soothe the pain.

"Where are you?"

"At the police station." I coughed again.

"Why? What happened? Are you all right?"

"Yes, I'm fine." I wanted to tell her about my plan to leave Cash, but after he told me there was a tracker in my phone, I didn't take the risk. I didn't know if the call was being monitored, too. "K, I love you. I'll call you right back."

"Chanel, please don't go!" I could tell she was crying.

"I have a meeting, okay? But I'll call you right back, I promise." I dabbed at my tears. Crying came easy to me now. I was a ball of emotion.

"No, you won't! Oh Lord." She was really distraught. "Please don't hang up. I had a premonition about you."

"Tell me about your dream later. I have something important to take care of." I sniffed. I didn't want to hang up but time was against me. The faster I spoke with Tone, the faster I could be on the road before Cash got wind of it.

"He is going to take your life!" she blurted out, which sent a surge of electricity through my body so powerful it caused me to drop the phone.

For seconds I just sat there in shock. The siren of a squad car racing past snapped me back into reality. Instantly, I remembered Cash had cops on payroll, so I pulled away from the police station like my life depended on it.

I chose not to call my sister back until I was a few miles down the road because she had freaked me out. Resorting to the last person I could trust in Ohio, I turned down a familiar block. Pulling up to my old house, I got out and rang the doorbell. I had to restrain myself from having a coughing spell. Looking from side to side, I made sure I wasn't being watched or followed.

Of all the places in the world, I felt like Dom's would be the safest. I hadn't spoken to him in over six months, but here I was, and I didn't know why. I had treated Dom like shit when he lost his job, and left him for who I thought was Mr. Perfect. Now I wished I'd stayed here and stuck by my man because he was as close to perfect as they came. It was a funny thing to realize too late what I'd had.

"What are you doing here?" Dominic asked after snatching open his front door.

I didn't say anything at first. I just stared at him. He was finer than I ever remembered him being. The fact that he came to the door with no shirt, black sweatpants, and no underwear, which advertised his package well, rendered me speechless.

"Dom, I'm sorry," I blurted out and began to cry.

"Your sorry ass is a little too late, and your tears don't mean shit to me anymore." He prepared to close the door, but I reached out and stopped him.

"Dominic, I'm in trouble! Cash is crazy. He beats me, and he is into some very illegal shit!" I cried.

"Sounds like you need to be talking to the police, shorty." He shrugged his shoulders.

"I can't go to the police. He'll kill me! I came here for your help, so please help me." I cried harder.

"Look, I'm sorry you aren't as happy as you thought you would be. I'm sorry that you're being mistreated, but you asked for this, so deal with it!" Dominic stared out toward the street in order to avoid making eye contact with me.

"Please let me borrow a few dollars for gas. I'll pay you back as soon as I get squared away." I coughed and batted my eyelashes, trying to play my last card.

"I don't have shit for you. I wrote you off the day you decided I was no longer good enough for you." He frowned and leaned in so close to my face it scared me. "I don't know where home is for you these days, but it for damn sure isn't here. Now get your washed-up ass out of here." With that, Dominic turned around and closed the door in my face. I just stood there for another minute or two, hoping he would open the door and let me inside.

Not knowing what to do, I walked off the porch and took a seat on the second to last step. I didn't have anywhere else to go because I'd burned almost all of my bridges. I only had $3 in cash and a half tank of gas. As I realized I was all alone, scared to death, and homeless, I contemplated my options.

Quickly I decided I was done with Ohio and ready to put this city in my rearview mirror. A weight lifted off me as I thought of my mother. She wasn't the best, but she would at least let me stay with her. I figured once I was back in the D, all I had to do was round up my old associates, and someone would have me on a plane in no time.

With a broken smile on my face, I decided Detroit would be my next stop. Pulling up to an Exxon station, I grabbed a bottle of water and a bag of Doritos, and I prayed my half tank got me within the city limits of Detroit.

Chapter Thirty-seven

Hopping off of I-75 after the four-hour drive, I called my mother, who was asleep at this hour.

"What's wrong?" she asked in a groggy tone.

"I'm on my way home."

She smacked her lips. "Chanel, you aren't a little girl anymore. You can't keep running from your problems." She was annoyed.

"I don't need a lecture right now, okay?" I was tired and irritable.

"Where are you?"

"On Chene," I said, which indicated that I would be pulling up in less than ten minutes.

"See you when you get here," she said, and I hung up.

Bending the corner, I pulled up to the riverfront building as a sigh of relief came over me. After being buzzed up, I took the elevator to the eighth floor and walked down the hallway. My mother was standing in the doorway, holding her pink satin robe closed. It took everything in me not to run into her arms like a little girl, but I did cry at the sight of her.

"What's wrong?" She actually appeared concerned.

"Mom, I'm in trouble and I'm scared." I cried on her shoulder.

"Come on in the house, and tell me what happened." She ushered me inside and closed the door behind us.

I plopped down on the burgundy love seat and began to spill the beans about almost everything I'd experienced over the past few months. I even told her about Cash's alleged involvement with robbing my bank and killing those people. I'd never spoken of it to anyone, but the burden was weighing heavily on my chest. My mom wasn't the best person to talk to, but right now she was all I had.

"Chanel, I know it's not easy loving a man like Cash, but you've got to try."

"How can you love someone when you're afraid of them?" I cried. I needed her to understand that I was literally scared to death of him.

"Don't you think you may be exaggerating?" She lit a Newport.

"Exaggerating?" I coughed. Standing, I pulled my shirt off and exposed the whips and lashes across my back, legs, and arms. "You were there. Remember these?"

"Put your shirt back on." She frowned.

"This is what he's done to me. Look at it!" I screamed.

"What do you want me to do?" She hunched her shoulders. "There is no use crying over spilled milk. The wounds are there, and they aren't going nowhere." She pulled on the cancer stick. "Now you pick up the pieces, and embrace them as a part of your story." She puffed.

"Are you fucking serious? That doesn't even make sense!" I snapped.

"Everybody has a story, and your scars are a part of yours. Women are strong individuals because we can bear a lot of burdens. We take things in stride and keep it moving. There is not a woman out here who hasn't been cheated on, hit on, or mistreated. You are no better than anyone else."

Porscha flicked her cigarette into the ashtray. "Now you can sit here and cry to me about your problems, or you can hit Cash in his wallet. For every pain you endure, you'll make a profit if you're smart." She stretched and put out her cigarette. "I'm going to bed. I'll see you in the morning." With that, she left me alone with my thoughts and a cup of tea to soothe my cold.

Minutes turned into hours, and night turned into morning. Sleep hadn't come easy for me that night. The nightmares of Cash were on repeat and caused me to toss and turn. Now daylight was creeping in through the mini blinds, so I placed a pillow over my head.

Just then, I felt something moving around in my bed, which woke me out of my sleep. I'd been trying to ignore it along with my urge to use the restroom for twenty minutes, but the hissing sound alarmed me. Opening my eyes, I tried to focus on what it was. Suddenly, I caught sight of another person standing against my wall.

Blinking rapidly, I recognized the figure as Cash, and I almost pissed myself. I squirmed around in my old full-sized bed, but I couldn't move. My hands and feet were bound to the bed frame. "What are you doing here, and where is my mother?"

"Your mother is all right. I'm here to collect what's mine. Did you actually think I would let you leave me?" He smirked.

"Cash, untie me," I demanded.

"I will, but first you have to learn a lesson." He walked closer and pulled down the comforter. I thought he was about to rape me or something, but I was dead wrong. On my left side there were two white mice, both of which were dead. On my right side there was a medium-sized boa constrictor sliding and slithering around my body.

"What the hell is this?" I was beginning to hyperventilate. I was deathly afraid.

"The two things I despise most in the world are rats and snakes, and you seem to be both!" he barked. "I expected different from you, Chanel, and you disappointed me."

"What are you talking about?" I kept my eyes on the snake, which also had his eyes on me. He was a tan brown with dark cross bands and was about three feet in length.

"You tried to rat me out yesterday when you went to the police station, and then your snake ass went behind my back to go fuck your old boyfriend last night. What type of mark-ass nigga do you take me for? Don't you know who the fuck I am?" he barked.

I wanted to know how he knew all of this, but I wouldn't dare provoke him by asking. Instead, I went right to work explaining and apologizing. "Baby, I would never rat you out! I was only at the police because I thought someone was following me. Remember you told me if I ever felt like I was being followed to lead their dumb ass straight to the police station?" I tried to jog his memory.

I watched as he rubbed his goatee. Just then the snake hissed, and I shivered. He slid up beside me and moved onto my arm and then across my stomach, where he stayed. I was scared to death, and it showed on my face. Beads of sweat began to trickle out of my pores and down my body until my bed felt wet. I wasn't sure if the moisture was sweat or urine, but the latter was probably more likely. I no longer had the urge to use the restroom.

"Okay, well, that explains that. But what the fuck was you doing over old boy house last night?" Cash frowned.

Swallowing hard, I decided not to lie about being there because I knew for certain that he knew I was there. However, I was about to lie about the reason for my visit. "That nigga called me and said I received some mail from the bank over there." I spoke softly and remained calm, although the snake was now so close to my face I could've kissed him. "I figured it was important and could be about me getting my job back, so I went." Turning on the waterworks, I cried, "Cash, I'm so sorry, baby. I didn't think it would make you mad. I was going to tell you."

"When was you going to tell me?" His voiced rattled the four walls of the bedroom. "When you fucking made it safely to Detroit? Your ass thought you could leave me and I wouldn't notice? Don't you know I see and hear everything?"

"I came here because I missed my mom and needed to see her. You have other females occupying your time anyway, and you made it clear to me that you don't want me." I shifted my gaze from the snake to Cash, who was pacing back and forth.

"I don't give a fuck how many other fucking females I have. Until I tell you I'm through with you, you need to wait around and play your goddamn position!" he barked, and I felt sick to my stomach. At this point, I realized he would never let me go. I was tired of fighting and going against the grain. It was his way or no way. I had to oblige because going against him would prove harmful.

"You're right, baby. Now please let me go." I sniffed.

"Who the fuck is your daddy?" He stood over me and waited for the answer.

"You are." The hot tears rolled down my face and onto the pillow.

"Who gives you your bread and butter, bitch?"

"You do."

"Have you learned your lesson?" His cold brown eyes stared at me, and I whimpered.

"Yes!" I cried hysterically as he began to untie me. Cash was moving around the bed like this boa was invisible, but I was still very aware of his presence. Just as Cash untied my feet, I shot up from the bed like a jack-in-the-box. The snake hissed. Obviously it didn't like my sudden movement. After a few seconds of the uncomfortable stare down, the damn thing turned its attention to the dead mice and went on to eat lunch.

Chapter Thirty-eight

Going back to Ohio was the last thing I wanted do, but I had no other choice. My trifling-ass mother had turned me in.

"Okay, we're out of here," Cash called to Mother, who was lying across her sofa like everything was velvet.

"Are you forgetting something?" She stood.

"How could I forget?" Cash reached into his wallet and grabbed a few bills. "Here's your finder's fee."

"Your bitch ass sold me out?" I looked on in disbelief as she counted $900.

"Rent's due!" was all she said, and she closed the door as we walked out of it.

I couldn't believe Porscha. I came to her in my time of need, and she turned me in. That day I learned a valuable lesson. I was born by myself, and I would die by myself. Nobody in this cold world had my back. It was time to look out for my damn self.

The ride home was uncomfortable to say the least, with no words exchanged among the three of us the entire time and not even the sound of the radio. I knew Cash was seriously contemplating something. I dozed off a time or two, and when I woke up the last time, we were back in Ohio, but Caesar was not taking us home.

"Where are we going?" I stretched and looked out the window, trying to get my bearings.

"Going to teach your bitch-ass ex a lesson!" Cash said coldly, and I felt sicker than usual. My lie about being called by Dom to pick up mail was about to put his life in jeopardy. I instantly regretted what I'd said earlier.

We pulled up to my old residence, and I sat frozen partly because I was saying a silent prayer for Dom and partly because I didn't want to get out of the car. I wasn't in the mood for playing witness to Cash's mayhem.

"What are you waiting for, an invitation? Get the fuck out of the car!" he demanded, and I reluctantly followed him and his goon. Once we were on the porch, Cash pushed me forward, and I stumbled a bit. "Ring the doorbell."

After a few seconds, Dominic swung the door open. "Didn't I tell you—" His words were cut off when he noticed my company.

"Didn't you tell her what, my nigga?" Cash asked while pulling a 9 mm handgun from his waistband.

Dom looked at me as Cash forced him back inside of the house. Caesar looked behind us to make sure we weren't being watched. Once he determined the coast was clear, he closed the door and locked it.

"What the hell is this, Chanel?" Dom begged for understanding, and I put my head down.

"Don't talk to her, my nigga. Talk to me!" Cash said with the gun still pointed at Dominic.

"Okay, then you tell me what the hell this is." Dominic stood tall like the man I knew he was. He didn't appear afraid at all. I wasn't sure if that was a good or bad thing.

"This is about you calling my girl to come over here last night!" Cash answered, and Dom whipped his head in my direction. I didn't say a word, but my eyes pleaded with him not to blow up my spot. I was scared to death, and I was sure he could sense it. "Next time she gets some mail over here, just send that shit back to the post office. If it's important, they'll find her."

"Yeah, my bad, homie. You got it!" Dom nodded his head in agreement. Just as I exhaled a sigh of relief for him not ratting me out, someone emerged from the kitchen.

"Baby, who was at the door?"

We all looked up to see the woman, and my mouth flew open. Standing there was Noel in one of Dom's sky-blue work shirts. A few buttons were undone, and her breasts were almost completely exposed. I was in total shock as she tried to apologize. "Oh, my gosh. I'm so sorry, Chanel."

If I could've taken the gun from Cash, I would've shot her trifling ass myself. Then Cash would've shot me for showing feelings for Dom, so I played it cool.

"It's all good, miss lady. We're the ones intruding." Cash smiled and winked at Dom, who shifted nervously. "Come on, let's go." He nodded his head, and we walked out.

Turning to get one more look at the perpetrators, I caught Cash twisting his neck to peek under Noel's shirt, and I cringed with a twinge of jealousy.

Later that night, Cash put a hurting on me that I wouldn't wish on my enemies for the stunt I pulled. He whipped me with an old extension cord from the time I stepped foot into the door until he got tired. My body was a mess, and I threw up a few times at the sight of the blistering open sores. Some sores were pink, but the others exposed my white flesh. I needed stitches ASAP.

"Cash, I need a doctor," I cried from the bathroom, where I was assessing the damage.

"Shut the fuck up," he yelled from the bedroom.

"I'm serious. Please take me to the hospital." My body looked as though I had been sent through a paper shredder. It hurt to breathe, sit, or stand, and lying down was definitely out of the question. "Look at me," I screamed

out in agony. "I will die if I don't see a doctor." I stood
over the couch, where he was lounging.

"Damn, you always need something, don't you?" He
rose up from the couch and flew into the bathroom. "You
are just one needy bitch!" he called out.

At this point, he could've called me every name in
the book as long as he got me to the emergency room.
I waited impatiently as Cash slammed the medicine
cabinet and a few drawers. I didn't know what he was
doing, but for some reason I was nervous.

"Cash, please come on." I damn near shit on myself
when I saw that he had retrieved a bottle of alcohol.
"Ahhh!" I screamed an earth-shattering scream as the fire
ripped through me. The pain was excruciating and too
intense. I guessed my body couldn't handle it, because I
fainted.

Chapter Thirty-nine

I must've been out cold for a day or so. When I woke up, I was inside a hospital room. "Rise and shine, sunshine," said an overweight nurse who spoke in a Southern accent.

"Where am I?" I stretched and looked at the keloids that now covered my entire body. Quickly I tried to hide them beneath the covers because I was embarrassed.

"You're at Mercy, darling. You've been here since Tuesday." She poured a cup of water for me.

"What's today?"

"Friday." She pulled the curtains back to let in sunlight. "Dr. Muzar will be in shortly, okay?" She didn't wait for my response before leaving the room.

I sat up and tried to get comfortable on the twin-sized mattress, but it was no use. The IV in my arm made it impossible.

"Ms. Franklin, I'm Dr. Muzar." The tall, well-built Caucasian gentleman spoke softly as he entered. "How are you feeling today?"

"I've been better." I licked around my crusty, dry lips to make them look better. My saliva was thick and smelly. My teeth needed to be brushed twice.

"Well, I'm here to talk about your test results." He took a seat next to the bed.

"Test results?" I asked.

"Yes. When you were dropped off in emergency the other day, we thought an emergency surgery was necessary. It originally appeared that several of your nerve endings might have been damaged as a result of the beating you endured. As a precaution, we test for pregnancy, all forms of hepatitis, HIV, and AIDS."

My heart skipped four beats as I waited for his diagnoses. "Lay it on me," I said and held my breath. With my luck and bad karma, I was bound to have something.

"Ms. Franklin, your labs came back positive for both pregnancy and HIV."

"Please tell me this a joke." Tears began to gather in the corner of my eyes.

"I'm sorry. I can't do that."

"Am I going to die?" Panic was evident in my tone.

"We all will die one day, but HIV is not a death sentence. With proper treatment and a medicine regime, you should be able to live a fairly long life." He patted my shoulder, and gave me some paperwork to read over about the diagnosis. "Do you have any questions?" he asked. When I didn't respond, he said he'd give me a few minutes alone and that sometime later a counselor would be around to speak with me.

No doubt I needed time to let the realness of my situation marinate. With tears running down my face, I wanted to die right then and there. I couldn't believe I had HIV. Not that long ago I had been living life without a care in the world, and today I'd received what I thought was a death sentence. Suddenly the room started to spin, and I felt like I was going to throw up. Desperately I scanned the hospital room for something, anything that could be used as a weapon, but I was too much of a coward to end my own life, so I closed my eyes and prayed the Lord would just take me now. For hours I sat and reflected on my lifetime of poor choices, and then I remembered that every action had a consequence. I had put out so much negative energy into the world that finally, I reasoned, it was only fitting to get a positive HIV test.

After crying myself to sleep, I woke up from a nap and called Cash. I didn't know why, but I needed to hear his voice. Maybe he could tell me that everything would be okay, maybe he would encourage me to take another test, or maybe he would just sit in silence with me on phone. I didn't really know what Cash would do, but I desperately needed him.

"Hello." He cleared his throat. It was 3:10 p.m., and he sounded like he was just waking up.

"Baby, where are you? I need you," I cried as soon as I heard his voice.

"Chanel, I'm asleep."

"I need you, Cash, please," I begged, feeling so alone and afraid.

"You are a big girl. You don't need me holding your hand." Without another word he hung up.

Later that day the hospital sent a social worker named Ric'quel to talk with me, and she explained that this was no longer the death sentence it used to be. "With medication, prayer, and a positive attitude, you could possibly live longer, Chanel." She patted my arm, only after asking if it was okay to do so.

"What about my baby? Will it come out sick?" Honestly the baby was the least of my concerns right now, but I did need to know.

Ric'quel went on to explain the new plan, treatment, and delivery procedures in place for positive mothers. "There is a very good possibility your baby will be born healthy, without the HIV virus," she said.

Although I genuinely appreciated her support and concern, I felt my days were numbered as well as my unborn child's. I couldn't bear the burden of guilt I would endure if he or she was born positive. Instantly, I once again regretted the way I chose to live my life. Had I appreciated the small things life had to offer, I may not have been in this mess. I wished I'd made Cash wear a condom the first time we had sex. I also wished I'd requested that Cash provide me with his medical information before I let him hit it raw.

My mind went back to that night in Cash's sister's basement, and again I felt nauseated. I was so eager to drop my panties for a nigga I thought could change my life, while the love of my life was at home waiting for me with loving arms. I had so many regrets about the way shit was turning out for me, but the biggest regret of them all was calling Dominic to tell him my status. I prayed like hell that I hadn't infected him with my risqué behavior.

Chapter Forty

After three more days of rest and recovery at the hospital, I was discharged. On the Uber ride home, I rode in silence. I ignored text messages and phone calls, choosing to contemplate my life instead. I came to the conclusion that Cash was the source of all my problems. Since I was going to die anyway, I might as well take him with me.

The bastard never sent a flower or called to check on me. He didn't even have the decency to pick me up from the hospital, and it was only twenty minutes from the house. His excuse, as usual, was that he was asleep. Something like that would normally hurt my feelings, but today it was the motivation I needed to kill the motherfucker.

After thanking my Uber driver for the ride, I walked into the house like a zombie. On autopilot, I went into the study and opened the cigar box that was on top of the mantel. The gun was right there, locked and loaded just like always. Next, I headed to the utility closet and grabbed duct tape and rope. I wanted Cash to be as scared and helpless as I was all those times he hurt me.

Taking each step made me anxious. I had never shot anyone, but that didn't deter me one bit. I was on a suicide mission. There was so much anger and hostility building up inside of me, I was about to blow up.

Pushing the door open, I crept into the dark bedroom. It was 10:30 a.m., but the heavy drapery prevented daylight from coming inside. Easing my way up to the California king-sized bed, I gasped. Lying beside Cash was Trina. The bitch was sleeping on my side of the bed and even had the audacity to be wearing my shit. I was caught off guard but not completely surprised. Cash was shit, and Trina had always longed for what I had ever since I met her. *Two for the price of one,* I thought silently.

With a smirk on my face, I went to work securing him and her trifling ass to the wooden bed frame. It was a good thing they were both heavy sleepers or else I would've been dead. Cash would've surely put the smack-down on my ass if he woke up, but I was prepared to take that chance. As I looked at Trina, my friend, I wanted to slap the taste out of her mouth, but that was too easy. This bitch needed to die. It didn't matter to me that Trina would be leaving a son behind. The bitch needed to learn that if you played in my kitchen, you would be burned.

Finally, they were both secured to the headboard and footboard. I grabbed Cash's cup from the nightstand, then went into the bathroom and filled it with scalding hot water. Next, I pulled the drapes back so I could clearly see where I was going to shoot. There was only one chance to get this right. I had no room for error.

"You snake motherfuckers better say your prayers!" I shouted at the top of my lungs after throwing the water into Cash's face. I was sick and tired of being sick and tired. There was no mega house nor luxury vehicle worth the pain he caused me. There were no purses or shoes, regardless of labels, worth the abuse I'd suffered both physically and mentally. I could do bad all by my damn self. I didn't need this nigga to add value to my life.

"Chanel, what the fuck is your problem?" he screamed, immediately awake as the hot water hit his face.

"You are my problem, and I'm done dealing with you." I smirked. He blinked rapidly, allowing the vision of me standing over him with a Desert Eagle to become crystal clear.

"Bitch, I will fuck you up if you even think about—" His words stopped there because I backhanded the shit out of him, causing blood to squirt from his lip.

"Shut the hell up! It's my turn to talk, and I'm the bitch with the gun, so I suggest you don't interrupt." I waved the big-ass weapon around in the air. He tried to move but the duct tape around his wrists and ankles prevented that. Cash didn't say anything, but the frantic look on his face was priceless. "Scared?" I laughed.

"Never that," he said like a timid little boy instead of the evil self-centered man I had come to despise. "Why are you doing this?"

"Because I've been shit on by you for way too long, and I'm tired." I began to cry.

"Nobody shit on you, Chanel. That's all in your head," he tried to explain, but I shook my head vigorously.

"Look at these marks!" I held my arms and legs out for him to see what he had done. He didn't stare for too long, just glanced at them and turned his head. "Then you got my friend in our bed!" I pointed to Trina, who had woken up.

"She is not your friend. If she were, she wouldn't be here." Cash shook his head.

"Chanel, let me explain." Trina panicked when she realized shit was about to get real.

"You can save that bullshit for somebody else. You're in my bed, with my clothes on, lying next to my man. There is no coming back from this." I paced the floor.

"Stop fucking playing and untie me." Cash tried shaking his hands free.

"I'm not playing, and this is no joke. I could've been your Bonnie, your ride-or-die chick. I could've been your wife and loved you forever. But instead you robbed my bank, got me locked up, beat my ass, fucked my friend, and gave me HIV. Why did you do this to me?" I sat down on Cash's oversized chair and wiped my running nose and watery eyes.

Trina's eyes popped out of her head. "HIV?" she repeated with a look of pure horror on her face.

"Yes, HIV!" I snapped. "You always wanted what I had. Now you got it." I laughed and cried at the same time. The look on her face was priceless, but it did nothing to alleviate my pain. "Cash, I asked you a question."

"I did what I did because you let me," was his cold and simple reply.

"Did you know you were positive?" Trina asked.

"Yeah, I knew." He smiled. "See, y'all let me in your bed too easy. Women like y'all are funny. If a nigga flashes a little dough, instantly your panties drop."

"I loved you," I screamed.

"Stop it! How can you love me but be engaged to someone else? You didn't even know me, Chanel, and you let me hit it raw! You did it because you saw dollar signs."

I didn't have a comeback, because he was right. In that instant I embraced the fact that I'd had the power to control my actions. I could've changed my situation with him but used every excuse in the book not to. In the end, I guessed I valued material things more than my own life.

"Bitches like you come a dime a dozen. Always screaming that independent shit but quick to hop on the first gravy train coming your way. While you were looking for a pimp, I was looking for someone to pimp! While you were looking for a trick, I was looking to trick somebody. I guess we found each other, huh?" He smirked. "I let you enjoy my lifestyle, and you let me enjoy your body.

The only fucked-up part is that all the places we've been and all the money we've spent won't matter in the long run because we won't be here to enjoy it." He laughed wickedly.

"You are a sick-ass person. I wish I had never met you." I began to cry. "I lost everything that ever meant something to me because of you."

"Baby, spit that bullshit to someone else. You only lost them because your selfish ass let them go. Now get me out of this shit before I fuck you up." He tried to shake loose, but the tape was too tight.

"Cash, it's over." I sniffed.

"Your ass won't be going nowhere. I own you!" He hawked a wad of spit in my direction. "From the hair on your head to the red bottoms on your feet, I own you." He tried shaking himself free again. "Nobody is going to want you, Chanel. Look at you. You're all used up—"

That was the last thing Cash ever got to say to anyone.

Aiming the gun, I pulled the trigger and shot him right between the eyes. Blood and brain matter flew everywhere. Trina screamed frantically. Not only had she experienced Cash's death up close and personal, but her face was covered with his blood and pieces of his flesh.

"Please, Chanel, don't kill me," she begged.

"Don't trip. I'm going to let you go, Trina." I smiled and cut her free. She practically fell over herself trying to gather her things off the floor and leave the room.

"Thank you, Chanel. I swear on my son's life I won't tell anybody what happened here," she hollered over her shoulder just as she reached the bedroom door.

"Hey, T," I called out as she put her hand on the door-knob. Before she could turn around, I pulled the trigger and shot that bitch in the back without even flinching. Pow! "They say never bring a knife to a gun fight, bitch." I watched as she dropped like a fly, and I erupted into uncontrollable laugher. She had stabbed me in the back, and I shot her in hers. Now that was some funny shit.

After getting myself composed and calming my rising heart rate, I reached beneath the bed and grabbed an empty duffle bag we used for travel. Next, I went over to Cash's nightstand and grabbed a small stack of money and then headed for the closet. Once in there, I pulled down a few shoeboxes. Inside each of them were small amounts of money. I didn't know where all of his cash was hidden, but I was damn sure going to take what I could find. Quickly I flew through the house, ransacking drawers, removing pictures from the wall, and flipping the mattresses in all the bedrooms, including the one Cash's dead body was lying in. I only found about $20,000 total, but that was good enough.

Chapter Forty-one

I ran from the house like a bat out of hell, tossed the duffle bag onto the passenger seat of my car, and pulled out of the driveway practically on two wheels. I didn't know where to go or what to do. I wasn't made for prison, but then again, in my condition I wasn't cut out to be on the run either. My options were limited. I didn't have any friends, and I couldn't trust my mother as far as I could throw her. That's when it hit me that the only person I had in the world was Kris, my sister.

On autopilot I drove to her house with tears streaming down my face. I was scared of what my fate would be but relieved that the bogeyman, my bogeyman was dead. I was thankful that he would never be able to darken my doorstep again.

"Chanel." Kris was standing outside removing groceries from the trunk of her car when she noticed me pull up. "Where have you been? I've been calling you for days."

I couldn't move or even speak. Seeing my big sister made me feel like a child all over again. Through my tears I watched as she closed the trunk and walked over to my car to open the door. I saw the look of horror in her eyes as she assessed the new scars all over my body as well as the hospital bracelet on my arm.

"I killed them," I whispered.

Without a word, she reached through my open window and wiped my face.

"Did you hear me?"

"Yes, I heard you, but don't say that out loud again. What's the plan?" Kris looked past me to the bag on the seat. I reached into it, removed about $3,000, and handed her the bag. She tried to hand it back.

"Kris, I'm going to turn myself in. I need you to keep that for you and Deona, and I'll need you to also put money on my books." Wiping my face, I sat up in the seat so she knew I was serious.

"Are you sure this is what you want to do?" Kris looked sad. "You do realize a charge like this could be life if you're convicted."

"I got a life sentence the day he gave me HIV, so either way I'm done for." I shrugged. Though I was sure my sister wanted to ask me to repeat myself, she didn't.

"Look at you." She pointed to my scars. "Can't we claim self-defense?"

"Probably not on a double homicide case."

"Chanel," was all she could muster as her shoulders dropped in defeat.

"It's okay. I'll be fine. Just take the money and put it up. I also need you to go see Dominic and tell him about my HIV-positive status. He needs to get tested, but I don't have the heart to be the one to tell him, especially with everything else that I'm dealing with." In all honesty, I was just being a coward. After all the shit I'd put him through, I still was too selfish to want to hear the hurt or see the pain that I'd caused him with my negligence. It was one thing to leave him for someone else. It was a whole other thing to leave him with a reminder as permanent as HIV.

"Okay, Chanel, I'll do that for you. Do you want to come in and shower or get something to eat before you turn yourself in?"

"No, I got something to handle first, but I'll turn myself in as soon as I'm finished." I opened the car door and wrapped my arms around my sister, something I hadn't done in a long time. "I love you, Kris."

"I love you too, Chanel. You will beat this, and I will be there for you every step of the way."

"Kiss Deona for me." With a face full of tears, I pulled away from my sister, got back into my car, and headed toward my next destination.

Epilogue

Fifteen Years Later

I'd left Kris's house that morning fifteen years ago and was on the run for about two and a half weeks. I knew I was going to prison, but I wanted to get an abortion before I got there. There was no way I wanted to bring a child into this world while handcuffed to a hospital bed. I also didn't want the baby to be a burden on my sister or end up in the system, which was why I never told her that I was pregnant or where I was going next.

After the abortion, I healed for two weeks and then turned myself in. It was no sweat off my back, and it didn't faze me one bit. In fact, I figured I'd only be in prison for a year or so tops because of my death sentence, but I was wrong. I'd been in the Ohio State Women's Prison for fifteen years now. After my lawyer proved temporary insanity for shooting Cash, the murder charge was reduced to manslaughter. I had also only received a five-year sentence because health records showed that he knowingly gave me HIV. However, my sentencing for the murder of Trina was life. I'm not going to lie—some days were better than others, but I was maintaining.

During my life sentence, I'd only received packages and visits from my sister and one letter from Dominic. It had come at the beginning of my bid. He'd been informed by Kris of my positive status and was writing to tell me his results. Thank God he was negative. He also told me that he and his new fiancée, Noel, were both

praying for me and that he'd forgiven me. He said that he
was grateful for the things I'd put him through because it
had made him a better man for her. Now isn't that some
shit?

My poor excuse for a mother had yet to reach out to me.
At first I was upset, but karma is a bitch. I'd heard from my
sister that she was just diagnosed with stage IV lung cancer.

Throughout my prison stay, I'd reflected on my life several dozen times. I wished I'd done things differently, but
if I had, I wouldn't have had this testimony. After my tenth
year on the inside, I was asked to join forces with the Save
Our Youth Organization. Their goal was to show troubled
teens how they could end up if they didn't get it together
fast. With my newfound faith and outlook on life, I happily
obliged. If I could save one person from the lifestyle I chose,
it would be worth sharing the intimate details of my story.

I watched as the group of rowdy teenage girls stepped
from the yellow school bus into the prison corridor.
Some of them looked tough. A few looked scared, and
three of them didn't have a clue. I shook my head at the
long weaves, revealing clothing, piercings, and tattoos
they were all too young to have.

"This is our future," Queenie, my cellmate, shook her
head in disgust.

"That's why they're here, so we can communicate to
them what we did wrong," I responded.

"You can't tell youngsters shit!" she added, and a few
other inmates nodded or spoke their agreement.

We continued to look on as the girls underwent the
customary greeting they received from the correction
officers. They were then given bright orange jumpsuits
and shoes without laces that resembled knock-off Vans.
I never took my eyes off of one girl in particular. She
looked all too familiar. She was the prettiest and most
stylish by far. I noted that the diamonds she was remov-

ing from her ears and neck were the real deal. Next, I glanced over her attire and paid special attention to the Hermès belt and matching purse she was handing to the CO, not to mention the Jimmy Choo boots on her feet. I smiled.

"Fuck you smiling for, lesbo?" she popped off when she saw me looking.

"I ain't no dike. I was just admiring your shit, that's all. You've got good taste." I winked.

"It ain't like you know anything about labels." She smacked her lips, and the CO stepped in between us.

"Look," I said, raising my hands in defense, "I was trying to compliment you, that's all. You remind me of a younger me," I explained.

"Girl, please!" she snapped. "Look at you and look at me." She flung her curly hair over her shoulders. "You look like a monster with all those scars." She referred to the wounds on my frail body that had eventually scarred over the years. Her schoolmates laughed and pointed. I was no longer the beauty I once was. I eventually turned into the beast no one wanted to look at any longer than necessary. Instead of feeling ashamed or embarrassed, I embraced my wounds as a part of my story, as Porscha would've said.

Without another word, I walked away and let her be for the moment.

Once the group of girls had taken their seats inside the cafeteria, we got our intervention underway. The whole time the other inmates gave their speeches, I continued to watch the young girl from earlier. I was sure I made her uncomfortable, but I couldn't help it. I was anxious to share my story and inspire her to learn from my mistakes.

Finally, it was my turn to take the floor, and I jumped at the chance. I knew my story would affect that young girl the most. Not only was she who I used to be, but she was actually Deona. Kristian wrote me several times explaining that she was following my path. Deona was dating older men who bought her expensive things, and she was also having unprotected sex. I advised K to send Deona to this program, and I'd counted the days until her group arrived.

As I took the floor, my eyes stayed on my niece. I would die before I let her get caught in the lifestyle. I had only a small window of opportunity, so what I said needed to catch her attention. Without further hesitation, I opened up and shared my life.

"Money is a motherfucker. It's good for changing lives and the people who live them. Some are changed for better, others for worse, but they are changed nonetheless. Money turns close friends into fast enemies and almost always buys you false admirers. I'm sure you already know the ones who smile in your face but really couldn't care less about you. Money messes with your mind and is known for making people do some crazy shit. It's funny, because people will give up everything for a chance to 'have it all.' Now what sense does that make? Hell, some people will sell their souls and their mamas, too, for a chance to taste the good life. Through my pain and tears, I must admit I was one of those people.

"Greed is a sin, and I was guilty of it. Not only did I lose the most important people in my life, I also threw away my blossoming career as well as my identity. On the road to riches I lost myself, my morals, and my common sense. I let a man change me in the worst way. It's sad that I didn't do it because I loved him, but because I loved what he could do for me. People say money is the root of all evil. I just had no idea. Maybe I was too busy popping tags to pay attention. However, now that I look back on it, there is no fur coat, diamond necklace, luxury car, mega house, or dollar amount worth the price of my life, which is ultimately what I paid to live the glamorous life.

"My name is Chanel Franklin, and this is my story."

The End